Mr Darcy
falls
in love

A *Pride & Prejudice* parallel companion

by **Noe** *and* **Cindy**

Congrats on Winning!

Have A Good Read —

This book is dedicated to everyone who loves
to read Pride and Prejudice as much as we do,
and to Jane Austen for that excellent story
with its unforgettable characters.

Noe

Sept. 30, 2013

Introducing Mr. Darcy . . .
let's begin this story:

Fitzwilliam Darcy, heir of Pemberley estates . . . to most, he is *Mr. Darcy;* to his friends, of whom there are few, he is simply *Darcy.* Most consider him to be proud and disagreeable -- his being wealthy and taciturn seems to be a confirmation of this notion.

He is now twenty-five years of age. Two years ago his father died, and he still feels the loss. His mother preceded his father in death some years earlier, leaving just himself and his much younger sister, Georgiana. Darcy, having been away at school and subsequently entering into adulthood, was not able to spend as much time with Georgiana as his familial impulses urged upon him. Hence, he now feels a loneliness that anyone in such circumstances would understand.

His sense of isolation is increased, however, by his lacking in those skills of social intercourse that most learn from their interest in being accepted into society. By nature, he lacked this interest, and by the indulgence of his parents, he was not urged to learn them. He is a man that appears to have everything, and yet longs for that most basic of human needs: *companionship.*

We find Darcy just as he was walking through the shops of London; he happened upon a young gentleman and lady debating in a friendly manner over something in the shop window. He could not make out from their actions whether they were husband and wife, or brother and sister, or just friends.

The gentleman, looking up and seeing Darcy approaching, turned to him and said, "Sir, I beg your pardon, my sister and I are in need of an arbiter, and as you are a man of fashion and taste as can clearly be seen, may we request your assistance?"

The young lady interrupted, "Charles, such a thing is not to be done without a proper introduction! What manners, to be stopping a perfect stranger to make such a request!" Then addressing Darcy, she said, "You must forgive my brother, sir; he has yet to master the art of proper decorum."

Charles then declared, "You are quite right, Caroline. Pray, excuse me, sir, for attempting to draw you into a quarrel between brother and sister without an introduction. My name is Charles Bingley and this is my sister, Caroline Bingley. It seems the two of us cannot come into the shops without getting into some difference of opinion over something or another, and if you would be so kind as to settle this disagreement, I for one would gladly submit to your word on the matter."

Caroline was about to utter another reprimand to her brother when Darcy said, "My name is Fitzwilliam Darcy, and if I can be of assistance, I shall be only too happy." Darcy felt a certain gratitude for being invited to be a part of some sort of family setting.

"Very fine, Mr. Darcy," started Mr. Bingley, "you see those shoes which are said to be the latest fashion from France? I am of the opinion that they simply would not do for an Englishman. My sister holds they would do for a man of fashion no matter the country. What is your view, sir?"

Darcy looked at the shoes, but was reflecting, "What pleasure is to be found in having a family with whom one can be involved, in such a simple controversy over shoes."

His pause was beginning to make Caroline feel embarrassed over their request, so she remarked, "Excuse us, Mr. Darcy, we had no right to involve you in such nonsense as this. We will simply move on and trouble you no more."

Darcy was not the sort to be open with strangers, but he was feeling the loss of family keenly at this moment; and there was something trustworthy and honest about Mr. Bingley that made Darcy immediately feel comfortable and familiar. His kind, happy face and his displaying all the warmth and openness of a friend or brother touched Darcy. "No, please, it is no trouble. My taking so much time to answer was only because I was considering the pleasure of having family with which to have such discussions."

Charles said in an empathetic tone, "You have no brothers or sisters, Mr. Darcy?"

"I have a sister, but she is more than ten years my junior, and my schooling and other matters have prevented us from enjoying one another's company. Consequently, conversations such as this with her are rare indeed."

Forgetting about the shoes and their disagreement, Charles responded, "In that case, Mr. Darcy, we are on our way to the *Three Lions* for lunch. Would you be able to join us?"

"That is very kind of you," and then Darcy uncharacteristically added, "I would enjoy the company."

The *Three Lions* was a short walk from where they were, and they soon were seated. "Do you live in town, Mr. Darcy?" Caroline asked.

"We have a place in town, but the family home is in Derbyshire -- the Pemberley estate."

"What a fine thing to have a place in the country and in town!" remarked Charles. "My father, who died a year ago, had intended to purchase a country estate; but alas, never did."

"My father has also recently died; I know what a loss that can be. My condolences to you both."

Charles and Caroline replied in a similar way to Darcy, then Charles asked, "You are master of Pemberley estate?"

"Yes, and thankfully I have my father's excellent example to follow. He prepared me well for this eventuality. And you, Mr. Bingley, are you the eldest son of your father?"

"I am the *only* son, Mr. Darcy. Our father made his money in trade, which is why we reside in town. My father liked the idea of an estate in the country, but his business kept him too busy to pursue his desire for country living."

"And your mother, is she with you?"

"No, my mother died a year before my father. Consequently, it is just my sister, Caroline, and our other sister,

Louisa Hurst, and myself. And what of your mother, Mr. Darcy?"

"We seem to have a great deal in common, Mr. Bingley. My mother likewise died before my father, leaving my sister, Georgiana, and myself."

Caroline asked, "And you are raising your sister? Is it a challenge to be solely responsible for her?"

"It is a serious responsibility to say the least, but my father had the good sense to bring my cousin, Colonel Fitzwilliam, in the case. So between us, we share oversight."

"Is the colonel married?" asked Caroline.

"No; like myself, he is single."

Caroline light-heartedly observed, "In that case, it was sensible of your father to bring in your cousin. Without a woman's wisdom to consult, it would take two men to manage."

"Oh, yes, speaking of the wisdom of women . . . those shoes in the window. Did you form an opinion, Mr. Darcy?" asked Charles.

Looking first at Charles and then at Caroline, Darcy said, "I beg your pardon, Miss Bingley, but I believe they are too flamboyant for most English gentlemen."

"It seems I made the mistake of not allowing you to answer when we first met, Mr. Darcy. Through the course of the meal, you and my brother have become confederates and have sided with each other."

"You may have something there, Caroline," laughed Charles, "but since the shoe was designed to be worn by a man, it seems we would be the better judges of what an English gentleman would find acceptable to wear."

"To be sure, and being outnumbered as I am here, you are quite safe to make such an assertion. So if you two *English gentlemen* would give me leave to hold my own opinion, I will be satisfied."

The two men nodded their heads and looked at one another with a smile. As the meal was over and Darcy was considering what an enjoyable time he had been having,

Charles extended an invitation for him to come to their home the following day for dinner, which was accepted.

* * * * *

Darcy was not the sort that made friends easily, but this day he happened upon Charles Bingley, whose easy manners and friendly countenance encouraged him to be less reserved. Seeing the bantering of Charles and Caroline, and then being allowed to be a part of it, was a sense of family life that Darcy had not much experienced. The fact that they had so much in common likewise made him feel a closeness with Charles that was unique for Darcy, and he was actually looking forward to having dinner with them.

Darcy's engagements with the Bingleys continued beyond this dinner. It seemed that his first impression of Charles Bingley had been well-founded, and their friendship grew steadily.

Chapter 1

In the course of three years, Darcy and Bingley's friendship has grown, as one might expect. Charles' modest, humble nature made the younger man look up to his friend. After all, the Darcys, though untitled, are one of the old families. Then there is Darcy's calm, steady, self-reliant approach to life, which to Bingley is a picture of dependability. Charles had grown quite dependent on him for guidance and would hardly make a move without conferring with him. Darcy, on the other hand, confers with no one.

Charles is now approaching his friend for just such a purpose: "Darcy, I am seriously considering the Netherfield property I wrote you about as a place to settle. I know you have not seen the place, but would you say I am being too hasty?"

"It is a small neighborhood, as I understand, and a single man with a large fortune such as yourself will be viewed by the ladies in the neighborhood to be in want of a wife. You are sure to cause quite a stir, if I am not mistaken. But may I ask, what sent you in this direction?"

"Well, Caroline and Mrs. Hurst are quite anxious for me to take a place so they can make it over as they like, and Netherfield Park seems to fit their description."

Caroline, who was in the room, could not help but remark, "Yes, Mr. Darcy, though my brother appears to want to hide what really brought him this direction by attributing his decision for his regard to my sister and myself and our keen desire to hang new drapery and rearrange furniture, his *true* motives are to be found in the great interest aroused in him by the reported beauty of the ladies of the area."

Among the reported beauties of the neighborhood are the Bennet family of five daughters. Jane, the eldest, and her sister, Elizabeth, were always the first to be mentioned in those reports. Bingley was interested in meeting these reported beauties, especially the Bennet sisters.

Darcy is not known as one for smiling much, but this speech, at least, brought what might be considered the beginning of a smile. Knowing Bingley's gregarious nature, he could well imagine his friend eager to see a pretty face, and the prospect of reported *beauties* would be an inducement indeed for him. Darcy, though, prided himself on being more rational and deliberate in his actions and feelings.

"Let us not trouble Darcy with matters that do not interest him, Caroline, but please do tell him of your being enraptured with the size of the dining-room and the cozy room on the west side for taking tea and enjoying small gatherings."

This subject was one that Caroline did not hesitate to take up, especially at the possibility of sounding sophisticated at the changes intended. Really, she would not miss the opportunity of impressing Mr. Darcy. He did listen, but he was not the type to look impressed if he was not, so the best Miss Bingley could get was polite listening.

However, there was a certain novelty to such conversation for Darcy. His was an estate that had been in the family for many generations, so the excitement of starting a lease which might in time prove to be the Bingley family estate for generations to come was something that had more than a passing fascination to him. The most he could boast of having purchased since inheriting Pemberley was a new landau to replace an aging one, or some number of horses, so the thought of being the one to establish a family estate such as this actually made him feel the honor in what his friend was setting out to do. Certainly, nothing could make him regret having Pemberley as his birthright, as well as all the honor of being thus situated since the distant past, but to be the man who makes the decision as to what future generations would call their legacy was something profound for Darcy to contemplate.

Indeed, he could not help but ask himself, "What have I done that might be remembered by those family members that will come after me?" This thought stayed with him till he and

Charles were alone, and prompted him to say, "Charles, I have been considering what a great moment in the history of your family this possibility of finding an estate that could be passed on through successive generations might very well prove to be for you."

"My, to be honest, Darcy, I had not considered it from that point of view; I thought of it only as a place to live as a country gentleman! You know, one of those necessary purchases one must make to live comfortably. But with what you have now brought up, I must say I am glad it is only a lease! I do not believe I could make a decision that would have such a lasting effect on my progeny without first testing out the place to see whether it is suitable for that legacy."

"It is wise, to be sure, to take the proper amount of time to consider such an important decision, but it has caused me to think of myself and what I may do in the future that could even closely resemble such a legacy. What I now have to pass on has been passed on to me -- what you are setting out to do will be marked in the family annals for all time to come. I have as yet done nothing by comparison."

"I don't agree with you, Darcy. Making the start is certainly a momentous thing, but how many great families have had the disgrace of giving up their legacy due to improper management of the inheritance? Your legacy will be your living up to the family standard and improving in your own way as you are able."

Mr. Bingley's other sister, Louisa Hurst, and her husband now entered the room, and the two friends were interrupted by Mr. Hurst asking if they would like to join them for cards. The men rose to do so, but Darcy made an excuse to linger behind, as he reflected on Bingley's words. He had known more than one great family that had been thus disgraced, and what had just been said made him feel all the satisfaction that could be his, this being a faithful steward of the Darcy legacy.

The conversation of taking Netherfield continued with great enthusiasm over cards, which made it quite clear to

Darcy that soon the Bingleys would be settled in Netherfield Park.

Chapter 2

Mr. Bingley, having now established himself at Netherfield, discovered he had settled into the neighborhood at an opportune time. The community was in high preparation for their annual Meryton assembly ball, which was to take place in a fortnight. Charles, therefore, could not help but reflect on the prospect of seeing the ladies that he had heard so much about, and felt with keen anticipation this approaching ball, to which he had received any number of invitations from his neighbors who were anxious to see him, or rather, have their daughters dance with him. Caroline and Mrs. Hurst, though, had little interest in associating with their neighbors until Charles mentioned his intention of trying to get Darcy to come.

Caroline quickly agreed, "Yes, Charles, by all means, you must endeavor to have Mr. Darcy attend! That of all things will make the evening tolerable. You must write immediately, asking him to come."

"No, no, Caroline. You know Darcy's disposition toward these public balls and dancing; he will not come if I just write. But if we go to town and ask him to come, we will be there to return with him and it will be harder for him to decline the invitation."

"That's a splendid scheme, Charles, let us leave tomorrow! I am sure with the both of us asking, he cannot refuse."

Arriving at Darcy's home the following day, Charles and Caroline were greeted warmly. "Charles, Miss Bingley, how good to see you. I had not expected your coming to town since you have just moved into your new home. The Hursts were well when you left them, I trust?"

"Oh yes, they are very well; thank you, Darcy."

"Let me ring for tea. Have you come for the shops?"

Before answering, Bingley again considered his friend's inclination toward dancing. It was not great, though he was a fine dancer -- all admired such a tall man moving so gracefully about the dance floor. He also knew Darcy's thinking toward these public balls and was not sure he could persuade him to come. He therefore began discreetly, "No, Darcy, we do not have to do any shopping, though now that we are here, Caroline may very well find some reason to go into some of her favorite ones."

"I had not the slightest notion of it, Charles, but now that you have put me in mind of it, I am sure I will."

Charles looked at Darcy and rolled his eyes. "Our real purpose in coming is to ask if you would please pay us the compliment of coming to look at Netherfield?"

Caroline, greatly desiring the opportunity of having Mr. Darcy near her, made her appeal likewise: "Indeed, Mr. Darcy, for we shall not consider ourselves as settled until you have been there."

Darcy, looking a bit puzzled, said, "Surely you needn't have given yourselves the trouble of coming all this way for that. You could have simply written to invite me."

"That is all very true, Darcy," continued Bingley, "however, we were hoping our being here to accompany you would serve as a greater enticement."

"Whatever could you mean, Charles? Of course, I will gladly come. As you know, I have had more than a passing interest in seeing the place and was only waiting for an invitation."

"Mr. Darcy, you need never concern yourself with such formalities on our account, for nothing would give us greater pleasure than to have you come unannounced at any time, wherever we might be," said Caroline. "We are fond of your company and relish the idea of the three of us going back together." Charles was glad Caroline spoke up as she did, for he was concerned that Darcy was heading in a direction that would make it difficult for him to conceal the ulterior motive for their coming.

Darcy, then addressing one of his own concerns, began, "Excuse me for asking, Charles, but can you arrange that we not always be in company, or be constantly asked out? I'm sure your new neighbors are anxious to get to know you, but the inhabitants of such a small neighborhood can be so irksome."

"Don't give it a second thought, my good man. I shall keep Netherfield as quiet as a tomb; and as to invitations, I will consider myself quarantined, just for you."

"But, Charles, you have forgotten about the ball," said Caroline. Bingley had to turn away to conceal his expression at this remark, for he was not quite ready to introduce the subject.

"Of course; thank you, Caroline, for reminding me." Then turning to Darcy, he began with a little apprehension, "Meryton is having their assembly ball, and as we have been invited and plan to attend, you could accompany us, and that will certainly account for our having none of the neighbors to Netherfield while you are there." He was not sure this sort of sideways reasoning would have its intended effect on his friend, and therefore waited rather anxiously for Darcy's reply.

"I will gladly come to see Netherfield Park, and since the ball will be but one evening, I should certainly be able to tolerate it, though it is a public ball."

Bingley had his private celebration at this apparent success, till he heard from his friend: "Charles, this ball and your invitation to Netherfield seem a great coincidence. Is there not the smallest possibility that it is more than that?"

"Darcy!" Bingley declared, smiling. "Are you suggesting I have resorted to trickery to get you to accompany us to the ball? Well, as you have already agreed to come, and my memory has just now become a bit clouded, I think I can safely say - *I really don't know.* But you are right, it does indeed seem quite a coincidence."

Chapter 3

Darcy did go to Netherfield, and as he was being shown about the place, he expressed satisfaction on the size of the rooms and their prospects. He especially admired the view from the breakfast room and commented, "This is indeed a pleasant place to start the day, Miss Bingley. The colors you have chosen highlight the natural beauty of the outside view." For Caroline, this was praise, to be sure, even beyond its real intention.

They were then called to tea, during which time Charles talked of riding out the next morning to show Darcy the grounds. All in all, Darcy's visit started very well, and the Bingleys were gratified with his appraisal of the place. For the next few days, the party at Netherfield enjoyed one another's company in various ways that only those with such estates can.

Nonetheless, and perhaps too quickly for some, the day of the assembly ball came, which found Charles in eager anticipation and his sisters declaring their disapprobation of joining with the townsfolk for such an occasion. Darcy's feelings were different from all the rest; he had his own concerns which belied his indifferent composure.

He felt an uneasiness growing -- that uneasiness he often felt on occasions such as these. He very much respected Charles; indeed he loved his good friend. But Bingley's manners and disposition were such that his own were sure to be put in the worst light. He certainly felt no desire to please anyone, much less to have the good opinion of the townsfolk of Meryton, but no one likes to feel awkward.

* * * * *

The evening of the ball arrived, and at first, those assembled were disposed to think well of the Netherfield party, for who would not be impressed at such fine dress, coupled with the stately manner in which they entered the room? Mr. Darcy particularly drew the attention of everyone by his noble way of carrying himself, his fine figure and handsome features being admired by both the ladies and gentlemen.

However, Darcy saw the most common dress and heard the most mundane conversations and merry-making that would set a fellow of such good breeding as himself into despair and disdain at the prospect of having to spend the whole evening there! As his disposition had grown worse from actually being where he did not want to be, Darcy became even less inclined to converse and make himself agreeable. It soon became clear: his ability to tolerate this one evening with composure was proving to be more difficult than he had anticipated. The trouble of the exertion was not worth the prize! Consequently, he offended everyone, and the speech about him made its way around the room, which only served to make him more disagreeable. It was a cycle that, once started, had no end.

Charles alone enjoyed himself, dancing and mixing with his new neighbors. One of the ladies in particular caught his fancy: the very *Miss Jane Bennet* whom he had heard so much about.

Still, upon seeing his friend standing alone, avoiding and being avoided, Charles approached to urge him to find a partner: "Darcy, what, pray tell, are you doing not dancing? I would have thought by now you would have warmed to the idea and ventured onto the floor."

Darcy was in no mood to comply, answering, "Charles, look about the room. There is no one that it would not be a punishment for me to stand up with! Although, as I have often seen happen, you have found the prettiest girl in the room for a partner. And I have done all the dancing I propose to do this evening."

"But, Darcy, you have danced only two dances, and those were with my sisters."

"I detest dancing with a partner with whom I am unacquainted. The absurdity of trying to make oneself agreeable to a stranger is a folly in which I choose not to participate."

Bingley, ignoring what his friend had just said, singled out one of Jane's sisters. "Surely your fastidiousness cannot include Miss Elizabeth Bennet. If you would but turn, you will see she is sitting just behind you, and I dare say you will find her an acceptable partner."

Turning that direction, Darcy fixed his gaze on her till she looked up at him, and then quickly averted his attention back to Bingley. Speaking loud enough to be heard even by Elizabeth, he said, "I grant her to be tolerable-looking, perhaps, for the undiscriminating; but you will observe, Charles, that she has not enough beauty or charm to tempt any other man in the room to ask her to dance. Should I be expected to play the prince for all such ladies thus ignored? Your time would be better spent in some other activity than trying to coax me out onto the floor."

Darcy had learned early in life to hide behind an appearance of haughtiness, reserve and fastidiousness to deal with uncomfortable circumstances such as this. Though it began as a facade, regrettably it had become a part of his character.

Somewhat embarrassed by his friend's unkind remark, Charles simply replied: "As you like, Darcy, but if it is all the same to you, I will enjoy the rest of the evening," and left his friend standing alone.

* * * * *

The evening finally came to an end and the Netherfield party found themselves back home. Charles declared, "What a lovely evening it has been! In the ways of a ball, I vastly prefer this style. There was none of the stiffness that accompanies some private balls . . . you know, the ones that have an air of formality which stifles getting familiar with those in the room."

"Bingley, you astonish me. Never have I seen a collection of people with whom there could not be found anything of any interest," Darcy said coolly, as he poured himself some sherry.

"Come, come now, Darcy, I have never seen such prettier girls or pleasanter people in my life!" Bingley protested.

As Darcy walked back to the center of the room and stationed himself by the fireplace, Caroline condescendingly observed to Louisa, "When will our poor brother ever learn a more discriminating taste?"

Darcy, taking up his own cause, responded, "Charles, you cannot seriously consider what we saw put on display tonight to be people possessing any fashion or beauty."

"I will allow you to have whatever opinion you would like on that head no matter how strongly I disagree, Darcy, but either your eyesight or your view of beauty would be called into question if you would not agree that Miss Jane Bennet is perfection itself in female form!"

"I will not quibble with you on the extent of Miss Bennet's attractiveness. She is pretty, but her always smiling is a definite detraction. Such a thing is not to be done by ladies of real fashion and sophistication."

"She smiles too much!" Bingley exclaimed. "Darcy, you do recall we *were* at a ball, not church! Heaven preserve us if a woman being happy at a ball is not permitted to be in fashion or refined enough!"

Caroline, for reasons her sister understood, would never contradict Darcy, especially on the subject of what is acceptable and refined, being every bit as proud and conceited as he was. She did venture here, however, to say a word in defense of Jane, whom she had found agreeable, for Jane's manners were both kind and humble. "Truly, Mr. Darcy, though Jane Bennet may smile more than one should, she is a dear sweet girl, and despite your declarations, Louisa and I would wish to know her better." Darcy made a bow and the conversation moved on to other subjects, and at length, they all retired.

* * * * *

Mr. Darcy, now in his apartment, found his mind going over the evening's events from a different point of view. His cool, unconcerned exterior would often give way to something that more closely resembled what he *could be* when he was alone. He thought of Bingley having encouraged him to dance with Elizabeth Bennet, and the manner of his refusal as she was so near kept entering his mind. There was something about his discourtesy on that occasion that plagued him. Though he would not admit to her being attractive, her happy countenance, sitting there in innocence while he spoke ill of her, was not sitting well with him.

Alone with these thoughts, he found himself drifting off into sleep with the image of the face of Miss Elizabeth Bennet before him.

Chapter 4

The next day, Charles and Caroline took Darcy into the town of Meryton. As they were walking through one of the shops, they heard the voices of Jane and Elizabeth. Charles moved toward them, happy for this accidental encounter, and said, "I thought it was your voices I heard; how very pleasant to see you! How are the Bennet sisters?"

Darcy and Caroline, having followed him, likewise said their hellos. There were the usual comments on the weather and what brought each of them into town. Bingley then added, "I see there is a café on the other side of the road. Do you have time to sit and take some tea?" Jane answered that they were in no hurry, so the whole party ventured across and sat outside.

"We came to take Mr. Darcy on a tour about the town," Bingley offered congenially.

"And what is your first impression of Meryton, Mr. Darcy?" asked Elizabeth.

"It appears to be a pleasant enough place," came Darcy's terse reply.

Addressing Caroline, Elizabeth repeated her question. Speaking in a supercilious manner, Caroline responded, "It will do for those mundane necessities of everyday living; but for clothes, I find one must go to London."

Elizabeth, being confronted with such a blatant attempt to express superiority, resisted the urge of exposing such an absurd remark, but at least had the pleasure of saying to herself, "But of course, since clothes are not one of those necessities of everyday living!"

Understanding the slight his sister had just given, though, Bingley added, "Speaking of clothes, I noticed some very fine-looking coats and hats in that shop over there. To make myself truly a part of the neighborhood, I really must buy something today. Can I count on the two local ladies to assist me in my admission into the Meryton community?"

Darcy was a bit envious of how easily Charles could convert such a moment into one that would further his acquaintance with Miss Bennet. It seemed to come naturally for him, and certainly showed his agreeable personality in a good light, whereas for Darcy, such openness and easy-going manners were a mystery.

"For such a noble cause, how can we refuse?" Elizabeth answered quickly, not wanting her sister to miss this opportunity.

From the start of their encounter, Darcy found himself observing Elizabeth with a critical eye. He thought to himself, "There is not an attractive feature about her. Her face has nothing to recommend it, and her figure lacks that sense of symmetry one finds so pleasing in the female form."

Was this because, in comparison to Jane, the majority of women would find themselves wanting, or was there something else at work here?

While shopping, Mr. Bingley purchased more than just a few items. He was determined, not only to make up for his sister's belittling remarks, but also to demonstrate his earnestness in making himself a part of this small community. Darcy, however, took it as Bingley's way of prolonging his time with Miss Bennet. However, it was soon time to part, so they all said their goodbyes and went their separate ways.

Now that the Netherfield party were in the carriage returning home, Bingley spoke of Jane: how she united in one woman a gentle and kind spirit, one that answered for what a woman should be, with the appearance of one that has all that is appealing to the eye and a modesty that no one could label false.

Darcy spoke his mind, "I dare say Miss Bennet is a lovely creature as you describe, Charles, but I suppose there was no more beauty to be spared for her sister Elizabeth."

Caroline laughed triumphantly, enjoying Mr. Darcy's wit at Elizabeth's expense, while Charles looked surprised at his friend. "You can't be serious, Darcy! She does not quite rival her sister, it is true, but Miss Elizabeth is a very fine-looking girl."

"I am sure what you are observing, Charles, is a passing resemblance to her sister, for whom you have an attraction, and this prejudices your opinion."

"I assure you, my feelings for her sister do not have the influence you suggest. My eyes see clear enough, and dare I say, better than yours, considering I bagged a greater number of birds than you last season."

At this reference, Caroline, with the authority of a mother that all women seem to have been born with for moments just like this, demanded that the men not enter into a debate about whose eyesight is better or who is the better shot, adding, "Men are always turning everything into some sort of competition." The two men, like obedient children, complied and began to discuss their evening plans.

Later, while dressing for dinner, Darcy began pondering over the discussion with Charles about Elizabeth. "Why am I so determined to find fault with her? I have seen the best and worst in women of both the high and middle classes, and have been unconcerned even with those that have put themselves forward so obviously to get my attention. With perfect indifference and complacency I have handled myself; why has my mind taken such a turn as this with her?"

Darcy considered the subject from every possible side, but found no answer. He did realize that he had to go back many years before he was able to recall being so occupied with a member of the opposite sex. Bingley, on the other hand, had been infatuated any number of times in their acquaintance. One thing he did conclude: he must wait for their next encounter and consider what his reaction to Miss Elizabeth Bennet would be then.

Chapter 5

Lucas Lodge proved to be the location of their next meeting, everyone having been invited for an evening's amusement. It was here that Darcy found he must make a retraction, as he discovered that there was an attractiveness to Elizabeth, especially *her dark eyes.*

He now found in himself a growing desire to know Miss Bennet better. This presented a problem, for in this setting, conversation was certainly not his strong suit. He therefore determined to covertly listen to *her* conversations with others. His skill as a discreet eavesdropper, however, left much to be desired, for he was soon confronted by her on this point in her friendly, teasing way:

"Mr. Darcy, you must offer your observations upon my urging Colonel Forster to give us a ball at Meryton. I know your satirical eye caught something worth mentioning."

Feeling he had just been exposed, Darcy rallied himself and made a reply with some composure: "I would say you have shown yourself to be like most young ladies. A ball always elicits an energetic display." He was, without a doubt, glad that Charlotte Lucas happened to be there to insist that her friend now play some music for the party, thus pulling Lizzy away. He was not sure how strong her powers of perception were; even though he was certain she was quite ignorant of his amateurish attempt, any further conversation may have uncovered his sense of surprise at her discovering him.

Darcy truly wanted to turn his attention elsewhere, but he simply could not. He watched her move to the piano and could look no other direction. He confessed to himself, "Charles was correct in reproving me in my remarks about Miss Elizabeth; my first impression of her appearance was much in error. Her form does indeed have a light, pleasantness about it. . . her playing and singing are creditable also."

After Elizabeth played a song or two and requests were being made for her to continue, she saw her sister Mary approaching the instrument in earnest. Lizzy did not want to deny her one of the few pleasures she could enjoy in such a gathering, and so gave up the instrument to her. Mary gave a serious attempt at a long concerto, after which her other sisters, Lydia and Kitty, who were growing restless of such non-activity, requested she play more lively music with which to dance. Several of the young ladies and officers then joined in a reel.

At this turn of events, Darcy could not help but heave a sigh and say to himself, "Why individuals would choose to pass the time dancing instead of spending it in meaningful conversation is an irrationality that betrays a lack of refinement." If he could have been more objective, he may have had the presence of mind to realize how absurd it was for him to condemn the one activity in favor of the other, as he did not engage in *either* of these when attending social affairs.

Being as absorbed in his thoughts as he was, he did not notice Sir William Lucas approach, until the latter began to speak of dancing: "What a lovely spectacle, young people dancing. It gives that air of refined society, would you not agree, Mr. Darcy?"

This, of course, was not a subject Darcy was in any mood to discuss, so speaking in a brusque manner, he observed, "It would permit an easy admittance into polished society, since savages dance as well."

Sir William, not knowing in what light to take such a comment, merely smiled. Noticing Bingley join the dancing, he said, "Your friend Mr. Bingley performs delightfully on the floor! I dare say your performance is nothing to blush at either."

Obliged now to say something, Darcy remarked, "You did see me dance at Meryton, sir."

"Indeed, and your skill is just as I stated. Do you often dance at St. James'?"

"Never, sir."

"Oh . . . surely that of all places would deserve the compliment!"

Darcy declared, "That is a compliment I avoid paying to any place, if I can."

This could hardly be taken in any other light, so Sir William, being the gentleman that he was, changed to another topic, which brought hardly a response from Mr. Darcy at all.

From across the room, Miss Bingley was watching Darcy through all of this, thinking she understood well the looks on his face. She was sympathizing with him at a distance, until Sir William stopped Elizabeth, who was just then walking by.

"Miss Eliza, can I not encourage you to dance? Mr. Darcy, this is surely an inducement for you to dance! Where else is such a partner to be found?" Sir William had taken Lizzy's hand and offered it to Darcy, and though it was unexpected, he was showing himself willing to follow through by beginning to reach for her hand.

Elizabeth, however, withdrew it. "Indeed, sir, I am not inclined to dance. I have not moved this direction to be noticed for such a purpose."

Darcy, believing her disinclination was from this having been a scheme of Sir Williams' rather than his own, declared his own willingness by asking straightforwardly, "Miss Bennet, will you allow me the honor of having this dance with you?"

Lizzy, turning to Darcy with an arched look, declared, "This is a day for me not to dance, Mr. Darcy; I determined it as I rose from bed this morning. So, except there be an order from the king, I must not break my vow of not dancing this day." She then moved on to the refreshment table.

Elizabeth's turning his offer to dance down only served to heighten his fascination of her. "For a woman to purposely miss an opportunity of making an impression with someone like myself is strange indeed, to say nothing of missing an opportunity to dance!" Now he was not only admitting her beauty, but he was also becoming more intrigued with the person.

Though Caroline could not be sure what had been said, the change in Darcy's countenance was clear enough, and gave her motive to begin making her way over to him, as she saw Lizzy walk away. Not realizing he was filled with thoughts of Elizabeth, Miss Bingley believed she understood his eyes to be expressing dissatisfaction for being in such company.

"Poor Mr. Darcy, how the insipidity of this gathering must be a torment for you."

Expecting him to agree and for them to have a cozy moment of enjoyment in disparaging their companions, she was surprised to be presented with something altogether different.

"Your conjecture could not be further from the mark. My mind has not the torment you suppose; I am much more agreeably engaged. There is a pair of very fine eyes and the face of a pretty woman that I have the great pleasure in considering."

Her heart quickened when she asked, "Whose eyes could cause such reflection?" She was thinking, of course, 'who else could he be meaning, but myself?' and greatly desired to hear him acknowledge it. His answer, though, caused her heart to take an altogether different reaction than she had hoped: with intrepidity, he stated that it was *Miss Elizabeth Bennet's.*

Surprise was the emotion of the moment for Miss Bingley. She had for some time had the vague opinion that Elizabeth could be a rival for the attention of Mr. Darcy, as any woman within his acquaintance would be considered such. But now, to hear him go from criticizing her, as he had been hitherto, to *admiring* her was too much.

She responded by summoning all the sarcastic wit at her disposal. "Miss Elizabeth Bennet! My dear Mr. Darcy, how well you have chosen for yourself! This, above all things, is a marriage that will be eminently celebrated."

"I fully expected you to be in raptures; the female mind has a convenient bent in that direction. A man cannot look at a woman without it all being settled in that instant."

Miss Bingley was not going to permit this to be the last that was said on the subject. "But, Mr. Darcy, you do your choice no justice. . . just think what a fine thing to have such a mother-in-law. What joy is to be yours, having her always at Pemberley! And to be sure, Eliza's uncles are in the same profession as your own uncle, the judge. Certainly their pictures must be hung together in the great hall. Why, in this you may have stumbled on a fine thing for all the great houses of the land -- to incorporate space on their own walls for the common inhabitants of the town to hang pictures of notable members of their families!"

Darcy tolerated it all with composure, then finally tiring of it, said drily, "If you are quite done with the recital of my future happiness . . ." and moved away.

Later that evening, alone in his apartment at Netherfield, Darcy could think of Elizabeth without being interrupted. He recalled her comment to Charlotte before sitting to the instrument: she had referred to himself and the Bingleys as persons accustomed to hearing the very best performers . . .

. . . and to be sure, he had heard those who were more accomplished at the instrument, but he could not recall a time when he had been so captivated by the performer.

Chapter 6

After being presented with both Darcy's admiration of Elizabeth and their brother's continuing favoritism toward Jane when they were all at Lucas Lodge, Caroline was today considering how best to discredit the Bennet sisters openly, yet also make it seem to be without malice. Nothing was more unbearable to her than to have Mr. Darcy feel regard for any lady other than herself, but the idea of his stated admiration of Elizabeth becoming an attachment was bordering on misery.

"Louisa," she cried, "we simply cannot stand idly by as Jane and Eliza Bennet maneuver and suggest their way into Charles' and Mr. Darcy's affections!"

Mrs. Hurst stood to pace, and in a moment said with a sly look, "Knowledge is power. We must invite Jane over to get better acquainted with her. You can be in no doubt as to how best to use the information we gather about their family relations and history."

With Caroline in agreement, the sisters now knew how to proceed against the two unsuspecting women. They easily comprehended how Jane, with her open heart, would be more than willing to relate all they needed to undermine both her own and her sister's standing in the eyes of the two men.

To that end, Jane soon received an invitation to lunch with Caroline and Mrs. Hurst. Her mother rejoiced at the prospect of her seeing Mr. Bingley, until learning that he and Mr. Darcy had been invited to dine with the officers. Mrs. Bennet, whose primary occupation was incessantly scheming to advance all her daughters' marriage prospects, encouraged Jane to accept the invitation, but directed that she go by horse instead of carriage, for it looked like rain, and thus her returning home would be delayed. Perhaps she would even have to stay the night, thereby ensuring that she would remain long enough to see Mr. Bingley.

As things turned out, Jane was more than delayed in returning, for it *did* rain on her ride over, soaking her completely. Hence, she found herself sick with a bad cold, and the Bingleys would not hear of her leaving until she had seen the doctor. They sent word to the Longbourn family that Jane would stay until she had recovered.

Alone together that evening, Caroline said to Louisa, "How utterly foolish of Jane to come by horse, and in the rain, no less! If our brother were not so taken with her, this alone should have made her fall in his estimation; but instead, he is beside himself with concern for seeing to her comfort."

"Though we cannot enter into our brother's tender feelings for her, we must nevertheless likewise demonstrate our compassion. For you see, by this means our laying before him her unsuitableness will not be viewed with any suspicion."

"You are quite right, Louisa. After all, my heart is touched by her being sick. I only wish she would have had the manners to have caught her cold after returning to her home."

Mrs. Hurst laughingly answered, "For a lady who could not manage to have a carriage in which to be conveyed to a luncheon, what else is to be expected? To say nothing of her father and mother allowing their eldest daughter to go to the home of neighbors, such as we are, in that manner!"

"Perhaps the father and mother were, in their own way, hoping to have their daughter established in some respect -- I am sure you will agree with me that Jane Bennet would do very well as a governess for any children you might have someday!" returned Caroline. "But seriously, Louisa, it was a splendid plan of yours, for we have learned enough of the Bennets to overcome even our brother's undiscriminating views."

"And what of Mr. Darcy's opinion of Jane's sister?"

"I can only suppose," stated Caroline, "that if Jane is nonsensical enough to ride over in the rain, her sister Elizabeth, who is not nearly so genteel, is sure to produce her own follies for Mr. Darcy to scoff at! And as we relate what we know on the subject of their connections, his regard for her *fine eyes* will not be able to overpower his revulsion."

* * * * *

Upon receiving a note from Jane the following morning, Lizzy, feeling for her sister, determined to go and see about her. Since she loved long walks and fresh air, she thought nothing of the *'barely three miles there'* and made her way to Netherfield on foot. It does not take much imagination to consider what becomes of a young lady's attire and appearance from jumping over puddles and stepping over stiles after a rain! It is in this state that Elizabeth entered the Bingley home.

The mere notion of a lady walking unaccompanied was shocking to Miss Bingley and Mrs. Hurst. Being ladies who deemed themselves elegant, their idea of a walk was a turn about the gardens, not a walk through the countryside, and certainly not after a rain! Elizabeth, arriving muddy and windblown, proved to them their view was correct.

A young lady looking *like so* was not a sight that people of fashion were accustomed to see in one who was allowed to be an acquaintance. Therefore, Darcy was at a loss as to why, in this state, her beauty was not only undiminished, but he could not deny how alluring she was to him at this moment. There was the censorious side of him that was also at work, however, which did not allow the present circumstances to warrant such an exertion on her part. Whether his sense of good breeding and fashion would overcome his growing fascination with Miss Elizabeth Bennet, as Caroline believed it would, was a question Darcy scarcely even considered.

Elizabeth was immediately shown upstairs to Jane, and while she was tending to her sister, the sisters downstairs were tending to Elizabeth.

Caroline ecstatically thought, "I fully expected her to expose her simple-mindedness, but not quite so blatantly nor so theatrically!" Seeing this as the opportune moment for putting into motion their scheme of discrediting her, she stole a knowing glance at her sister, and began, "Whatever could she be thinking, coming all this way unaccompanied, looking as she did upon arriving? How revealing this is of her character -- this sense of conceited country independence, so clearly without concern for what is proper decorum!"

Charles objected to this assessment. "It shows a concern and attachment to her sister that is to be admired," he stated boldly.

Caroline sneered, "Surely, you are not of the same opinion as my brother, Mr. Darcy? You would not wish your sister to make such a spectacle of herself?"

"No, of course not," he replied simply.

Miss Bingley, though, hoping for more, and not being gratified with this reply, moved closer to him. Thinking herself only to be heard by Darcy, she said in a low tone, "I imagine this crude display of hers will have cast a pall over her *'fine eyes'.*"

"What you call a crude display, I would describe as a morning's exercise, which I would hasten to add, actually brightened her eyes in my view," Darcy said for all to hear.

Caroline laughed, as if to suggest he had spoken in jest, and moved back to the middle of the room. She then returned to a subject that she was certain would have a firmer footing: "Their uncle, Mr. Gardiner, actually lives within walking distance of his warehouses -- they live in Gracechurch Street! What can be said of that? Does not its very name carry a sense of dignity? Can we not all name the great men who have come from there?"

Mrs. Hurst chimed in, "It is a street among all the other undistinguished streets of London where all manner of undistinguished people live -- that very sort of melancholy dreariness which all great cities must of necessity have."

"Yes, but you overlook, Louisa, just how essential such common people are for the everyday workings of such a great city. We now have the uncommon good fortune to be able to say to our acquaintances *'we know some persons that live near Cheapside!'* Would that not be a distinction for us among them?"

Charles could not listen without defending Jane and Elizabeth. With even more courage than before, he stated, "How dreadful the day when our worth as individuals is measured by our relations! I, for one, am not in the least altered in my good opinion of them on this account." He was alone in his stand, however.

Darcy insisted, "Bingley, in their situation and with such relations, their prospect of marrying well is greatly affected."

Charles made no reply to this, but Caroline, at least, heard something to make her smile.

Chapter 7

Later that day when the ladies went upstairs to see Jane, Bingley ventured to take up a subject that had been on his own mind and heart for some time. It was that of *love and marriage,* which he began in this way:

"Darcy, would you say that money should determine the affairs of the heart, or should love?"

"What is the meaning of your question, Charles?"

"Earlier you mentioned that the Bennet sisters have little chance of marrying well because of their lack of fortune and connections. This I am sure you would say holds true for anyone, be they male or female, and that leads me to ask the question: should *money* or *love* determine the affairs of the heart?"

"Love is an emotion," began Darcy, "that must be governed by the mind. Therefore, for reasons of practicality and reasonableness, a person does well to consider carefully before allowing his heart to give in to feelings of love."

"So you allow no room for love to be the reason? I have always supposed love to be one of the strongest things that the world has ever seen!"

"No, you quite mistake my meaning, and you also have failed to take a certain fact into consideration."

"And what fact is that?" asked Bingley, intrigued by his friend's supposition.

"In the world, there seems to be an opposite to everything -- a perfect equal, as it were, only opposite. In the case of which we are speaking, there is *hate*, which has exerted its power in deeds both great and small, and sad to say, is equal in force to *love.*"

"Yes, you are quite right, Darcy; I did not take that into consideration . . . but you spoke of me mistaking your meaning?"

"So many people believe that we are powerless when it comes to love. Let us take the opposite, *hate*. It is perfectly reasonable to believe that we will meet with someone that we hate. When this happens, we are expected, as gentlemen in a civilized society, not to give free reign to this emotion, but to control *it* or *ourselves*, whichever way it might best be said. If it is true of hate, should we not do the same with love? We should exert control of such emotions out of consideration of the consequences of not doing so."

"I follow your reasoning, and your argument is powerful, but since hate is so harmful -- even destructive -- in the context of which we speak, rightfully it should be controlled. And to be sure, love -- without regard for what is right and good -- could bring harmful consequences. But, please remember, Darcy, we are referring to whether we should allow that money be what determines with whom one falls in love."

They were called to tea, which ended the conversation.

However, Darcy, who had been feeling smug at the end of his speech, was shaken from this perch, as Charles' question continued echoing in his mind: '*Should money be what determines with whom one falls in love?*'

He wondered, "Is a lack of fortune to be rated the same as one would a deficiency of character? or some other real evil?" Try as he might, he was unable to call himself to his own sense of self-composure on this subject.

Chapter 8

For the few days that Elizabeth was there under the same roof with Darcy, he found there was something about her spirit and wit that was unique among her sex. He became more and more intrigued by the lady, but he also grew concerned that his partiality for her was beginning to show. It was at least apparent to Caroline, who continually teased him about the Darcy name being connected with such a family as the Bennets. She dwelt with enthusiasm on what would likely be the most potent destroyer of attraction: to have *Mrs. Bennet* for a mother-in-law!

If Darcy had any doubt just how potent Mrs. Bennet could be to that end, he had only to wait till her arrival with her two youngest daughters the next morning. Elizabeth, wanting her mother to make an assessment of Jane's condition, summoned her to Netherfield. This caused a concern on the part of the mother, who came straightaway; but seeing that Jane was in no real danger, Mrs. Bennet now felt easy to proceed to do whatever she could to promote a match with Mr. Bingley and her eldest daughter whilst being there.

Everyone was gathered in the drawing-room to hear the report of Mrs. Bennet and the apothecary, who had arrived at the same time. "Jane was not well enough to be moved home" was the unanimous conclusion of the two, although the mother's reasons were slightly different than that of Mr. Jones. Satisfied that her daughter would be staying awhile longer, Mrs. Bennet quickly moved the conversation away from Jane's condition, to praising Jane's sweet temper, and then on to country living.

"Country living, and Netherfield in particular, must have its attractions for you, Mr. Bingley. I dare say you will be in no hurry of quitting the place."

"I find myself quite happy here, though if I would be off, I would be off in a moment. It is, I suppose, my nature that what I do is always done in a hurry."

Elizabeth observed, "That is the exact picture I have of you, Mr. Bingley!"

"You have seen me through on this short acquaintance, I see, Miss Elizabeth."

"Some characters are more easily made out, and yours is one."

"What a pitiful chap I must be, to be so readily understood. Perhaps there is some way of finding a compliment in it." Darcy, who was intrigued by the subject, was moving closer to the two of them.

"Characters that are more intricate may offer more of a diversion, but that has nothing to do with how estimable one such as yours is," Elizabeth said.

"Thank you, Miss Elizabeth, for finding the compliment. However, I would not have taken you for a studier of character. I had always supposed such a student to be less active and past midlife! This must offer some easy entertainment for you."

Darcy now had to join in the conversation: "The country must be a very limiting place for this, seeing that it is so confined and there is little in the way of diversity in its society."

Turning to him, Elizabeth replied, "Quite as you say, but people themselves change, so there seems to be something new to observe constantly."

This pleasant discussion was now interrupted by Mrs. Bennet, for she was bent on taking anything Mr. Darcy said as an affront. In an ill-mannered and disrespectful tone, she attacked him with, "Sir, you give the country no credit! There is just as much to be found in the country as in town, I assure you!"

Darcy was certainly accustomed to being teased by Caroline, but to be reproached in a manner such as this was *shocking*; indeed everyone in the room felt it. He gazed upon her a moment and turned away, making no reply. This was just the beginning of Darcy witnessing the truthfulness of Caroline's taunting remarks about the mother, for Mrs. Bennet continued exposing herself to be coarse and offensive in manner.

She next turned to Charles, "Mr. Bingley, I know *you* consider country living exceedingly above that of being in London."

Glancing with concern first toward Darcy, he said, "I can find myself pleasantly situated in either, as I can see the advantages of both."

"That is because you have the right disposition. . . that gentleman thinks nothing of the country!"

The mortification of Elizabeth over her mother's ill manners was as one might expect, and addressing her, she politely contradicted, "Indeed, mama, you are mistaken; Mr. Darcy was making no slight of country living. He only meant there are fewer people to be met with in the country than in town, and that is something you must acknowledge as being true."

Then to move away from this topic altogether, she asked about Charlotte Lucas. This effectively changed the subject, but her mother continued to embarrass Lizzy no matter what the topic.

By now, Darcy, who had determined to be only a disinterested listener, heard Elizabeth make a comment that drew him from this posture. It began with Mrs. Bennet rambling on about Jane and some fellow of a much earlier acquaintance, who was showing an interest and had written some poetry verses to her.

Elizabeth, seeing what her mother was about, then stated impatiently, "Thus ended his affection. I wonder who first discovered that writing poetry would result in driving love away!"

It was clear that the statement was made to put an end to her mother's garrulousness; nevertheless, to hear a young lady describe poetry in that manner drew an impulsive response from Darcy: "Poetry, I have always believed, *nourished* love -- not the other way around."

Elizabeth, surprised to hear Darcy speak, replied, "That is the case only when the feelings are strong and established, rather than just an inclination, in which case, a short poem -- or worse, a sonnet -- would drive love away entirely! There appears to be something very unclever in resorting to poetry in the early stages of love."

To be sure, Darcy was no poet, but to be in the presence of a young lady expressing ideas such as this was singular indeed. He contemplated, *"What new surprise will come from her? Will she next declare flowers to be of no value in promoting the feelings of a man for a lady?"* As he smiled at Elizabeth's speech, an additional thought crossed his mind, *"How are the feelings of a lady such as this to be won?"* This musing required that he turn away and look out the window, in order to dismiss it as quickly as it came.

When Mrs. Bennet finally left, Elizabeth went immediately upstairs to Jane, for she did not want to endure the looks of the two ladies of the house after such a demonstration from her mother.

With all the Bennets removed from the room, Mrs. Hurst declared sarcastically, "Mrs. Bennet is the picture of refinement and good manners!"

Her sister responded, "To be sure, Louisa; the man that marries one of the Bennet girls will certainly have a mother-in-law over whom to boast. Would you not say, Mr. Darcy?"

He made no reply, but fully understood her meaning. Not being satisfied with this, she continued, "And of all the uses to which Miss Elizabeth can put her *fine eyes*, she employs them in the study of character! I most certainly agree with her, people do change so much -- it is clear her mother has become more vulgar in just this short time of our acquaintance!"

"Indeed," laughed Louisa, "her study of character has not aided her in learning the ways of a real woman of fashion."

The two ladies found great amusement at the expense of the Bennet women, while Darcy, to whom most of these comments were directed, remained aloof. He would not join them in their berating of Elizabeth and her mother. What he saw of Mrs. Bennet, however, was enough to give him pause. The abuse of Mrs. Hurst and Caroline did have this effect as well: he felt pained for Elizabeth, seeing how embarrassing it was for her to endure her mother behaving in such a way. Although he felt empathy, he was not interested in making a defense of her against such pretentious persons as Caroline and her sister, however.

He had his own struggles about Elizabeth to contend with, and these feelings were making him very uncomfortable.

Chapter 9

As Jane's health improved, Elizabeth was allowed to spend more time downstairs with the others, and indeed, even Jane herself joined them after a time. To Lizzy, the satisfaction of seeing her sister given the warm attention of Bingley was almost worth the trouble of enduring his sisters.

On one evening, Elizabeth was asked to join the group at cards. She responded that she would prefer a book, which led Bingley to this observation, "I am amazed at the patience of young ladies, to be so accomplished as they all are."

"All young ladies!" was Caroline's objection.

"Yes, indeed, *all.* What young lady is there that does not paint tables, cover screens, and make purses? These are lovely accomplishments, I dare say."

Darcy expressed his disapproval, "With such a paltry list as this, you are perfectly right, Charles, although in my estimation more would be required for a lady to deserve the description. I can only count half a dozen such women in the whole range of my acquaintance."

Miss Bingley, always seeking to be Darcy's confederate, said, "As can I, I am sure."

Elizabeth uttered cynically, "Mr. Darcy, you make me half frightened to ask for your list of just what makes a woman accomplished."

Caroline, wanting to demonstrate to Darcy how alike they thought on the subject, hurried to answer first, saying condescendingly, "My dear Miss Eliza, for a woman to be esteemed truly accomplished she must greatly surpass what is commonly to be found. She must possess a thorough knowledge of music, singing, dancing, and even be well-versed in the modern languages. Of course, there must be that special something in her air and manner of walking, tone of voice, proper address and expressions."

To this, Darcy added what he felt was most important: "And there must be something more substantial . . . the improvement of her mind by extensive reading."

Elizabeth listened to this extraordinary list perfectly composed in countenance, and then pointedly said, "It is a marvel that you know six such women; I would doubt there being a single one."

Darcy responded, "What a surprising comment you make upon your own sex, not allowing for such women to exist."

"My statement was not meant to be severe on womankind; rather, it was a reference to the list of accomplishments you deemed necessary before bestowing the title of *accomplished.*"

Mrs. Hurst and Caroline both cried, "Miss Elizabeth, we assure you there are many among our acquaintance that fit this description."

They chose the wrong person with whom to be so contradictory! Unintimidated, Elizabeth said, "How strange then, your first agreeing with Mr. Darcy of knowing only six such women, to now knowing many."

The consternation on Miss Bingley's face was as far as this was taken, for Mr. Hurst called their attention back to the card table. It was necessary, though, for Darcy to hide a smile as he said to himself, "How often I had wanted to point out Caroline's contradictions in her efforts to make herself agreeable. It could not have been done more ably just now."

* * * * *

For the remaining days, many a conversation was had between Elizabeth, Bingley, Darcy and Caroline on various topics. Even a bit of teasing took place between Caroline, Elizabeth and Darcy on the subject of 'taking a turn about the room.' During these occasions, Darcy admired how well she endured the rudeness of Caroline and Mrs. Hurst. He was very impressed, when engaging her in some repartee, at how equal she was in defending her views with such cleverness, even against his own.

An instance of this occurred in the evening of the very day Mrs. Bennet had come to Netherfield. Darcy declared that Charles had been making an indirect boast when he told Mrs. Bennet that 'he could leave Netherfield in the turn of a moment.'

Charles retorted, "Do you write down my words, Darcy, in order to use them against me in moments such as this?"

"Oh, Charles!" cried Caroline, "do be serious. Must you carry on this way?"

"Be serious? When being called to account for a statement that was made in the morning, which one would certainly have forgotten by evening? But if you would have it so, then let me affirm, Darcy, that I would indeed be off in a moment, had I the inclination."

"I dare say you would, Charles, and if, while you were mounting your horse, a friend were to ask you to stay, you would just as readily dismount."

Elizabeth broke in, "Mr. Darcy, in finding fault with your friend, you have instead paid him a compliment."

"Your defense of me is quite admirable, Miss Elizabeth, for there is not one in a hundred that can take Darcy's statement and make it a reference to my sweetness of temper. Although, I might be better thought of by him if I were to ride off leaving this supposed friend behind."

"Would Mr. Darcy find more rational meaning in your being obstinate in sticking to your first decision?"

"Being obstinate might very well be considered more rational by Darcy, but that is something he would have to say for himself."

Darcy could hardly keep quiet at this: "I would first point out that it is not I who have used the word *obstinate*. However, be that as it may, what great merit is there in acquiescing to a friend who has offered no reason for Bingley to alter his plan? As it is presented by you, Miss Bennet, the mere asking of a friend should take precedence over the reason for his leaving."

"The appeal of a friend, and to yield to it, is of no merit with you then, Mr. Darcy?"

"To submit without reason seems to do no justice to the requester nor to the one yielding. Surely a person is not expected to be always changing his mind simply because a friend asks."

"Is not the weight of friendship and affection reason enough? Whoever they are, must a person wait for arguments in favor of not leaving, from the request of someone that is highly regarded, before yielding? We will have to wait for a full set of circumstances in the case of Mr. Bingley before concluding what his actions would reveal, but do you think less of a person because his regard for a friend moves him to alter his plans in a moment?"

"You are failing to take into account that not all friendships carry the same weight; our attachment to everyone we might call a friend is not the same. Would we not do well to be more particular on these points, as well as what the reason for the planned departure is, before continuing?"

This was a bit too much for Bingley, who disliked anything that resembled an argument. "Have we not had enough of this imaginary departure of mine, or that of anyone else?"

Darcy smiled and said, "Of course, you are right, Charles, and I had better finish my letter."

After some time had passed, to the astonishment of Elizabeth, Darcy asked her to dance when Caroline was playing a lively Scottish tune on the piano forte. His eyes had been keenly fixed on Elizabeth, who seemed to be ignoring him, and he felt that now seemed as good a time as any to ask her to dance. At first, she gave no reply, but after his repeating the offer, she declined.

"This is the second time she has turned me down, and with an apparent attempt to affront me. How *does* she manage to disappoint and intrigue simultaneously?" he thought. There was a mixture of feminine sweetness and uncommon sauciness in her that captivated him beyond his ability to comprehend.

"Would I still be struggling with these feelings if her station in life was higher?"

The man that had recently declared to Bingley, "*Men should not be rendered powerless by love*" seemed powerless over his growing admiration for Elizabeth Bennet; and for Darcy, this was something new and quite distressing. So caught up was he in this conflict, he was left without perception of the feelings of the lady, for Elizabeth had developed a decided *dislike* of him. She considered him ill-tempered and disagreeable. To be sure, she was too fine a woman to express such feelings; but just as certainly, she gave him no encouragement in the established ways of men and women in matters of the heart.

* * * * *

Jane was finally well enough to go home, which was a relief to Elizabeth, for she was despised by the ladies of the house. It brought relief to Miss Bingley, because where matters of the heart are concerned, any rival will be unwanted, and her feelings of jealousy were growing, even though Elizabeth was unaware of the gentleman's interest in her.

Darcy was also relieved and was able to rally himself enough to ignore Elizabeth in such a way, he was sure that if she had some inkling of his inclination, it would be put to an end by his actions on this last day of her being at Netherfield.

Indeed, as Jane and Elizabeth were escorted to the carriage by Bingley, Darcy made it a point to be absent. However, he was drawn to the window by an urging that would not be suppressed. As he saw her from this safe distance, his mind was filled with wonder at how Elizabeth, a person of no rank or consequence, could enthrall him so.

Every effort any other lady had made to make herself pleasing to him had the opposite effect. He felt contempt at being the object of any lady's wiles and arts. This sort of social sport was something Darcy had not become adept at.

The falseness of it all caused him to protest inwardly, "How is a man to know with whom he is becoming acquainted?"

In Elizabeth, though, he found a young lady unimpressed by who he was, someone who cared more for character, and who had a wit not often found in her sex. Oh, it could be said that she would not answer for his description of a truly accomplished woman. . .

. . . but just as truthfully, it could be said, he had never met her equal.

Chapter 10

Charles had promised to give a ball as soon as Jane was well. The ladies of Netherfield, on first hearing of this, did not consider it with pleasure. But at the prospect of showing the locals just how a ball is to be done, they took up the project in earnest. As a consequence, Darcy was confronted with the prospect of seeing Elizabeth again soon, and in such a setting as a ball, where more would be required than just a civil acknowledgement.

This gave rise to a most unusual debate in his mind. "Should I ask her to dance at this public affair, or should I continue to ignore her? Not to ask her might seem an attempt at insulting her, and such a slight as this does not seem appropriate . . . but if I ask too soon, it could give the appearance of being eager to dance with her. Of course, I *have* asked her to dance twice and have been refused on both occasions, so if I ask a third time, will it seem I am pursuing her? . . . no, it is a ball after all, being held in *my* particular friend's home, surely I must ask her to dance . . . but I should do so after the dancing has been underway for some time, so it will appear to be a simple gesture of dancing with an acquaintance, and not give her or anyone else a reason to think more of it than that."

Darcy did not consider what such premeditation on the simple act of asking a lady to dance implied about his feelings for the lady; he was only too glad to have worked out a scheme that he could be comfortable with.

Bingley, looking for an excuse to see Jane, approached Darcy with the idea of doing his duty and calling on the Bennets to see how their eldest daughter was feeling.

"Do you not think that it seems the proper thing to do, Darcy?"

"Indeed, Charles, it does."

"Then, will you do me the favor of accompanying me?"

Darcy felt it would do him good to see Elizabeth in this way before the ball. After all, he was confident that he was the master of his emotions and could meet Elizabeth with indifference. So they rode out on this beautiful day that would best be spent out-of-doors.

On this very day, Jane and her sisters had taken their cousin, Mr. Collins, to see their Aunt Phillips in Meryton. The Bennets had received their cousin as a visitor from Kent, he being the rector of Hunsford, under the patronage of Lady Catherine de Bourgh. The Bennet manor was entailed to the next male heir, this very Mr. Collins, which would leave the women of the family with nothing at Mr. Bennet's death.

Riding through Meryton, Bingley and Darcy came upon Jane and her sisters involved in conversation with an officer, a clergyman and another gentleman, so they rode toward them. Although Darcy felt he was prepared for meeting Elizabeth, there was someone in the group that he was *not* prepared to meet.

The fellow's name was George Wickham, and the very sight of him made Darcy's face fill with contempt, which no one noticed but Elizabeth. Darcy obeyed his instincts and prompted his horse to move on at once, though Bingley was still in conversation with Jane.

Observing that his friend had gone ahead, Bingley felt compelled to follow after him. Upon catching up with him, he at first was determined to mention his friend's rudeness, till he saw that Darcy was perturbed.

Before Bingley could say anything, Darcy began with agitation, "I beg your pardon, Charles, for leaving so abruptly. I know it was quite discourteous, but when I caught sight of that man, George Wickham -- for he is no gentleman and I will never call him such -- I could not tolerate a moment in his company!"

Bingley responded in an understanding and sympathetic manner, "So this is the Wickham from your childhood that you've told me about?" He added unconsciously, "He certainly is striking in appearance, I must say."

"Yes, and his charms are equal to his appearance! However, he is an unprincipled scoundrel in equal measure to his looks and charms!"

These words were spoken with more feeling than a person was accustomed to hear from Darcy, even his good friend Bingley, whose kind heart went out to him. He knew that his friend was truly disturbed at this development, and knowing Darcy was not one for dwelling on such things openly, they simply rode on in silence.

When the two gentlemen arrived at Netherfield, Darcy expressed a desire to continue out-of-doors. Bingley rode on to the stable, and Darcy located a comfortable place under a great tree that afforded a very pleasing vista, although the view did not interest him. He wanted to be alone and was not in any mood for Caroline's teasing, if she was so inclined, as she often was when she knew he had been in company with Elizabeth.

His mind was full of the perverseness of *that man,* George Wickham, not only being in the vicinity, but also his becoming acquainted with the Bennets. Any thought of Elizabeth being imposed upon by such an unscrupulous person did not enter his mind, for every thought was overthrown by the shock of simply seeing Wickham. It now seemed more possible than ever that Darcy would not only hear of Wickham, but also see the man. He did have a momentary impulse to leave the area out of revulsion at this looming prospect, but he quickly resolved to ignore Wickham's presence as one ignores a yapping dog behind a fence.

"After all, Wickham is nothing to me, and he is forming an acquaintance with persons whom Bingley is getting close to, not I," he said to himself.

He began to think he had given him too much thought already, but when one's feelings have been so deeply affected as Darcy's had in the past by Wickham, it would be impossible to do otherwise.

Chapter 11

The day of the Netherfield ball arrived, and at the house there was plenty of bustling around. The two men were being applied to for their respective opinions, and wherever it was possible, Caroline was sure to defer to Darcy's. The men felt all the need of making the place presentable, they just cared less about it than the ladies.

Finally making some excuse that took them from the commotion, Bingley and Darcy retreated into the library, each sitting in his own easy chair. Bingley, filled with eager anticipation for the evening's amusements, especially the prospect of spending so much time with Jane, began to ramble on about his plans for the evening.

Darcy pretended to listen, but his mind was occupied with the probability of George Wickham soon being under the same roof. He knew Charles could not exclude him from the general invitation extended to the officers, so he would just have to endure it. Added to this, there was a growing concern that he had not considered at first seeing Wickham; he began feeling uneasy about *Wickham* becoming acquainted with Elizabeth.

He now found himself struggling with his two resolutions - - ignoring Wickham, and conquering his feelings for Elizabeth. How could he not think of Elizabeth being taken in by Wickham's charms? Although they had been introduced, it did not necessarily follow that they would be in each other's company very much. Hence, Darcy concluded that any more consideration on the matter at this time was fruitless, and he must wait till the ball to observe for himself without further conjecture.

Bingley ended their hiatus in the library by a suggestion that they go to the kitchen, for he knew the cook had been preparing a most refreshing punch from a selection of his favorite berries. The two gentlemen spent the rest of the time before the ball making themselves useful in whatever way the ladies deemed necessary.

That evening as the guests began arriving, the family properly positioned themselves at the entrance in order to greet each one as they were directed into the drawing-room. Darcy, though, placed himself in an adjoining room. Being most uncomfortable at this sort of thing, he remained there until he saw that an ample number of persons had arrived, and then quietly slipped into the drawing-room. Since the people in general did not care for him, he was in no danger of being spoken to, leaving him free to make concealed observations about Elizabeth and Wickham.

When he first beheld Elizabeth, he was unable to see or notice anyone else. He began to rouse himself, however. "I feel like a silly schoolboy smitten by seeing his first pretty girl. What nonsense all of this is!"

He resolved upon moving to another part of the room and putting thoughts of Wickham and Elizabeth out of his mind, or at least attempting to do so. Caroline, though, noticing what direction he was looking, put her own predetermined plan into motion. Not wanting to lose the advantage of being near him, she stepped to his side, and taking his arm, requested, "Mr. Darcy, you must spare me from being asked to dance by one of the local men -- or worse, one of the officers!" Her feigning to be a lady in peril did not move him, but he was glad of the distraction.

Caroline spent most of the dance reproaching Charles: "It was abominable of my brother to have such persons into our home! I do not believe he will ever apprehend the need to be discriminating in his taste. I will be glad to be mistress of my own home one day, so that proper preference on who enters will be exercised. Being only the sister, you know, it is difficult to have one's opinion given much weight. As you were witness to, I exerted myself toward that end, but to no avail; Charles was determined to be generous in his invitations."

"It seems he was directed in this by his not wishing to offend by excluding anyone," Darcy offered in a half-hearted attempt at defending Charles.

"And this is the very thing of which I speak! People of consequence care little about offending people such as these."

Miss Bingley truly did not understand Darcy; she felt comments such as these would appeal to his sense of superiority and make it clear how similar they were. But he was not interested in a haughty wife that would only get more puffed up if she were to become mistress of Pemberley.

After the dance with Caroline, Darcy moved aimlessly about the room. It became clear to him that Wickham had not come; now he recalled his scheme of asking Elizabeth to dance. Though he was perturbed at himself by what he deemed to be juvenile behavior earlier, Elizabeth held an attraction for him; and whether he would admit it or not, he was not going to let the evening pass without dancing with her.

He therefore approached as she happened to be speaking to Charlotte Lucas and applied for her hand in the next dance. Elizabeth, taken by surprise, would have declined the application, but did not. It seems the atmosphere of a ball predisposes all young ladies to accept an invitation to dance, even someone as keen as Elizabeth, for she certainly would rather not stand up with him. Having received her acceptance to the request, however, Mr. Darcy excused himself immediately to await the start of the set, and soon enough, they found themselves together on the dance floor.

Darcy was not conscience of the looks and whispers of many in the room as he was observed escorting Miss Elizabeth Bennet to the dance floor. Everyone there recognized her as one of the finest women in the area; still for Darcy to single her out, the compliment was apparent to all.

In an effort to demonstrate his indifference toward her and this entire arrangement, Darcy began by being silent, and at first, Elizabeth was just as determined to be silent for the two dances. Soon, however, the absurdity of not talking while dancing struck her, and then her mischievous nature took hold

... she considered there would be some amusement in actually obliging him to speak.

"This is an excellent dance for the number of couples on the floor," she began, and then made any number of witty references to it.

"Indeed," was all Darcy would say in response. This only served to fuel Lizzy's playful disposition.

"There is a certain responsibility one accepts upon asking a young lady to dance, Mr. Darcy, and as I have started a topic for conversation, I believe it now falls to you to say something in return."

He smiled, "I am perfectly ready to say whatever it is you wish to be said."

"That is convenient, for it would appear quite strange to be silent for a whole half an hour. But I would not wish to tax you beyond your ability, and since something has been said between us, we can now be silent for the next ten minutes."

More was at work here than just Darcy's wish of being seen as unaffected by her. He found his powers of trivial conversation sadly lacking, and his purpose in asking Elizabeth to dance was unraveling before his ineptitude, for her quips were making him feel uncomfortable with his laconic attitude.

He now became desirous of starting a topic of conversation and, as often happens when one is in a situation reaching for something to say, he introduced a subject that would better have been left alone ... "Do you often walk into Meryton?"

Elizabeth could not resist using this opportunity of seeing how Darcy would respond to the subject uppermost in her mind. Since their fateful meeting that day in Meryton, Wickham had informed Elizabeth that he had been raised with Darcy at Pemberley, because his father had the management of that estate. He further told her that Darcy had, by virtue of neglecting his father's will, reduced him to his present state of relative poverty, instead of giving him a valuable family living when it became open. This intelligence had served to make Elizabeth's opinion of Darcy go from bad to worse.

"Yes," she replied archly, "the day you saw us, we were making a new acquaintance, a *Mr. Wickham.*" It had the effect of drawing upon his countenance the same disdain she had observed the first time. She saw this discomfort and was not proud of herself for causing him pain.

There was a moment's hesitation, but at last Darcy spoke, trying to sound composed, "Making friends for Mr. Wickham has always been easy; keeping friends has proved to be more of a challenge for him."

This comment drove the feeling of regret she had felt towards causing Darcy any pain away, for she believed it revealed his meanness as related by Wickham. With strong feeling, she replied, "The loss of *your* friendship is something he will suffer from for the rest of his life!"

In this situation, Darcy did not handle himself well. He had not anticipated being confronted by Elizabeth with the subject of Wickham, nor was he prepared for her willingness to defend him. As they parted, he felt his own disappointment keenly. It was all the more disturbing as he had intended the dance to be a demonstration of his indifference, if not for others to observe, at least for himself.

Now, instead, he found he could think only of Elizabeth. Darcy could forgive her feelings in defending Wickham, because he knew how the man could appeal to people, especially a lady. His ability to manipulate persons and situations was something Darcy had seen before.

Walking to a window to get some air, his mind returned to his teen years and the time that he had confided to Wickham his interest in getting to know a certain *Emma Elliott.* Darcy's nervousness, coupled with the stiffness of his manner, was holding him back from speaking to her. To show up Darcy's inferiority in such matters and to spite him, George had demonstrated just how easy it was for him to do what Darcy *wished* he could do himself. Before he knew what Wickham was doing, Emma had become infatuated with *him.* Darcy recalled just how painful it was to see Emma's hurt and scorn, when Wickham, tiring of this game, told her falsely that it was all related to a dare presented by Darcy.

He could recall many such occasions where Wickham used his natural talents to make Darcy feel inferior. All this had the effect of deepening his reticence. It also caused him to develop greater pride in his rank than he would have been inclined to by nature; in effect, he reasoned: "Wickham may have been blessed with *that,* but I have *this.*"

Darcy's father, seeing this and not knowing its true source, felt it only proper that a *Darcy of Pemberley* should sense the family's position, and so encouraged it. In addition, Darcy gave himself over to improving his mind and controlling his emotions to avoid exposing himself to the pain of these situations. This only served to create a greater appearance of pride and prejudice. Now, whereas he had rejoiced in the success of his personal efforts and the comfort and safety it brought, this night he wished he had directed his energies towards improving his abilities at social intercourse.

After spending enough time in self-reflection, he moved away from the window, only to see Bingley with Jane, which was the case for most of the evening. Seeing Sir William Lucas, Darcy recalled his earlier mentioning the commonly held view of Charles and Jane being married sometime in the near future. Indeed, his was not the only voice to be heard on the subject. Knowing Bingley's open-hearted manner and Mrs. Bennet's expressed desire to do anything so that her daughters would catch the attention of a rich man, he began developing a deep concern for his friend.

With this intelligence in mind, he decided he should try to discern the strength of Bingley's interest for Jane, as well as Jane's for his friend. This brought some much needed relief to him, as it gave him employment for the concern of someone other than himself.

It was in this activity that he spent the rest of the evening.

Chapter 12

The next day found Bingley leaving for London on business. When he had quitted the house, Caroline and Mrs. Hurst approached Darcy in a most distressed and agitated state. Their brother's continued and increasing regard for Jane Bennet had gone far enough, and the sisters determined it was time to put an end to it!

"Mr. Darcy, you simply *must* assist us on a mission requiring immediate action!"

"In what way do you need assistance?" he asked. Caroline always seemed too eager to appeal to Darcy on any subject great or small, and it usually had the effect of drawing an inaudible yawn on his part; but on this occasion, he found she was raising a subject that was already occupying his own mind.

"On the matter of Charles and Jane Bennet. She is a lovely girl, to be sure, but to be a match for our brother is ridiculous! Do you not agree? And last night, to have the subject talked of by people in general, especially that obnoxiously vulgar Mrs. Bennet -- and in our own home, as if the matter had already been settled -- it is too much to be borne!"

"Yes," replied Darcy, "the subject was much talked of last night, and Charles seems quite taken with her. I find myself deeply concerned about it as well, but I do not think he would have made an offer without consulting me. In matters of great importance, Charles always talks things over with me. I believe we are not too late, but we must follow him to London, whereby we can make good use of this momentary separation."

Therefore, Darcy and the rest of the Netherfield party set off to London the very next day behind Mr. Bingley. They felt it best on initially seeing him that they simply say the ladies wanted to take advantage of this opportunity to go into town themselves and hoped they could stay for a few days instead of hurrying back, as Charles had first intended. Of course, he welcomed their company, although he was surprised at their sudden appearance. But whenever he was applied to by his sisters, Charles was always ready to oblige them, even though his heart, on this occasion, was strongly tugging him back to Netherfield.

After having concluded his business, however, Bingley could talk of little else than returning there. All the while, the three conspirators were stealing knowing glances, and to own the truth, there was a look of concern on all their faces, as they had testimony before them that their task was not going to be an easy one.

Taking Darcy aside, Miss Bingley implored, "We must act to prevent my brother from entering into such an alliance! The thought of us having such coarse relations is positively maddening!"

Confessing his own concerns about his friend, Darcy replied, "Yes, I can see he has grown quite attached to Jane Bennet. The idea of Charles being so close to the influence of Mrs. Bennet -- heaven only knows what entanglements might await him! In addition to that, I am convinced Miss Bennet does not really love your brother, but is being pushed into this relationship by her mother, simply to raise the family's prospects. And I am determined that Charles not enter into a loveless marriage." The two ladies readily agreed with Mr. Darcy's assessment of this matter.

Hence, later in the afternoon, after they had quitted the dining-room and were having coffee, Darcy thus began the subject: "Charles, may I speak frankly to you on a matter that is of serious concern to the three of us?"

Looking at his friend and two sisters earnestly, he replied, "Upon my word, how solemn the three of you look! Pray, what is this all about?"

"Our concern involves you and Miss Bennet. You may not be aware that at the ball, the subject of the two of you being soon married was considered as quite settled. You have not made her an offer of marriage, have you?"

"Oh, Darcy, you know very well how people will talk about matters that do not concern themselves. But, no, I have not made her an offer; I would not do so without discussing something that significant over with you."

Caroline was on the verge of expressing her views with all the strength that a sister with her disposition can, but when she heard the business was not as far along as was feared and saw her brother's willingness to talk things out with Darcy, she held her tongue and allowed him to continue.

"I agree with you, Charles; people often speak of things that are not their business. But those types of busybodies were not the only ones talking about the subject. Rather, persons very close to the case were expressing themselves quite decidedly. Mrs. Bennet was heard to say how advantageous your marriage would be for Jane as well as the other Bennet girls, stating emphatically that 'they would be introduced by you to other rich men.' In truth, our great concern is that Jane is being pushed into this simply to bring up the fortunes of the family."

"Really, Darcy, is this the first time such a thing is heard of, a mother trying to make a match for her children?"

"No, not at all. Only consider what you and I were talking of just the other day, your establishing a legacy for those to come after you. With such connections as the Bennets, would you say your future would be made more secure?"

"Darcy, please, you are being too dramatic in the effect such a marriage alliance can have."

"Charles, this is not meant as an affront to you, but your sisters have often mentioned how your sweetness of temper and open-heartedness can make you forget some responsibilities you owe to yourself and your family, both the present and that to come. You must not close your eyes to the potential stress upon your resources that marrying into a family with little fortune can have. If you could but envision having as sisters the youngest Bennet girls, not to mention someone as ridiculous as the mother, intruding into your life, and what grief that would bring! Understand, I am not speaking of the annoyance of having Mrs. Bennet's ill-mannered ways near you -- your temperament may tolerate such a mother-in-law. In particular, I am referring to what schemes she may try foisting upon you in an effort to improve the situation of her younger daughters."

"Surely, you do not believe me so weak as to not be able to stand up to a mother-in-law."

"I am quite ready to grant you are capable of that, but now add the strong desire of wanting to please a beloved wife whose voice would certainly be joined to her mother's, and I assure you, you would not be the first man who could not."

Charles, becoming agitated, stood and turned away in a gesture of objection to what he was hearing.

Darcy continued, "If you doubt how difficult it could be, Charles, only consider how your heart is worked on when your sisters ask something of you -- can you honestly think your heart would not feel the same pull?"

"Indeed, Charles," cried Caroline, "but with Louisa and me, you have persons who are interested in guarding you. With Jane under the influence of her mother, you will not have that same concern for either yourself, or even -- dare I say? -- our family's welfare."

The vision of ruining the family prospects by such an alliance as portrayed by Darcy, who Charles would take as eminently qualified to address such a subject, coupled with the more established and greater feelings he had for his sisters than he felt at this time for Jane, was beginning to work on him.

Darcy, though, felt the expressed evils of such a match might be done away with somehow if simply left at that, so he decided to introduce what he believed was, for Bingley, an even weightier reason: "Charles, there is one other thing that troubles me to a greater degree than what I have already pointed out."

Charles exclaimed, "There is something that troubles you more! What could be worse than possibly blasting my family's fortune and reputation?"

"It has to do with Miss Bennet's feelings toward you."

At this, Charles looked directly at his friend. "What is this you have to say, Darcy? Please, tell me what it is that concerns you so."

"Let me ask: would you want to marry someone who did not truly love you? Someone who would be marrying you only for your fortune and what it can do for her family? Would you not want as a wife someone that loves *you*, and not one that is being pushed into this relationship by a scheming mother?"

"I believe Jane cares for me and is not the sort to be mercenary, as you describe."

This response made Darcy feel certain that he was right to cover all his concerns about the match. "I did not describe her as mercenary; her mother, on the other hand, I would. Unfortunately, I do believe Jane to be motivated chiefly by a love for her family, and not you."

"Darcy, you must be mistaken. I believe Jane cares for me and the case is not as you describe."

"Oh, to be sure, she is exceedingly flattered to be singled out by you, especially when every unmarried lady in the town had entertained hopes of being so. But consider how unanimated her countenance is even when she is with you -- she appears to be someone doing her duty, and not one whose emotions are roused. In short, she is not as moved by you as you are by her."

Caroline once again spoke up: "Charles, the entire time that Louisa and I spent with her, you were not the subject of her conversation, and a woman truly in love cannot help but speak of the object of her love. She admired the furnishings, and the grandeur of the house, and how fine it would be to be thus situated, but really, she had very little to say about you."

Mrs. Hurst confirmed the saying, and with all the warmth of a sister added, "My dear Charles, you have one of the most tender hearts that beats in a man; the one thing you should have is a wife that loves you for this. If you married Jane Bennet, certainly you would have a wife with a mild disposition, but I'm afraid it would be one that would not give you what is most cherished in marriage -- her heart in return."

As the three continued talking, Bingley's regard and reliance on Darcy's judgement, combined with his ductile nature, began to convince him that Miss Bennet's regard for him was not what he had made himself believe it to be. This, coupled with their other points of concern, was such that Charles had to sit. His previous agitation was giving way, his strength was drained. A quarter hour more and it was completely done: Bingley could take no more, and as a true gentleman, he thanked them for the trouble they had taken to speak to him and retired for the evening.

Charles did not know just how devious his sisters could be, and it was not in his nature to suspect that their intelligence about their private conversations with Jane was not true. The sisters spent some time triumphing over their success in keeping their brother and themselves out of a degrading alliance, and had absolutely no feelings of compunction over their actions.

But Darcy, having spoken what he believed to be true, found no delight in seeing the pain on his friend's face. He did find comfort in saving his friend from the designs of such a woman as Mrs. Bennet, however, for he really believed this was all *her* doing.

* * * * *

The next morning found Bingley out-of-sorts, as one might imagine. His sisters, though, were in such high spirits it was difficult for him to bear. Feeling for his friend, Darcy exerted himself to draw the ladies away under some pretense of wanting their opinion on a new hat he was contemplating to pair with one of his coats. The scheme worked well enough for Bingley to finish his breakfast in peace, though he did not have much of an appetite.

After breakfast, Darcy asked if he would like to take the morning air and stroll into the park that was in easy distance. Bingley, truly distracted, replied, "No thank you, I feel encumbered indoors; I shall walk to the park."

Mrs. Hurst and Caroline were amused by their brother's response, but Darcy understood the meaning and suggested that 'it is a fine day for it,' only asking 'if he would like some company, or would he prefer to be alone?' Bingley wished for the latter, and so took his leave.

Darcy likewise felt the need to leave the company of Caroline, as he was not in the mood to be the object of her attention. He simply did not have the spirit for it, knowing his friend was in pain. To be sure, he felt that he had done a real service for his friend, and considering the shortness of the acquaintance, he didn't think it would be long before his friend returned to his old self.

Of course, if Darcy had underestimated the strength of Bingley's attachment, then his calculation of the depth and duration of Bingley's pain would not only be in error, but the benefit of his service to him could rightly be called into question. Darcy would therefore have to wait and see just how much time would pass before Charles would return to his old self.

Chapter 13

As the days passed, Bingley could at least not *look* so forlorn, which was comforting to Darcy, who was leaving town shortly. Before his departure, however, Caroline informed him of having learned that Jane Bennet was in town. She felt it wise to conceal this news from Charles, and Darcy agreed. The more time that passed with Bingley not seeing or hearing about Jane, the better it would be for him to forget her.

Darcy's cousin, Colonel Fitzwilliam, was to meet him soon in London, and from there the pair were to pay their annual visit to their aunt, Lady Catherine de Bourgh. They did not begrudge their duty to their aunt, but neither was it an occasion that gave them the greatest pleasure; so it was convenient that they do their duty together, as they often managed to do.

The colonel came later that week, and after spending the night, they rose early the next morning to travel by carriage. During the first part of their journey through the city, the cousins were not much in the mood for conversation. But when they found themselves out in the open countryside, they were then inclined to enjoy some catching up, as it had been some time since last they had seen one another.

Close in age as they were, they had much in common, except that Darcy, being the only son, had inherited Pemberley estates and was therefore independent; whereas, the colonel, being the youngest son, did not have the same resources at his disposal.

After talking for some time about pleasant things, Darcy mentioned that he had seen George Wickham, who was well-known to the colonel, and related that it was clear that he had not improved himself either materially or in his character.

To this the colonel responded, "Why is it that men of that sort never seem to learn that their misconduct will continue to reap the same results? A person with any sense would not take so long to comprehend that."

"I do not believe the problem is with sense," said Darcy. "I would call it a lack of moral fiber. It takes a lack of good morals to proceed down such a course to begin with, and from what I have observed, men of that sort tend to get worse. If they learn anything, it is how to be more devious."

"I must concur, because it seems that nothing -- not even the love of a good lady -- affects their conduct. I have often wondered at the bad choices many young ladies seem to make when it comes to marriage to such men."

Taking up this new subject, Darcy said, "It seems that even when presented with good sense, many will not take it up, whether man or woman. But I am glad to say that I was recently able to be of service to a good friend on that very point." For some reason he was unsure of, Darcy felt he should keep the good friend's identity to himself.

"Really, how so?"

"My friend was forming an attachment with someone that was sure to bring him misery; but thankfully, I was able to bring him to his senses before he had become too entangled in his feelings for the lady."

"What was the cause of your concern, Darcy?"

"Let me just say, there were things about the lady that he was not thinking through. Men are often in the habit of not thinking when their heart has been touched. Obviously, there is a certain amount of pain associated with that sort of separation, but far less than what he would have experienced if I had not prevented him from establishing such a connection."

Being as close to the subject of Elizabeth as he now was, Darcy could not help but mention her, though not wanting to reveal there was any connection between what they had been discussing and Elizabeth. So changing the subject, he said, "This calls to mind, on the subject of ladies, I met a truly unusual young lady recently. She is lovely, to say the least, but she is remarkable in other ways that make her truly fascinating."

"Oh, really -- *fascinating?* -- whatever do you mean?" The colonel's interest was aroused at the mention of a lovely young lady; but to hear *Darcy* speak of a lady in terms of admiration was unusual indeed.

"To begin with, you know how young ladies are always stumbling over each other whenever a single man with a fortune or title is in the room? They are so eager to make themselves agreeable that their conversation becomes insipid and dull. This you will not find with Miss Elizabeth Bennet. She has a ready wit and powers of observation that are most intriguing, and even challenging."

With warmth of feeling, he continued, "I must say, Fitzwilliam, when she sits down to the piano forte and sings, she has a way of pleasing a whole room. To be sure, she is not the most accomplished at the instrument, and her voice has not been trained by a professional tutor, but nevertheless, she has a most pleasing talent for entertaining in that cozy environment after dinner."

"What of her family, Darcy?" the colonel asked, interested in probing further.

Darcy hesitated in answering this, not knowing how to begin or even how much to venture to say on the subject. He could talk of Elizabeth with real delight and respect, but the subject of her family always seemed to give rise to such a contrast of feelings. To him, it was unjust that she should have such a family. He determined to answer in this fashion: "Her family, unfortunately, is of no consequence. Her father is a gentleman, but no more. The family living is entailed away from his children, and therefore, their circumstances are not promising."

"That is unfortunate!" cried the colonel. But wishing to change the tone of the conversation because he could see the lady's situation affected Darcy, he added, "If she is as you describe, cousin, I wonder -- could we manage for her to be at our aunt's? For such would be a welcomed diversion!"

This prospect made Darcy smile, though it seemed impossible. He, however, had failed to consider that the possibility was very real. The two traveled on, discussing first one thing and then another, till they found themselves approaching the grounds of Rosings.

Chapter 14

Arriving there late in the afternoon, they were welcomed by Lady Catherine with effusions of pleasure mixed with recommendations on what they ought to have done for their journey.

This left them not knowing whether to return her expressions of pleasure or express their determination to follow her advice. The seeming predicament did not last above half a moment, as the great Lady quickly moved on to instructions as to what they should do next to prepare for the evening.

Before they were able to quit the room to follow their aunt's directives, however, she added with an air that showed she had just realized her orders were making the cousins neglect her daughter, Anne, who was concealed behind her mother -- "Darcy, Colonel, you have failed to take notice of Anne."

"Yes, forgive us, cousin Anne. It is lovely to see you again." She made them a slight bow, and the two were then off to dress for the evening.

Darcy, in his apartment, reflected on one aspect of the visit that always troubled him. . . his aunt continued in her determination that he and Anne form a marriage alliance. He had never entertained such a foolish concept for himself, and could recall how he felt when his mother and Lady Catherine would speak of it when he was a young boy. His spirit would always rise at such a prospect, and through the years it had hardened into a resolve.

Thankfully, his mother would notice the concerned look on young Darcy's face after Lady Catherine would speak of the plans to him directly, and she would always console him with promises of his being free to marry whomever he chose. She was always more inclined for her son's happiness than any disappointment to herself or her sister.

Perhaps if Anne had been more amiable, active, and attractive, these charms would have worked at weakening his initial objections as they grew up, but such was not the case. Their being so different, she held no attraction to him, and he held none for her. So at least between the two, Lady Catherine's references had the same effect, although in Anne's case, she would not have the will to go against her mother's schemes, should Darcy be of a mind to make the alliance.

Darcy's musings were interrupted by his noticing the hour and the need to go down for supper. He now hurriedly joined the party.

The conversation at table consisted of what would not pass for conversation anywhere else. Lady Catherine was talking on from one subject to another without any seeming connection. Her nature would not permit her audience to blissfully ignore what was being spoken, for she did demand attention, and there would be the occasional statement that required the appropriate exclamation.

In addition, she was always sure to depart from her ramblings on these occasions by drawing Darcy's attention to Anne in one way or another. Tonight it was in this manner: "Darcy, do you not think that the color of Anne's gown suits her?"

"Yes indeed, madam. Anne, your gown is quite becoming." Darcy had learned to address both his aunt and his cousin; otherwise, the aunt would continue her efforts for Darcy to speak to Anne directly.

The colonel, recognizing the subject did not suit Darcy, took it up, to Darcy's relief. "Yes, Anne, the color is of the turquoise family, if I am not mistaken, is it not?"

Anne, who was quite ignorant by means of her being both dominated and spoiled by her mother, looked at the colonel as if he had just spoken Greek. This, of course, was of little consequence, because Lady Catherine took up another subject, which put an end to any semblance of conversation.

After dinner, Darcy expressed a desire to stretch his legs. The colonel, being of the same mind, took the added precaution of ensuring that it would be only he and Darcy by asking Anne if she would like to join them. She promptly replied that she had no such desire, as the cool night air certainly would cause her to catch a chill.

The colonel knew that if they had merely expressed their intention, Lady Catherine would insist that Anne join them. Now, of course, Anne had already expressed her disinclination and would not be forced to do what she did not want to do, and the two men could enjoy the exercise and conversation.

Out in the open air, the men were more inclined for the exercise than the conversation. The quiet and cool of the night was a welcomed relief to the rattling of the carriage and the constant monologue of their aunt. The cousins knew the place well and followed their favorite paths.

Soon the silence was ended when the colonel asked Darcy, "How long do we intend to stay this visit?" The question seemed appropriate since the reality of the dullness of the place was brought forcibly back by the night's events, or rather, non-events.

"Not long, Fitz; perhaps a fortnight or shorter. I am sure there is something that needs our attention elsewhere."

The colonel smiled and added, "It is odd that Aunt Catherine developed the habit of talking in such a way as she does and your mother did not."

"Perhaps it was because my mother was not a great talker that created our aunt's need to talk. In any case, I am glad my mother did not feel she needed to always be saying something. But when she did speak, she was always well-worth listening to, and I must confess, Fitz, there are times that I wish I had her as a counselor now. Not to mention, as you well know, her presence would be a great blessing for Georgiana."

The colonel, turning the subject somewhat, mentioned in a tone of feeling for his cousin, "I am sorry, Darcy, that our aunt continues in this scheme for you and Anne. Knowing your feelings and those of our cousin on the matter, I am glad that you are in a position to make your own way without feeling a necessity to give more serious consideration to the match."

"Thank you, Fitz, I know your concern is genuine, and I appreciate how you help me when the subject comes up. It is very gallant of you."

"Think nothing of it, old man; I hate to see you distressed in those awkward moments. Not to mention, perhaps our aunt will have pity on me and direct Anne towards me!"

That drew a chuckle from the two, but Darcy, thinking of his cousin's circumstances, asked in a more serious tone, "Would you truly consider marrying Anne?"

"To own the truth, *yes*; but such a thing is easy to say when the prospect does not seem possible. You know, Darcy, I do not begrudge my situation as the youngest son. I am still young and do believe there are opportunities around every corner, so if the prospect of marrying Anne were to become real tomorrow, I do not believe I would be so quick to say yes."

Darcy responded, "Fitz, do you think that if I made my feelings clear to our aunt, your position might be more clear in your own mind? After all, with our aunt always mentioning it, it is hard to consider things from any other point of view."

"To be sure, that is quite true. But as it stands, it is as if I have a certain freedom that I would not have otherwise."

"Freedom? What freedom could you mean?"

"With our aunt intending Anne for you, there is not much chance, with her limited society, that she would form an attachment elsewhere. In this way, I can consider her held safe. And at present neither of you looks upon the match agreeably, so the option of trying for Anne at some later time seems plausible. If, in the meantime, something more appealing would present itself, I would be free to pursue that."

Pausing momentarily, he continued, "I know the whole thing sounds like a dreadful calculation, especially when there should be something of romance when one is talking of marriage. Our society tends to make those of us in my situation be more calculating than romantic, though. In any case, Darcy, if you should change the way you feel about the match with

Anne, please do not let my ramblings prevent you. As I said, I am young and there is much living to be done even in my present situation."

As his cousin spoke, Darcy felt strongly for him, and vowed in his heart that if there was ever anything he could do for Fitzwilliam, he would do everything he could in his behalf.

But at the same time, this talk of marriage and romance . . . there was some vague feeling of uneasiness, like a distant sound that one cannot make out clearly, though it sounds familiar.

Chapter 15

The next day brought Mr. Collins to Rosings at the earliest possible hour that could be considered civilized. In his mind, he was driven by what seemed proper respect to the nephews of his esteemed patroness.

The colonel and Darcy had risen early, intent on a morning ride. They had, therefore, breakfasted and were taking coffee before their morning exercise. Lady Catherine had likewise risen with her nephews, whereas Anne always took her breakfast in her room. So it was in the breakfast room that Mr. Collins' presence was announced and Lady Catherine applied to as to whether he should be allowed in.

"Mr. Collins, our parish rector, has come directly to pay his respects to you," she informed the gentlemen.

"I say, madam, it is a good thing we rose early if we are to receive such a visit," was the colonel's response.

"Mr. Collins knows his duty on that head and is never negligent." Mr. Collins then was shown into the room and Lady Catherine made the introductions: "I believe, Darcy, the two of you are already acquainted."

"Yes, madam, we have met."

Mr. Collins made his bows and began, "You must excuse me for calling at such an early hour, but I felt it incumbent upon myself not to waste a moment in paying my respects to her ladyship's nephews."

He was interrupted here by the Lady as she interjected, "I believe, Darcy, you are also acquainted with Mrs. Collins and her visiting friend, Miss Elizabeth Bennet."

At hearing the name, the colonel turned with a start toward Darcy, whose face also shown with surprise. Their aunt, catching the reaction of the two, cried, "Is it such a strange thing that someone known by you would also be known here?"

"No, not at all, madam," replied the colonel. "It is just that we had been talking of Miss Bennet in the carriage yesterday, and now to find that she is here is a pleasant surprise, that is all." He was quick to add, "By all means, Darcy, we should follow Mr. Collins' good example and go straightaway to pay our respects to the ladies." Saying this, he quickly turned for his hat and was ready to go.

Mr. Collins, having been paid such a compliment, and eager to show his wife and Elizabeth how they were to be thus honored, just as quickly turned to lead the way. Darcy, who had the impulse to say and do what the colonel had, was still trying to collect himself, and could only manage to say in a confused manner, "Yes, of course, by all means."

Weeks ago, Lady Catherine had been irritated when she was informed that Elizabeth was acquainted with Darcy, and now she was all the more so at seeing the reaction of her nephews to the mention of her name, and to know that they had been talking of her on their way to Rosings. For, although her proud nature demanded that Anne was safe, her womanly nature gave her cause for concern; but there was nothing she could do about it at the moment.

Having made their way outside, the colonel, putting his arm around Darcy's shoulder, whispered excitedly, "This is certainly a positive turn, wouldn't you say?" and he quickly marched ahead of the other two. All the while, Mr. Collins was ecstatic at the idea of his being an example for these great gentlemen to follow, as well as the distinction of having them into his humble abode!

Darcy merely followed, his mind full of thoughts. "I have made the determination to put her out of my mind, yet I find myself always thinking of her, and when possible, talking of her. My scheme of putting distance between us should have worked to enforce my determination, and yet here she is! It is as if a secret wish deep inside has brought her here!"

The three gentlemen walked on -- the colonel leading the way, excited at the prospect of meeting Elizabeth, while Mr. Collins was eagerly wanting to keep up with him, but not wanting to disregard Darcy, who was lagging behind. This gave the appearance of his being the least interested, although each step closer was creating a disquieting sensation in Darcy that proved, of the three, his feelings were the *most* deeply affected.

Before entering the Parsonage, Mr. Collins said, "Please, sirs, permit me to enter ahead so as to alert the ladies within of your kind solicitude in visiting, and allow me to announce you into my humble abode properly."

As the gentlemen were waiting, the colonel smiled at Darcy with great anticipation. But Darcy's mind took another bend: he was struck with the glimmer of hope that he would find Elizabeth much altered, or that his imagination had enhanced her appearance and charms, and seeing her would remind him of the reality.

Among the commotion created inside by their announced arrival, he now heard Elizabeth's voice, and the effect of its sound did not bode well for his glimmer of hope . . . at once, his heart was divided between longing for her sight and that wish of finding her perfections much exaggerated!

* * * * *

He did not find Lizzy altered at all, for she was every bit as he remembered, and thus his determination of putting her out of his mind was crumbling. Those in the room, except for Mr. Collins and the colonel, saw his silence as incivility and pride. No one, though, knew the tumult of emotions that existed within that calm exterior.

The visit did not last long, but it was long enough for the colonel to form an opinion of Elizabeth, and as the two cousins were walking back to Rosings, he was full of praise for her. "This is truly capital, Darcy! Miss Bennet is indeed all you described, and her being here will add considerably to the pleasures of our visit with our aunt, wouldn't you agree?"

Darcy, at ease with his cousin, responded, "To be sure, where Miss Bennet is, there is always a pleasant distraction."

He wanted to say more, but held himself from it. He respected the colonel's opinions, and there was a certain comfort in knowing that his cousin had formed the same view of her. This caused him to entertain the thought that what he was feeling was only admiration and not something deeper.

The colonel's happy spirits were beginning to show on Darcy, so that by the time they entered Rosings to be met by their aunt, seeing their happiness in having visited Miss Bennet seriously disturbed her. She resolved immediately not to have visits from that side any time soon.

It was convenient for Lady Catherine that her resolve and that of Darcy was, for the present, working together. She found comfort in his not going to the Collins' home the next few days, even though the colonel made several visits there. But Darcy's resolve had something much stronger working against it, and even though he stayed away from Elizabeth, his *mind* was often there.

Unfortunately, the colonel, unknowingly working in opposition to Darcy's resolution, would come from visiting at the Parsonage and relate his continuing satisfaction with Elizabeth. "You really should accompany me next time, Darcy! Your preferring solitude to pleasant company and lively conversation puzzles me exceedingly."

"You are quite right, Fitz, I apologize. I have been preoccupied and felt ill-prepared to be good company."

"I have noticed you looking out-of-sorts. What is it that is concerning you? It does not have to do with Georgiana, does it?"

"No, not at all, she is doing very well. I just had a letter from her and she sent her regards to you . . . there are some personal matters that I am trying to work through, that is all. I had not expected that it would be so complicated, but as you know, such is the way of things. Nothing is as easy as one first expects."

"Yes, to say the least. But is there not something I may be of assistance with? It would be very rude of me to be enjoying myself when I could be of use to you."

"You are very kind, pray do not concern yourself. It is such a matter that has required only my thinking things through, and just when I feel I have resolved it, my mind takes another turn."

"Oh, I understand, but I have always found that when I have become too wrapped up in thinking things over, it helps to back away and take a fresh look after some diversion. And in our present situation, I can think of no better diversion than a visit to the Parsonage."

Darcy agreed with his cousin, all the while thinking how difficult it is to live by his private determination regarding Elizabeth when his cousin kept unwittingly urging him in a direction that would overthrow the whole thing. Their planned visit turned out to be unnecessary, however, because after a week of Darcy not showing any interest in that direction, Lady Catherine felt she could now have the Collinses and their guests over. The invitation was extended at church that Sunday.

Chapter 16

Having Elizabeth at Rosings was strange for Darcy. The room was familiar and Lady Catherine's attention to himself was as well, but never had he met with such a sight in that room that so stirred his emotions! Darcy, while listening to his aunt, found himself often looking involuntarily in the direction of Miss Bennet. A week had passed since last he saw her and heard her pleasant voice, with the occasional hint of laughter. Seeing the colonel engaged with such ease in conversation with her, and she with him, made him wish at that moment that he could do the same. Darcy's looking over at them so intently finally drew the attention of his aunt.

He was most sorry for it, because she could be so insolent, which is exactly what happened in this instance, as she demanded that she be let in on the conversation. Learning that they were talking of music, Lady Catherine declared herself to be the greatest lover of music, even proclaiming her own excellence at performing, had she but learnt!

Pausing in her praise of herself, she inquired, "Tell me, Darcy, how does Georgiana get on with her playing?"

"She plays remarkably well, madam. I dare say it would be difficult to find her equal in someone her age."

"You must tell her, then, of my instructions to practice and not neglect it, for it is by this means alone that she will excel."

"I assure you, Lady Catherine, she requires no such admonition. Her diligence in practicing is a model for anyone wanting to become proficient."

"Well, I see I must write her and give the needed encouragement; no one could convey my sentiments with their due weight besides myself." Continuing to speak as if she was a maestro, to Darcy's mortification she turned her attention to

Elizabeth, and directing again that constant practice was essential, she said:

"I told Miss Bennet that since Mrs. Collins has no instrument on which she can practice, she is welcome to come every day to play on the piano forte in Mrs. Jenkinson's room. It must be *every day,* Miss Bennet, for anything less will be of no use, and your playing in that room will not be disturbing the rest of the house with your practicing."

Elizabeth could see Darcy's embarrassment at his aunt's behavior, though he bore it well, but it did give her a moment's pause. She did not expect it of him; of the colonel, assuredly, but she felt Darcy and Lady Catherine were too similar for him to react in this manner to his aunt's conduct.

They were shortly afterwards called to dinner and the seating arrangement at table was just as in the parlor. Lady Catherine began her efforts to have Darcy and Anne at least attempt at saying something to one another. Charlotte, being placed perfectly to observe this, could not but think of Lizzy, and how such a sight would delight her fancy in the folly of human behavior. For Darcy, dinner at Rosings had never been so painful or slow, but it finally was over.

As they were returning to the parlor, Darcy heard Fitzwilliam say to Elizabeth, "Miss Bennet, may I remind you that you promised to play for us after dinner?"

"If you would be so kind as to escort me to the instrument, I will attempt at not making you regret having remembered."

The colonel was in real anticipation, seeing that everything else Darcy had said of her was not exaggerated. Indeed, he was delighted at her first choice of song, a melody that was well known to be a favorite among many of his acquaintance. Colonel Fitzwilliam could immediately see that Darcy was correct in his assessment of her talents.

As she played, Darcy was still being monopolized by his aunt, but he was not going to allow the rest of the evening to be as the start of it had been. During dinner, he had determined to enter into conversation with Elizabeth, and he was as good as his word. He interrupted his aunt with, "Pray excuse me, madam, but I have been neglecting the other guests," and at that, rose and moved toward the colonel and Miss Bennet.

Walking across the room, he felt a calm, a sense of reassurance. Perhaps it was because his cousin was there and he knew that any lapses would be taken up by him. Or was it that, since she was playing and singing, conversation would not be the main objective?

Upon his approach, Lizzy teased him by saying, "Have you come all this way to frighten me, Mr. Darcy? . . . especially since you have informed us of your sister's fine playing? Nothing is so intimidating for one as inept as myself to be compared with others, you know! Although, being thus threatened, I feel I may rally myself so as to be equal to the challenge."

A pleasant conversation ensued, with the two of them entertaining Colonel Fitzwilliam with a brief discussion about Darcy's conduct at the Meryton assembly ball, Lizzy citing his dancing but two dances as an example of his behavior there.

Darcy entered into the subject with the same sense of lightheartedness as Elizabeth, offering this as his excuse: "I knew no one but the two ladies that I had accompanied."

"Well, Colonel, it appears your cousin has not yet comprehended that it is altogether possible to be introduced to others at a ball."

Darcy had joined them, wanting to have his share of conversing with Lizzy, but had not considered he would become the principal subject! Nevertheless, he found himself acknowledging, "I am rather unskilled at such socializing with strangers."

Lizzy, turning to the colonel, said, "Dare we ask why a man such as he, with sense and education, would feel ill qualified to recommend himself to strangers?"

To this, Colonel Fitzwilliam replied, "I believe I can answer for it, Miss Elizabeth. Knowing my cousin as I do, I would say he does not give himself the trouble."

Darcy now spoke for himself, "I do not have the talent which some people, such as the colonel, possess of conversing easily when in company with those I do not know, for I cannot catch their tone of conversation or appear interested in their concerns. The world in general, I admit, seems to do so easily."

Elizabeth laughed at this, and said, "I spoke earlier of my ineptitude at the instrument just as you have mentioned your own. I, though, am willing to accept that my being less skilled at playing is my own fault, for I have not practiced as those others who do excel."

Bowing in acquiescence, Darcy said, "Concerning myself, I will acknowledge the truth of what you have said. But as for your playing, the colonel, I am sure, will agree there is little lacking. Your playing has always given us great pleasure." This did not portend well, for just as he had said it, he noticed his aunt moving toward them.

Lady Catherine quickly brought an end to any further pleasant talk by coming to the instrument and offering her supercilious opinions once again, which proved to be nothing more than critical observations of Elizabeth's performance. Despite her interference, Elizabeth would turn to the colonel and ask what else he might wish to hear, not being at all intimidated by her ladyship.

It was at one of those moments that Darcy spoke up, to her surprise, and asked, "Do you know the delightful English country song that speaks of a beautiful girl out in the garden?" He wanted to add, "I could not help but think of that tune when I saw you in the garden near the church today."

Though he did not say it, Elizabeth saw something in his look as he made his request that caused her to hold her gaze on his face, as it had been rendered unfamiliarly soft and appealing. The evening continued on in this manner, with Miss Bennet at the instrument until the carriage was called to take them back to the Parsonage.

Having bid farewell to their company and goodnight to Lady Catherine and Anne, the colonel and Darcy walked upstairs together to their apartments, with the colonel commenting, "What a pleasant evening it was, 'eh, Darcy?"

"Indeed it was."

"It is just as I said, you needed some diversion to help get your mind off the deliberations that were keeping you so occupied. Did you not find this evening helpful to that end?"

"Yes, Fitz, I found that some things became much more clear as a result of the things that occurred tonight. What about you? Did you find Miss Bennet's playing to your liking? You did seem to be enjoying yourself."

"I will tell you this, knowing that I am speaking only to you -- I have never been *half* so well entertained in that room before!"

"Nor have I," rejoined Darcy.

Chapter 17

Darcy, feeling encouraged by his having managed himself tolerably at the end of the evening, went to visit the Parsonage the next morning, expecting to find all the ladies at home. However, upon arriving he learned that Elizabeth was alone; consequently, all the confidence that last evening had imbued him with was left at the door. After expressing his wish of not interrupting her privacy, she politely invited him to come in and sit.

Elizabeth's congenial nature moved her to initiate a conversation, "When last I saw you in Hertfordshire, Mr. Darcy, you and the Bingleys left suddenly after the ball. I believe Mr. Bingley first left and then you and the others followed; is that not right? They were all well when you left London, I hope?"

"Yes, they were very well, thank you, and your recollection is correct."

"Your leaving in that manner put me in mind of the conversation we had back then -- perhaps you remember as well -- about Mr. Bingley quitting the place in a hurry? To see even you follow his example does not speak well for your side of the argument we were having, Mr. Darcy," she teased.

Darcy merely smiled, while looking a bit embarrassed, but made no reply. Lizzy attempted again, but being confronted with Darcy's curt responses, she soon dropped the effort and assumed a posture that indicated, if any further conversing was to take place, Darcy would have to do his part.

Comprehending this, he observed, "Lady Catherine has done a great deal to this house upon Mr. Collins coming into Hunsford."

"Yes, that is so. Mrs. Collins has shown me the alterations made, and I might add, your aunt could not have chosen a more grateful person with whom to be generous."

"Speaking of your friend, I must observe how well Mr. Collins has chosen his partner."

"I agree. For Mr. Collins to come across the one woman of sense and understanding that would accept him and make him happy, as well as be happy herself, is one of those pleasant coincidences of life."

Darcy next hit upon the subject of Mrs. Collins being situated in close proximity to her family and friends, and inadvertently turned the conversation in a direction that would move him to do and say something that would astonish both Elizabeth and himself.

He began, "There is, I might think, some benefit to her being within so easy distance of her family."

"Mr. Darcy, it is nearly fifty miles! I would certainly not say she is near her family; and besides, I would not have considered distance as being one of the advantages of the match."

"I would suggest your point of view is that anything beyond your own neighborhood appears far," he said in jest.

"Well, speaking of Mr. and Mrs. Collins, I believe it would be safe to say, though they have a comfortable income, it is not such that would permit frequent journeys at this distance. If it were half as far, then they would probably take your view of it being an easy distance," adding thoughtfully, ". . . but speaking for myself, I would say it *is* possible to be settled too close to one's family."

Hearing Elizabeth express this idea of being settled too near her family excited in Darcy a reflex of drawing his chair closer to her and saying warmly, "I can see that of you -- it is what I would imagine, that you would prefer some distance from Longbourn!"

Elizabeth looked up, surprised at his moving closer and his change of tone, which caused Darcy to draw back, being astonished himself by what he had just done and said. Taking up the newspaper, not only to appear indifferent to his comment but also to hide his embarrassment, he asked in a detached voice about her impressions of Kent.

Just then, Elizabeth noticed Charlotte coming up the walk and announced, "Mrs. Collins and her sister are home, Mr. Darcy."

He stood up in anticipation of their entering, and said, "Mrs. Collins, Miss Lucas, I arrived not knowing you were away from home, and I apologize, but I must now take my leave."

"Indeed, you need not leave so quickly! May we not get you some tea?" Charlotte offered politely.

"You are very kind, but thank you, no; I really must be off."

Darcy was glad to be out of the house, and decided to take a longer way back to Rosings. He needed to consider the meaning of what had just taken place with Elizabeth, having no idea that, at the Parsonage, Elizabeth and Charlotte were also trying to make out what his motives were in visiting. If the ladies had been able to ask Darcy himself, it would not be likely that he could have presented them with a coherent answer, for he was trying to sort his own thoughts out, as his heart was feeling things his head was not ready to acknowledge.

This was only the beginning of many such visits that Darcy and his cousin would pay to that humble abode. Sometimes they walked thither in pairs; other times it was one or the other.

Chapter 18

On one such occasion when the cousins ventured there together, the ladies were in a particularly lively mood. The colonel took the opportunity of entertaining them with tales of life in an assignment that had taken him to a coastal town of little credit.

"Believe me, for what passes for the opera or theater there, one would do just as well watching children at play." Darcy, as usual, was having difficulty joining in, but the colonel, in an effort to include him, prompted, "Darcy, you remember the town of which I speak, for you spent three days with me there."

"Yes, I believe I do recall," he said, surprised to be addressed.

To this brief reply, Colonel Fitzwilliam responded jokingly, "Please, Darcy, restrain yourself, for you are in danger of monopolizing the conversation!"

Everyone in the room enjoyed the ribbing, and even Darcy smiled, but still continued as a quiet observer. The colonel had often seen Darcy like this and knew him to be greatly affected by whatever company he was in; he therefore saw nothing to make him suspicious. At times, he did find it odd, though, for Darcy to put off leaving Rosings so many times; but as long as there was the company of Miss Bennet, the colonel was in no hurry to leave.

Privately, Darcy truly enjoyed observing Elizabeth during those visits to Hunsford. He had become captivated with her independent disposition and manner of easy playfulness. He considered, "What a contrast there is between Elizabeth and my aunt and cousin Anne! Lady Catherine is haughty, brash and impertinent, and Anne is insipid and self-absorbed. But Elizabeth can converse on subjects both great and small, and even debate with Fitz . . . which, considering the colonel's extensive education, is no mean feat!"

Darcy's admiration grew steadily, and he found it impossible not to esteem her, when in her presence, and could scarcely think of anything else when he was not. Though he said little when in company with her, there was the wish to speak -- so much he wanted to say. As a result, he looked at her a great deal, continually watching her every expression or turn about the room.

"If only I had that ability of entering into conversation with her as easily as I have observed Fitz do, or seen Charles do with Jane!" he sighed. "But, no! I find myself always behind in conversations, and just when there seems to be something I can say, before I am able to bring myself to speak, the moment has passed. When we are alone, there is at least the luxury of not having to vie for a part . . . of course, when we are alone, I am still challenged with what to say, but at least then I might say it."

He suddenly hit upon the idea of noting what time of day and which direction she would take her exercise. Deciding to take advantage of her being alone on her walks, he met her, not once, but *three* times. Darcy could see Elizabeth's surprise and that she was at a loss to understand his meeting her this way, but he was nevertheless determined to carry his intention through, even ignoring her hints of wishing to be alone. She seemed to become accustomed to ignoring him while they walked, for she did not trouble herself to speak to him, and therefore much of the time they were together on these walks was spent in silence.

It happened on one occasion, however, that Darcy ventured to say, "Miss Bennet, I recall you walking alone to Netherfield when your sister was ill, and here at Rosings I find you again walking alone as a regular part of your activity. What accounts for your fondness of this solitary pursuit?"

"One cannot always be alone when it is most desired, so I take advantage of this particular retreat as it affords me that opportunity. Besides, being alone in such surroundings, one is free to make observations that are of interest to oneself without explanation or interruption. Or if so inclined, I can forego all observations and just be happy with life."

That last thought caught Darcy's attention: "You appear to have a great penchant for being 'happy with life,' as you put it."

"Do I indeed? Are you being severe with me, Mr. Darcy, or is this a sincere observation?" Seeing that it was her privacy that had been interrupted, and it was Darcy, of all persons, being the one to invade it, she put all tact aside.

"I am not mocking you, Miss Bennet; it is just that I have been accustomed to meeting with persons who seem to believe that being dissatisfied with everything is a mark of good breeding."

"It seems to me," Elizabeth said with a quizzical look, "that to go through life dissatisfied is a mark of being spoilt and a waste of a most valuable gift from above."

"Indeed it is, and one might add, a sort of tragedy."

Elizabeth was puzzled exceedingly at this speech, for she would have put Mr. Darcy himself in the category he had just mentioned.

* * * * *

Another occurrence, after meeting her as before, began with this question: "Miss Bennet, do you find Hunsford to your liking?"

"Yes, Mr. Darcy, it is a pleasant enough place," she replied tersely.

Undeterred, he continued, "I have noticed that you seem not to perfectly understand my aunt's house. Perhaps when next you come into Kent, you will find yourself better acquainted with it."

"I will certainly own to not being accustomed to a home as grand as Rosings, as you well know," Elizabeth said with a wry smile.

Miss Bennet was, of course, ignorant as to what the comment 'she would be better acquainted with Rosings' was referring. Darcy, on the other hand, understood its meaning all too well and was once again confounded at his giving way to this sort of expression. Though obscure to the hearer, they exposed enough of his partiality as to make himself quite uncomfortable.

On the third meeting, Darcy was to introduce a subject that would render Elizabeth speechless: Having already discussed the day's weather and the various flowers they had encountered that morning, the two were walking in silence for several minutes, when Darcy abruptly asked, "What do you make of married life, now that you have been witness to the Collins' happy union?"

He had found it difficult to look at her during these discussions they had on their walks; however, not receiving a reply, he turned toward her. Seeing that the question had made her uncomfortable, he quickly added, "Forgive me for asking such a question with regard to your good friend, I meant no impertinence."

Now he felt clumsy and stumbled for a reason for the question. "I . . . recall on one of my visits to the Parsonage your commenting on the match being a good one."

"Yes, of course," was Elizabeth's reply, and without answering his question, she quickly moved to another subject. "Do you always stay so long with your aunt?"

He remarked that his stays were often determined by things he could not always control -- in this instance, of course, he was referring to her being there. Thankfully, there was no need to try to find another topic, for they found themselves at the gate in the pales opposite the Parsonage, and parted ways.

* * * * *

For his part, those walks with her were very satisfying. To be with such a lady in such surroundings was a new experience for Darcy, but everything he felt with reference to Elizabeth was new.

While thinking over her reaction to the subject of the Collins' marriage, Darcy was sure that she had been overwhelmed by it. After all, for any lady to hear the word *marriage* when being addressed by someone such as himself would surely have such an effect. He paused in his contemplation to recall his own determination not to pursue a relationship with her, but found that to speak the word *marriage* in the presence of such a lady as Miss Bennet likewise has its effect on the man . . .

Darcy could no longer deny that the feelings of his heart had overcome the reasonings of his mind.

Chapter 19

Darcy was aided in this new direction he had been taking by his belief that Elizabeth was of a mind to accept him, should he make an offer. Though the thought of actually saying the words, "Will you be my wife?" still came with a struggle, he now believed the agony of not asking would be even greater.

Regardless of that, he could not avoid the sense of degradation that would come to his family name being connected with hers. The reproof that would come by way of some in the family was also echoing in his mind. At times, he believed he could summon the strength to stop these feelings for Elizabeth; but when a young man has developed an attraction, coupled with strong admiration for a lady, all the strength is in the other direction.

He even recalled the conversation he had with Bingley weeks earlier. "At that time I was master of myself," he thought reproachfully. "My reasoning was sound, my logic convincing... . . . but if I am to be honest, even then my heart was forcibly arguing against me as it is now! That is why I had nothing to say to Bingley's last statement about love for someone who is not well-stationed in life. . . later I was able to convince him about Jane; *myself*, I cannot now convince about her sister."

Darcy had gone full circle again on the subject, and thought it best to put off coming to a decision about whether or not to make an offer to Elizabeth, and to judge what course to take by what would occur when next they met. She and the Collinses were to come to tea this evening, so he would not have long to wait.

When the party from the Parsonage arrived, however, Elizabeth was not among them. Mr. Collins informed Lady Catherine: "My cousin Elizabeth is unwell, your ladyship. I believe she took too much sun today. As you know, young ladies are often prone to overdo such activities, only to find out that they had done so too late."

In truth, what had caused Elizabeth to decline accompanying them was a conversation she had with the colonel earlier that day. They happened upon each other whilst walking through Rosings park, and among the topics of conversation was Darcy's boasting to Fitzwilliam about 'having lately saved a good friend from a most imprudent marriage.' The colonel made it clear that 'no names or any other particulars were given, but he took Darcy to be referring to a friend of his named Bingley, since they had been together recently, and Bingley seemed to be the sort of chap that would get himself into such a scrape.'

When Elizabeth inquired what reasons were given for his interference, the colonel replied that he understood 'there were strong objections to the lady.' Lizzy asked for more details, not revealing the intensity of her interest in the matter, but the colonel had only been told as much as he then related.

Now she was in no mood to see Mr. Darcy, knowing the greater share he had played in separating Bingley from her sister; her dislike for him crystallized into something much stronger, and she excused herself from attending the evening at Rosings.

"Ladies of good breeding know when exertion is due even when unwell. For Miss Bennet to be absent from such an invitation is exposing herself to her unfortunate upbringing," was Lady Catherine's unfeeling reply.

Charlotte dearly wanted to speak up for her friend, but she knew that to let the subject drop was the wisest course, because Lady Catherine would soon move to a new one and Elizabeth would no longer be the subject. The colonel seemed to have had the same thought, for Charlotte could see him restraining himself from likewise defending Lizzy. Their wisdom was proved right, as Lady Catherine proceeded to inform them of just how much sun is necessary for good health.

Through all of this, Darcy was contending with his own thoughts and feelings about Elizabeth, unrelated to exposure to the sun! He felt he had been prepared to meet with Elizabeth and be rational so as to judge aright his feelings as well as hers, but not seeing her had a transforming effect that he was absolutely unprepared for.

He was not sent into a panic, but the force of emotion that rushed in on him settled the matter that moment. The loss of seeing her, of hearing her charming voice this evening, brought acutely into focus a life without her in it. The clarity this brought to him moved him with the determination of a man in love.

"Forgive me, Lady Catherine, Anne, but I must excuse myself. Please, Mr. and Mrs. Collins, Fitzwilliam, I beg to be excused." With that he turned to leave, and though each one made some polite inquiry, their expressions simply followed him out of the room.

♥ ♥ ♥ ♥ ♥

Now outside, his feet found themselves walking the path they knew well, while his head was occupied with his need of securing the prospect of being always able to see and hear Elizabeth, and not re-live that sense of loss he had just experienced.

On reaching the Parsonage, the satisfaction that accompanied seeing her and hearing her say his name as he first entered the house and asked after her health fortified his intent in coming. But he began pacing about the room in silence, not certain how he wanted to begin and trying to gather his composure, with Elizabeth silently looking on, at a loss to understand the man. His behavior always seemed odd to her, but there was a certain agitation that he was displaying now that rendered his actions uncommonly odd even for Darcy.

Finally, his heart and mind being united in purpose, he turned, and facing her, declared outright, *"I have made every effort, but have found myself overpowered by my feelings for you. My admiration has turned into an ardent love that I must now confess to you."*

Elizabeth was rendered speechless with disbelief upon hearing this! Her face registering the astonishment of the moment only served to make Darcy feel all the more encouraged to proceed.

"I have for some time been denying how strong my feelings are for you, and indeed, I have exerted myself to do away with these sensations. Despite this, the consciousness of what a reprehensible match it would be on my side was not even sufficient to suppress them. Hours I have spent, telling and retelling myself how such a connection with your family would be a degradation to the name of *Darcy*! I would look at you, seeing your beauty and attractions, and remind myself of how inferior you are, to be a match for me."

His certainty of being accepted was obvious to Elizabeth as he stood confidently before her, with far too little romantic sentiment and far too much pride in his words and manner. What an odd mixture of feelings she was experiencing! She was conscious of the honor of such a great man as Mr. Darcy having expressed his love and admiration, but her anger was rising simultaneously almost with every word from him.

He continued, "Yet, notwithstanding how shameful it appeared to me to have my heart thus involved -- much less to express my feelings and entertain some idea of making them known to you -- the strength of my attachment has grown to the point that I can no longer conquer it . . . so I *must* ask, with full knowledge of how profound a wound I am inflicting on my name . . . *will you do me the honor of becoming my wife?"*

Elizabeth was somehow able to compose herself creditably before responding: "Women, of course, are expected to accept any eligible offer of marriage regardless of their feelings, and an offer from one such as yourself could hardly be viewed as otherwise. However, I am unable to follow the established mode of women. I have no wish of causing you distress, Mr. Darcy, but I cannot accept your proposal. If this causes any pain, surely the sentiments you have described so clearly, that have kept you from expressing yourself sooner, should make any discomfort of short duration."

Having been certain of her accepting him, it was now *Darcy's* turn to be astonished, and he stood silently looking at her, until finally he could speak. Controlling his resentment, he protested, "You mentioned the 'established mode,' but I am sure whether one is accepted or refused, it is expected to be done with a certain amount of civility!"

"Mr. Darcy, you amaze me! I was quite at a loss as to whether I should even make an answer to your proposal just now, or if I was to be merely offended by your remarks upon my family and myself! It would have taken a woman lacking sense to the greatest degree who could rejoice at such a proposal. If you deem my refusal as uncivil, I know not in what light you would classify your own words in making the offer!"

Darcy's formal education had taught him how to express himself well, but his lack of social education was undermining his efforts here. No lady would wish to hear in a marriage proposal such words as *degradation* and *reprehensible* being used with reference to the match! He had used such strong terms many times in an effort to do away with his feelings for her. Whereas, such terms were not successful in ending *his* feelings, they certainly had their effect on *hers*!

It should be noted, Darcy was not accustomed to being thrown off balance as he had been this evening, first with her absence at Rosings, which brought on this rush of emotion, and then her refusing his proposal in so decided a fashion. Hearing Elizabeth refer to being insulted by his remarks irritated him. His station in life being so far above her own -- how could she be offended by his acknowledging the obvious? His pride was getting the better of him, and he would not recover.

With his remaining silent, Elizabeth found she could not stop herself, as she continued, "The unpleasantness of your offer is one thing, but the ugliness of your part in ruining the happiness of my beloved sister Jane is something else . . . can you deny your part in this affair?"

"Deny it?! I have rejoiced in my success and have only wondered why I could not reason the same way with my regard for you -- it appears I have been kinder to Bingley than I have been to myself."

At hearing this, any other lady might have demanded that he leave, but Elizabeth was now provoked to go further: "How cruel -- to rejoice over dashing the hopes of two people in love and inflicting sorrow by destroying their future happiness! This is what you have grown to enjoy, it appears -- how grand was your celebration when you withheld what was due to Mr. Wickham -- ruining his future and leaving him to fend for himself?!"

Darcy certainly had not expected to hear *Wickham* mentioned in his effort to propose to Miss Bennet, and he was too emotional to make much of a reply on this subject. "As you describe me here, I am made to look like a man with faults too grievous indeed. I am left to suppose, though, that if I had not spoken truthfully of my scruples that held me back from . . . rather, as you say, had I done what is the 'common way' with men and women, and only spoken sweet words to flatter you, then perhaps you would not have had your *pride* hurt. But such things are to me the very nature of falseness, and I abhor such deception!"

"You are mistaken, Mr. Darcy, if you suppose that the mode of your declaration affected me in any other way, than as it spared the concern which I might have felt in refusing you, had you behaved in a more gentlemanlike manner! You could not have made me the offer of your hand in any possible way that would have tempted me to accept it." At this, Elizabeth saw him wince, but was too heated to consider it beyond notice. "I have such a deep dislike of your arrogance and conceit, I could never be prevailed upon to marry you!"

The last nail had been driven home! He was totally undone in his bid for her hand; all that was left was for him to wish her well and take his leave.

* * * * *

If he had a sense of humor, he might have laughed at how absurd a twist this evening had taken. But humor was not Darcy's way of dealing with things. He felt his honor and reputation had been sullied by her assertions involving Bingley and Jane, and even more so regarding Wickham.

Hence, Darcy determined to write a letter in which he would be able to command her attention without distraction; and through a letter he could consider his expressions more carefully. So, although she did not return his love, he felt he could at least recover *these* from her. Though unquestionably overwhelmed by his desire to vindicate himself, however, Darcy could not help but be haunted by her words which echoed in his mind . . .

"Had you behaved in a more *gentlemanlike manner.*"

Chapter 20

Darcy felt comfortable with pen in hand, and now being called to duty to defend his character, the blank sheets of paper he had gathered were inviting him in earnest.

He felt it best to defend his actions with reference to Bingley and Jane first. The thoughts flowed from his mind to pen with serious intent, as he imagined having Elizabeth before him, listening. How satisfying the feeling of communicating his viewpoint on this situation involving her sister, in which she believed his actions to be without virtue! He thus began:

Miss Bennet,

Please do not be concerned that I am attempting to make another offer to you, as if my pride could not countenance a rejection; certainly neither of us would like to continue that conversation. Rather, in your making clear how distasteful you found my proposal to be, you also leveled two accusations against me which, although differing in their nature, nonetheless, would not only make my character out to be a very cold-hearted individual, but really even worse. For that reason, I feel I must put forth the effort to address these offences. I trust your disposition, as well as your superior intelligence, will allow there being another side to any story and that justice demands it should be heard. So with the belief that you will give this your kind attention, I have chosen to write this letter, in the hope that, after you have read it in its entirety, my actions and motives will be understood.

I shall begin with the lesser charge, not meaning lesser in its significance to you, but less egregious. You have concluded that, despite the feelings of both your sister and Mr. Bingley, I did all I could to separate them. If you would but recall of what short duration the acquaintance of the couple was, surely you cannot imagine that my purpose was to inflict pain in separating them. Bingley and I have had a long standing friendship, and Charles' natural modesty has developed into his confidence in me and my judgement. While at the Netherfield ball, hearing the report circulating by persons of such good character as Sir William Lucas - that Bingley's attentions to your sister had everyone expecting a marriage between the two - I began to take closer notice of their behavior, and in doing so, became concerned about Miss Bennet's apparent lack of feeling for him. To be sure, she was pleased by his attentions, but from what I could see, her sentiment was not stirred to that same sense of participation as was my friend's. The placidity of her demeanor was such that, as acute an observer as I am, I saw nothing to convince myself that her heart had been touched. Although I admit that I desired her to be indifferent, it was not that, but rather, my impartial conviction which led me to this conclusion. I must acknowledge that, as you are better acquainted with your sister and are on more intimate terms, my perceptions could have been mistaken; and if it is so, I can well understand the strength of your resentment.

However, in addition to this, your family's abhorrent shortcomings had to be considered. I am not here addressing your family's want of connections. Obviously, for Charles, your undesirable connections could hardly be as important a concern as for myself. This was an obstacle that I was only able to overcome by the sheer strength of my attraction for you. No, it is with regard to this - I beg your forbearance, but I feel I must once again pain you by recounting your mother's lack of proper decorum, which was so frequently on display, as well as the actions of your younger sisters, being allowed to run riot and uncontrolled by your father. These evils my friend had not given due weight. For whatever it is worth, I must say that you and your elder sister have, unlike the rest of your family, always conducted yourselves as worthy models for any to follow. Be that as it may, although Charles had believed your sister returned his affection with equal regard, I earnestly and successfully convinced him of her lack of feelings for him and the undesirability of pursuing the match any further.

I must admit to one part of my conduct in Bingley's affairs which I am not satisfied with - that I concealed from him your sister having been in town, of which he is still unaware. Being informed of it by Miss Bingley, and because I was unsure that sufficient time had passed to permit their meeting without her being able to rekindle his interest, which I was certain was her intention, I kept it from him. I realize that this disguise was perhaps beneath me; however, it was done with the best of intentions for my friend's welfare.

This, madam, is the account of my actions in this regard, and though the motives that governed me may, by your account, seem inadequate, they were in the service OF a friend, and I certainly cannot apologize for acting AS a friend.

He would now turn to the subject of Wickham, which required a pause . . . how much should he relate about his dealings with him, especially with someone who had been so influenced by him as Elizabeth had? A partial explanation would not do; to leave some things unsaid could invite Wickham to fill in the gaps with his own falsehoods. After reflecting on Elizabeth's character, he felt more at ease, and proceeded to unfold to her the following:

Now as to my dealings with George Wickham, I must present to you the whole of our history. He and I grew up together as young boys, he being the son of the man my father had entrusted with the charge of Pemberley estates. As you have come to know, Wickham is as amiable a person as one could meet, and such has been the case since his youth. My father, therefore, grew very attached to him. In fact, Mr. Darcy did all he could to further his advancement, even generously providing for a gentleman's education at Cambridge. He intended him for the church and promised a valuable family living be given him when it became vacant. Mr. Wickham, you see, had every right to expect such a livelihood.

When my excellent father died, having continued to have the highest opinion of George Wickham to the very end, he directed in his will that I fulfill his wishes in this matter, and I was prepared to do so. However, being acquainted with Wickham's vicious propensities and his want of principle - which he had always been careful to conceal from my father - I knew he ought not be a clergyman. As things turned out, before the living became available, Wickham haughtily denounced any interest in the church or the position should it ever even become available, and chose to forego what had been promised him in lieu of a lump sum payment of three thousand pounds. This was given him, and I thanked heaven that I was spared the predicament of placing someone of a character such as his in the church. He declared an interest in studying law, which I hoped he would follow through on, and all appeared to work out to everyone's satisfaction.

However, three years later, Wickham, hearing of the availability of the position after the death of the incumbent, and having squandered his money in a life of idleness and dissipation, applied to be allowed to have it.

His circumstances, he implored, were exceedingly bad, his study of the law unprofitable, and he insolently suggested that since I had no other person to provide for, and it was my father's intentions that he have this position, I should therefore bestow it upon him. In view of this further proof of the inappropriateness of his being a clergyman, and the fact that he had already been given compensation that he had deemed appropriate, of course, I refused his petition, and his anger with me was commensurate with the degree of his plight. Considering the foregoing, I trust that you will understand my steadfastly refusing his entreaty and every repetition that was made. With this, Wickham left in resentment and all acquaintance between us was dropped; it seemed it would be the last I would hear of him. That, however, did not prove to be the case.

Before continuing, Darcy found it necessary to put his pen down and go to the window for air. What he would next reveal not only raised his ire, but also caused him to *shudder* about what could have happened. Refocusing on his main purpose, he gathered his composure, and returning to the desk, continued:

George Wickham next obtruded into my life in a way that, once explained, will expose you to the extent of his unscrupulousness. What I am about to relate is a circumstance I wish to forget and would never tell a soul; but I now feel an obligation to relate to you, Miss Bennet, and have no doubt of your secrecy in the matter:

As you may recall, my sister Georgiana is ten years younger than myself, and as her guardians, Colonel Fitzwilliam and I placed her in the care of a woman we thought to be of high character. We provided an establishment for Georgiana and Mrs. Younge in London, unaware that she was acquainted with George Wickham. Mrs. Younge then arranged a meeting between the three in Ramsgate, where she and Wickham connived to recommend a marriage bond between himself and Georgiana. It agitates me even now to say that Wickham almost succeeded in eloping with Georgiana, whom he was able to convince of his love for her, and persuade that she was in love with him; she was then but fifteen years old. His chief object was, of course, her fortune of thirty-thousand pounds; it could certainly be supposed that he also wanted to revenge himself against me. Having been informed by Georgiana of the intended elopement, I was, thankfully, able to stop it. I am certain you can imagine my reaction to this, and my repugnance of Mr. Wickham. My dealing with the matter was as decisively as my love for Georgiana had worked up in me, and Wickham took his leave immediately. I had not seen him again until the recent meeting in Meryton, of which you are aware.

My hope is, Miss Bennet, that you will acquit me of cruelty toward George Wickham. For verification of these matters, I can direct you to Colonel Fitzwilliam, who is joined with me in the execution of my father's will, and by this was, of necessity, involved in all the particulars. I will arrange for the colonel to be accessible to you, if you feel such confirmation should be necessary.

I now close with my best wishes for your health and happiness ~
Fitzwilliam Darcy

The retelling of this instance was indeed painful, but there was satisfaction in informing her of Wickham's true character. Darcy was not sure just what Wickham had told Elizabeth, but he put his confidence in the truth.

As he ended the letter, signing his name, he was confronted with a sad thought: he had looked forward to writing to inform his sister of his engagement to Miss Bennet. However, he was not one for sentiment, and would, therefore, not dwell on such a disappointment. So, sealing the letter, he would wait for the morrow to find Miss Bennet out on her solitary walk and place it directly in her hand.

The letter was closed and sealed; he wished his *feelings* could be as easily closed and sealed. But this night would be spent in reliving the scene at the Parsonage, and from that to a certain eagerness for the morning to come, so he could place the letter in Elizabeth's hand and have it read, so that her sense of justice might clear him to some extent.

READ AN EXTENSION OF THIS CHAPTER
at the end of the book

Chapter 21

Darcy had requested of his servant that he be called and awakened early and that coffee be brought, as he wanted to be off before the others would be aware of it. He had no wish of encountering them and meeting with inquires that he was not equal to dealing with, lest it be discovered just how troubled he was.

At being roused from sleep, he was glad he had asked for coffee instead of tea! As he sat on the side of his bed clearing the haze from this fitful night's sleep, the aroma of the coffee was having its effect by clearing his mind. With that, he rose, and directing water be poured into the basin, he began preparing himself for the task ahead. As if time had been rushed along, he now found himself outside, letter in hand.

His steps were directed to a particular sort of grove that afforded a view of the Parsonage, which also had the advantage of concealing him. He wanted no one to see him by chance, thus ruining his opportunity. The earliness of the hour confirmed he would have to wait before Elizabeth would venture out.

Waiting as he was, he began to condemn himself for not being the master of his emotions. "Were it not for my weakness in this, I would not now be here in an effort to clear my name, ensconced among the trees like some highwayman." His mind then turned to Elizabeth's words -- "Had I behaved 'like a *gentleman'*, she said! Yes, indeed! If I had, perhaps I would not now be doing penance."

Then rousing himself, "This will not do, I will not meet her feeling regret! . . . what I am doing must be done, honor and duty to my family requires it and I will not weaken my position with such melancholy reflections!" Little did Darcy know how intense these *melancholy reflections* would become, for at this moment, he had something like a '*cry to battle*' keeping them from him.

He had prepared himself to wait through most of the morning, but it was not necessary. Elizabeth likewise had a restless night, and so sought fresh air and exercise immediately after breakfast. Darcy moved along the grove as she walked down the lane. When she was near enough, he stepped out, though still being a little distance from her so as not to startle her. He saw her catch sight of him and turn in the opposite direction, but his long legs and quick pace brought him close enough to call her name. She therefore stopped and turned to face him.

Darcy truly made every effort to be and sound composed; to this end he had rehearsed carefully what to say, albeit just a brief sentence. He held out the letter and recited his line -- "Will you do me the honor of reading this letter?" -- but of course, no actor would have applauded his delivery.

Elizabeth, being ignorant of his struggles, thought he seemed cold and haughty, especially as he made a slight bow, quickly turned, and walked away. But he had delivered the letter, and what would come of it was now in her hands.

As he proceeded down the lane, he could not think; he was only aware of the ground meeting the soles of his shoes. He *did* feel, though: he felt, in giving Elizabeth the letter that contained such personal accounts of himself and his sister, that he was opening his heart up just as he had when he proposed to her. And for Darcy, this was not a comfortable feeling.

He was glad, however, that this meeting with her had been out-of-doors and before him was the walk to Rosings, which he could take at a pace that was dictated by the way he felt . . .

. . . a sense of both nervousness and relief upon handing over the letter.

Chapter 22

Having to walk to Rosings was good for him; his emotions had an outlet, so that, when he arrived within the grounds, he felt much more composed. The colonel saw him from the window and went directly out to meet him.

"Darcy, is all well? You must have gotten away very early. We had all thought you remained upstairs, till the servant informed us you were out."

"Yes, all is well, Fitz. For some reason, I felt a sense of confinement and needed to be out in the fresh air. But may I ask a favor of you, and will you do me the added honor of not inquiring beyond my request?"

"Certainly, old fellow, I will ask nothing; and if I am able, your favor will be done," came the colonel's earnest reply.

"Would you make yourself available at the Parsonage, so that, if Miss Bennet is of a mind, she can ask you about our dealings with Wickham?"

"Wickham! That scoundrel?! How could Miss Bennet know anything of him? Oh, yes . . . forgive me, Darcy, consider the question rhetorical. Should I go straightaway?"

"Let us go together," was Darcy's response. The prospect of seeing her after she had read the letter was his impulse. Would he be able to discern a change in her hard feelings toward him?

"If Miss Bennet has been taken in by Wickham, I welcome the opportunity to be of service to her," the colonel thought to himself, for he truly admired Elizabeth and was acquainted thoroughly with Wickham's devious ways. The thought that he had somehow misled her was enough to move the colonel with purpose.

Arriving at the Parsonage, they were invited in and informed that Elizabeth was out on her morning walk. As they were being seated, Charlotte, considering the attention the gentlemen were demonstrating toward Lizzy by coming to call, was pleased for her friend. Mr. Collins saw only that his humble abode was being thus honored, especially considering the gentlemen were to be leaving the next day. With Elizabeth out, the talk primarily revolved around the gentlemen's plans of leaving Rosings.

Darcy said nothing, but the thought of Elizabeth coming through the door any moment began to overpower him. He felt his being there was putting himself too forward, and that it would surely make Elizabeth uncomfortable, especially after her initial response at seeing him earlier that morning. With this in mind, he rose suddenly, made his excuses and farewells, and began to depart.

The colonel, not knowing if he should likewise leave, was caught by Darcy. "Please, Fitzwilliam, do not feel you must leave also. I have some things to do and must get to them before our journey back to London. You really must take your leave of Miss Bennet. I will see you in an hour or so."

That was clear enough for the colonel, so he stayed. It had been above half an hour when he suggested to Mrs. Collins that he would walk out after her. That scheme was thought better of, since she could arrive from the opposite direction that he would take. At last, an hour passed and he could wait no longer. As he was making his way to Rosings, he stopped on some rising ground and took one last look around, and still he could not see her.

When he entered Rosings, the colonel found Darcy and Lady Catherine together with Anne. On seeing him, the Lady cried, "So, you deign to spend your last day with your relations?"

"I apologize, Aunt, I lost track of time." And coming toward her, he spoke so well in his gratitude to her, it made her alter what she had considered a slight, and in a softer tone, she said, "Young men are too prone to forget time; women, on the other hand, are always better aware of it."

The two gentlemen excused themselves to finish packing, so that the rest of the day could be spent uninterrupted with their aunt and cousin. They wanted to speak of what had taken place at the Parsonage, but had no time. Yet, Darcy could sense that the colonel did not see Elizabeth, for if he had, he would have been in a more lively mood when he came in the house.

The next morning after having breakfast, the cousins took leave of Lady Catherine and Anne, assuring them of their looking forward to their next visit. Now in the carriage, the colonel could confirm what Darcy had sensed, that he was unable to see Elizabeth and could offer no intelligence on that head.

"I must say, Darcy, this is the only disappointment to an otherwise very agreeable visit here."

Darcy was deep in thought, and therefore only heard a reference to some disappointment, so it required that he ask, "Of what disappointment do you speak?"

"Come, come, Darcy, I am referring to not being able to speak to Miss Bennet about that confounded Wickham, and being prevented of taking my leave of her properly! I so wanted to see her one last time."

Darcy was not of a disposition to hear Elizabeth talked of throughout the four hours of their journey to London, so he simply replied, "Indeed," and then added, "I say, Fitz, I am dreadfully tired. Would you consider me a terrible bore if I closed my eyes?"

"No, not at all." In fact, the colonel soon found himself drifting off to sleep.

Darcy had intended this simply as a ploy of putting an end to the topic of Elizabeth. It was easy enough to keep the colonel from talking about her, but to keep himself from *thinking* about her was not so easily mastered. Before closing his eyes, he turned to look back at the place he was leaving, with a feeling of uncertainty, unsure of Elizabeth's reaction to the letter. Through all his adult years, he had been so careful to guard his heart, and now this sense of emptiness was overtaking him. The calm, pragmatic approach to life, combined with his self-assuredness that had served him so well, had failed him in this most important juncture of his life. He felt like a man that had risked everything in hopes of great returns, only to find his confidence had been ill-founded. Instead of holding everything, he held nothing.

However, he was more tired than he realized, and Darcy soon likewise drifted off to sleep.

* * * * *

When only a few miles from town, they were roused from their slumber by a bump in the road, and both exclaimed their surprise at how much time had passed. This was followed by the colonel's mentioning his father and older brother waiting in town to talk to him about a proposal which, according to their communication, was in a fair way of materially advancing his situation.

"Why did you not mention this before now, Fitz?"

"The letter only came yesterday, and occupied as we were, there was no time to tell you. Besides, I wanted to avoid Aunt Catherine and her particular observations on its contents."

"That was very wise of you; but did your father give no details?" asked Darcy.

"No, only what I have told you just now."

"If you don't mind my saying so, Fitz, I wonder at your not being in greater anticipation to know what it is."

"Darcy, my position has always been to have as low an expectation as possible. I know how far my father's reach can be in society, and if I were to entertain ideas in that direction, I could be greatly disappointed in what is presented. When one is being offered some assistance, nothing could be more shallow than to appear disappointed. Not to mention, this may be nothing more than an introduction to a rich ageing duchess, or something of that sort."

Darcy laughed at this, but also knew there may be some truth to it. "Well, then, it sounds as if you have adopted the best approach on this matter. But let us hope instead for a young, beautiful, rich woman seeking to marry a good name here in England."

"Now, Darcy, you are introducing things my way that may truly set my mind to wander! But whatever it is, it is kind of my father and brother to think of me in that way. They could do nothing at all, which if I am not mistaken, is what generally happens in such a case."

"Well, whatever it is, you have not long to wait. But I have given directions for the carriage to stop at my home first; I should amend that, so you are not detained."

"No, no, Darcy, you are very kind, but we will be within blocks of your address first. By all means, let me not keep you in this carriage any longer than need be."

"As you wish."

As the carriage was approaching Darcy's home, Fitzwilliam saw something in him that he had seen ever since yesterday morning. He knew Darcy well enough to notice it. At the start of the trip, he assumed it was merely tiredness, but now he felt sure something else was at work.

Hence, as the carriage came to a stop and Darcy said his goodbyes and well-wishes for his meeting with his father, the colonel added this parting remark: "Darcy, something seems to be troubling you. If you have need of a confidant, I will be only too glad to help."

"Yes, Fitz, I am well aware of that, and thank you for your concern."

They warmly shook hands like the good friends they are, which made Darcy feel more than just a little appreciation for his cousin, and wish from his heart that there would be good tidings awaiting the colonel.

Chapter 23

Darcy was glad to be in his own home again. Being in company had grown tedious for him after the emotional turmoil of the past couple of days. He was greeted by his servant who, opening the door for him, proceeded to take his things and make him comfortable. "Would you like some tea, or perhaps brandy, sir?"

"No, Jenkins, thank you. But I would like some soup and bread. Please send to the cook for some."

"Right away, sir."

"Wait, Jenkins, on second thought, let me go. I would like to see the cook myself. I may find something else while waiting for the soup."

"As you like, sir."

When the master is away, there is a certain feeling of freedom that all servants have, and Darcy's are no exception. But they truly loved their master and it was a pleasure to have him back home. Darcy felt comfortable in the kitchen; the cook, Mrs. Merryweather, had been a favorite of his since his youth.

"Welcome, master, you are a sight for these eyes of mine! There was some talk of you coming, but we had expected your return days ago. You look tired . . . here is fresh bread. What else can I get you?" she asked with concern.

"I would so much care for some of your oxtail soup to go with this bread."

"I had a notion my lad would want something of that sort, so I already made a pot! But, sir, make your way to the dining-room and let us serve you in a proper manner."

"Mrs. Merryweather, if it is all the same to you, I would prefer to have it here. The smells in your kitchen are a touch of home that I sorely need." Darcy felt what might be called hunger, but the emptiness could just as well have been something else.

"To see you at that table again would do my heart good, Master Darcy! This way I can tend to you myself."

The old cook knew her lad well and had seen that forlorn look more than a time or two. However, after setting the table for him, she proceeded about her business as if she did not catch his melancholy mood, knowing that if he wanted to talk, he would do so in his own time.

As Darcy was eating, he found that at least part of the empty feeling was hunger. But then his attention was drawn to the little tune the cook was humming. "What is that melody, Mrs. Merryweather? I have heard you hum it all my life, and yet I have never heard another living soul carry that tune."

"Nor will you, master. That is a little song my father made up for my mother. The little song had a very few words that declared Lucy to be so pretty that she is beautiful. You know, Master Darcy, I have a few days on me and have seen a thing or two, but I never saw a man who loved his wife more than Dad loved Mum. Everything she did was declared to be the best that could be done. Oh, they had their disagreements as everyone has, but just seeing them together, all knew they were the happiest couple to be found. And that sense of love and devotion was as strong as ever, their whole life together."

Darcy was touched at the description of such a pair of lovers, and he could not help but feel pangs of conscience. The description of such loving and admiring words, contrasted with the language he used to present his suit to Miss Bennet, served to chastise him. He felt he had better change the subject. "Mrs. Merryweather, you do your parents proud. And I must say, a man could travel across all of England and France and not meet your equal in the kitchen."

"Oh, Master Darcy, you are too kind," she said, and continued in her motherly fashion, "It is good to have you here with us again."

Darcy finished the last bit of soup and again thanked Mrs. Merryweather. He then made his way to the study, and as he looked at some of the books about him, he was reminded of the conversations the colonel and Elizabeth had on some of these very works -- Fitzwilliam, trying to sound brilliant by quoting what some of the professors had said on the subject without revealing his source, and Elizabeth responding in her uniquely clever way.

His mind returned to Elizabeth's reaction to his proposal ... had his letter had any effect on her? Since she did not avail herself of the opportunity of talking to the colonel, he wondered: was that a sign that she accepted his statements without need of corroboration? or was she determined to think ill of him regardless?

It was now late in the afternoon and he had not changed. He felt inclined for some freshening up and a stroll through the neighborhood. Having been nourished, he exchanged his traveling clothes for evening attire, and felt as if he had likewise removed himself from the events and feelings at Rosings. Stepping out into the brisk evening air, he found it was a capital idea to get out.

As he walked along, he saw a lovely young woman stepping into a carriage. She did not notice Darcy, but at the sight of her, he was taken with the concept that he could now have been an engaged man. His newly revived self made him consider the subject from a *new* point of view:

"I would have welcomed the prospect, for I was in earnest when I made the offer. But since she declined, why should I consider myself the loser? She is the one that had the most to gain by the match, not I; it follows that I would be the least unhappy, and she all the more! I have to suppose that the more she has contemplated what she threw away, she must now be full of regret!"

Being dispassionate seemed to suit him better. Let reason win out. Look at the occurrence objectively and see the sense in not lamenting the outcome . . . With this new anthem sounding in his mind, he returned home.

Chapter 24

Darcy found that the anthem to which he closed his eyes had become discorded and muffled when he opened them again.

He could see that sweet face and her playful smile. Her eyes bright and alert were so clear to him, it was confusing. When she would tease him, her face took on such a pleasant aspect, but he also recalled the look on her face and in those eyes in her reply to his proposal. How correct she was in declaring he had not behaved like a gentleman! Now instead of fierce independence, in his mind he was full of self-reproach and the echoing of Elizabeth's words on that occasion. And again he wanted to know what her reaction to his letter had been.

He had to think of something else . . . but when he thought of *Fitzwilliam* and wondered how his meeting with his father had turned out, he thought also of *Elizabeth* -- how the colonel was taken with her. He could hear Fitzwilliam speaking his praise of her, and thinking of the colonel, and how he hoped his situation would soon be improved, made him likewise consider Elizabeth and her sisters being in a similar situation, needing relief. This comparison served to increase the absurdity of his high-minded thinking and words toward Elizabeth and her family, which led to yet another mortifying similarity: the insolent behavior of his aunt with that of Mrs. Bennet.

"How embarrassed I was at Rosings by my aunt's conduct, just as Elizabeth was with her mother's at Netherfield. If my aunt's situation was reversed with Mrs. Bennet, would she not be considered just as foolish, ridiculous, and senseless? Why should money, or the *lack* of it, render a person's conduct more -- or less -- improper?"

These thoughts followed him from the bed, where they started, down to breakfast. After he had eaten, he asked for paper and pen. "Jenkins, send this note over to Colonel Fitzwilliam and wait for a reply."

The message read:

> *Fitz, would like to know how things stand with you.*
> *Can I come see you? Are you at liberty to talk?*
> *Darcy*

An hour later the servant returned with this reply:

> *Darcy, I am not at liberty to talk.*
> *But think: 'young, beautiful and wealthy!'*
> *Will contact you when I can.*
> *Now there is much to attend to.*
> *Fitzwilliam*

"This is pleasant news indeed!" Darcy thought. "Fitz, being happily married and . . ." Darcy had to check himself here. The colonel's material situation may improve by this match, but it did not follow that he would also be happy. Many a marriage has not turned out so, despite whatever material advantage there might come with it.

These thoughts would not have presented themselves so strongly or quickly had Darcy reason for joy himself. "Surely a man with Fitz's disposition and good breeding would lead a woman to love and respect him," he thought. And yet, here again he could not help but think of how happiness in marriage depends not just on the *one,* but on the *two.*

He had believed his proposal to Miss Bennet would make her happy, but his memories on this point were all too clear. Her words he continued to hear again and again: *"You could not have made me the offer of your hand in any possible way that would have tempted me to accept it."*

"I refuse to accept that my history on the subject of marriage proposal should doom good ol' Fitz. So I will leave it to him and this 'young beauty' to make happiness as they can." Darcy shook his head, as if he were a dog shaking the water off its coat; but alas, he could not so easily remove Elizabeth's words and the self-reproach they brought.

He had to get out of the house! He wished he was at Pemberley so he could go for a ride in those familiar surroundings. However, he had to get out, resorting to a walk; to where he knew not. He did not want to see his friend Bingley, as that would necessitate seeing his sister also; going from a woman that was disgusted with him to one that fairly threw herself at him was a swing of the pendulum too far at this time.

The contending that had started indoors continued out-of-doors. "She was expressing feelings of injury of the female kind, because my words and actions were not romantic. My honesty was not what a lady would like to hear on such occasions."

He sat down on a nearby bench. "No, Darcy, that will not do as an excuse for yourself."

He stood up. He ran his hands through his hair. "My words and actions were offensive regardless of the subject being discussed!"

He sat down. "I was so convinced that a woman in her situation would consider an offer of marriage coming from me as a gift from above, that I proceeded in pride and conceit."

He stood up. "This is not about romance! It is just as Miss Bennet said, *I did not behave like a gentleman.*"

He took a few steps to lean against a nearby tree. "A real gentleman considers the feelings of others regardless of their station. I have examples of such excellent behavior in Fitzwilliam and Charles. I had been used to think their actions were a consequence of their situation being so different from mine . . . Fitz has always had to be concerned about who he pleased, being the youngest son as he is. And Charles, being raised outside of society before his father came into his fortune -- it seemed only natural he had not yet learnt to be discriminating in his taste. But really, it is I who founded my actions on a very selfish premise . . . I am afraid Miss Bennet knows me better than I give her credit. That evening at Rosings while she played the piano, her reproof was *correct* . . . I have not given myself the trouble to learn how a *real gentleman* behaves in society."

With this perusal of his actions under such an honest light, he sat down once more.

Chapter 25

Darcy now became determined to make a better person of himself, to do away with self-interest and pride and make a go of showing an interest in others. This proved very helpful to him, as it gave him a constructive outlet. Further, he had now come to grips with at least one matter that had been weighing on him -- the arguing with himself about his share in the debacle that was his marriage proposal. He felt now he could put this behind him and come out as a man that had learned a valuable lesson.

He began to look at this matter as being comparable to his school days, when he had taken a difficult class. He recalled, "During that time I would think not just of the subject, but also of the teacher. However, once the lesson was learned and the class completed, I would remember the education and the teacher would no longer be thought of." Darcy resolved to take the lesson of doing away with selfish pride to heart and forget his teacher, *Elizabeth*; but forgetting *this* instructor would be a far cry from forgetting a stodgy old college professor.

He felt that he could now visit Charles and his sister. To that end, he sent a brief note:

> *Charles, I am back in town and would very much like to call on you tomorrow after lunch.*
> *Darcy*

Charles' response exhibited his usual exuberance:

> *By all means, come.*
> *Come sooner. . . today even, if you can.*
> *Charles*

Caroline wanted her brother to mention how she too was anxious to see him, but he was not one for writing and could not see what difference it would make to include her eagerness in his note. As he told his sister, "I have given him leave to call sooner. How am I to know if he did not set his visit for tomorrow after lunch because his own business requires it?" The argument was too sound for Caroline to make a reply, especially when all she really wanted was her name to be a part of the appeal.

Darcy, on receiving the message, smiled to hear from his good friend and note his eagerness to see him again. But as there were things that needed attending to that he had neglected and could now give the proper attention, he was to go the following day, as planned.

* * * * *

On drawing near Bingley's home, a thought of his resolution of showing an interest in others entered his mind. "But I am on such terms with Charles that it need not be an issue here; and besides, the one thing I do not want to do is give some kind of encouragement to Caroline Bingley."

As he entered their home and was introduced into the sitting room, Charles rose promptly and approached him with warmth and kindness, shaking his hand heartily. "It is good to see you again, Darcy! I can see that you are well. How are Georgiana and your cousin, the colonel?"

"Everyone is well, thank you, Charles; and it is a pleasure to see you, and you, Miss Bingley. But where are Mr. and Mrs. Hurst?"

Caroline answered for her sister: "They have been called away on some business of Mr. Hurst. I really do not know how you men can put up with having to be called away from friends and good company for this 'necessary business,' as it is put."

"Caroline, you are making light of the word *necessary*. I believe if you will but consider the meaning of the word, you will have your answer," protested Bingley.

"Oh, Charles, you can be so tiresome," and turning her attention to Darcy, she added, "Did you leave your aunt well? And what of her excellent daughter, Anne?"

To anyone that knew, it was clear that Caroline would never have spoken so highly of Miss Anne de Bourgh if she had known that *she* was intended for Darcy. But this is how ignorance shows its face.

"They were both well, thank you," he answered.

"But you stayed longer than intended, if I am not mistaken," returned Charles. "Is that not so? Your visit must have been a pleasant one. One will always lose track of time when happiness fills the days." Charles could not know that he had hit on a subject that would touch Darcy as it did.

It cannot be said whether the look in Darcy's eye was observed or went unnoticed. His mind caught on the word *happiness*. "Happiness?" Darcy repeated. "Yes, certainly, there were times of happiness." He had to change the subject. "I am sorry I did not come sooner or let you know I was back in town, but there were things I needed to attend to that prevented me from coming."

"You mean 'necessary' things," Caroline interjected. That bit of humor was a welcomed interruption for Darcy.

"Yes," cried Charles, *"necessary*! Now you may congratulate yourself on having learned the lesson of the day! Come, Caroline, we have not even asked Darcy if he would have tea."

"Yes, that would be welcomed, thank you, Charles."

The conversation over tea was of little interest except to the three. But Darcy, looking at Bingley, could not help thinking of how he had separated him from Jane. This, accompanied with hearing Elizabeth's account of what pain it had caused Jane and his intimate knowledge of how it had affected Charles, was beginning to make it difficult for Darcy to stay focused on the light-hearted conversation taking place.

Thankfully, Caroline turned and asked Darcy, "Would you please go into the shops with us and be of assistance in choosing colors and fabrics for Charles' new suits?"

Bingley added, "Yes, Darcy, do come. You know what sort of a fool I am in such matters, and Caroline only serves to irritate me."

Being up doing something was just what Darcy needed. "I will be glad to. I have also been meaning to look for a new hat; this scheme will work for us both."

"And then you must also take dinner with us, Darcy, for we have missed your company, and with Mr. and Mrs. Hurst away, the three of us will have an excellent time at dinner." All were in agreement, and to the shops they proceeded to go.

As the material and colors for Charles' suits had been chosen, it was time for Darcy to look for a hat. Looking at one and then another, Caroline would urge him to consider one of her choosing. This definitely did not please Darcy, for he knew his own mind and did not enjoy having this much involvement from another person.

She actually chose one that appealed to him very much, but considering how he would have to be reminded that *she* chose it for him every time he wore it, he felt it would be too high a price to pay even for so fine a hat. Hence, he had to say, "No, it seems I will not find one today. Since it is beginning to get late, should we not proceed home?"

Over dinner, Charles asked Darcy when next he would be at Pemberley. "Within a few weeks . . . I must say, I long to be back."

"Indeed, who would not cherish the thought of calling Pemberley home?" Caroline observed.

Charles then said, "Darcy, am I being too forward in asking if we could come for a few days? It is a perfect time of year to be out in the country, and Netherfield . . . well . . . it would be kind of you to receive us at Pemberley."

At hearing this, Caroline was filled with anticipation for Darcy's response. He observed this, but also noticed how Charles had faltered at referring to Netherfield. Sensing the reason for this, he felt for his friend and was eager to assist him, and thus responded with a warm invitation.

To own the truth, Darcy could not hear a reference to that area without feeling something himself. This was one of the main reasons he wanted to go to Pemberley. In an effort to redirect both Charles' and his own mind, Darcy addressed

Caroline: "Which of the grounds of Pemberley do you enjoy the most?"

"The area outside the breakfast room delights me very much. What a pleasure it would be to have such a view every morning!"

Charles, joining in asked, "Would you not enjoy a stroll by the stream? The natural beauty along that walk is impressive."

"Oh, Charles, honestly! Such traipsing about into nature is not for the refined lady. That sort of thing is for women of a more common and menial makeup, like Miss Eliza Bennet. Scampering about the countryside seems to be what she was made for!"

If Miss Bingley had gone to school to be educated about how to work against her own interest in the affairs of love, she could not have been more skilled at it! Charles could not hear such mean talk about people whom he thought well of without defending them.

His defense was not needed, though. Darcy responded quickly and with feeling, "I had not the impression that ladies taking exercise would put them in such a category as you propose. Tell me, do you hold the same view of ladies being out riding?"

Caroline's disposition was not one of mildness; she was mean-spirited and prone to retaliate. She therefore went working further against herself by retorting, "Mr. Darcy, pardon me! I see Miss Bennet's *fine eyes* still seem to have an appeal for you! Her experience out in the wild has evidently taught her how to bait a trap with some success. Or perhaps I should give the credit to her mother for teaching her gaggle of penniless daughters how to appeal to young men, even those who are not in uniform! What is to become of superior society if those whose relations could fill all of *Cheapside,* as Charles once noted, are allowed to be ladies worth admitting into one's acquaintance?"

Charles could not be silent at this speech. "Really, Caroline, is this sort of talk necessary? My only comfort is that Darcy is like a brother to me and will extend forbearance on your taking such liberties with him."

Darcy, who was about to say more than he really would have wanted to on the subject of Elizabeth if Charles had not reproved his sister, merely said, "Of course, Charles, such things are said to each other among family and friends. Let us not give it another thought. It is late now and I must be off. Thank you for dinner."

"But, Darcy, we have not had coffee."

"No. If it is all the same, Charles, I really should be getting back to attend to some paperwork before the hour advances too much more." With that, the carriage was called for, and he left.

"Caroline, what possessed you to speak so of Miss Elizabeth Bennet? and to Darcy?"

"And why is Mr. Darcy so ready to defend someone like *her*? Someone that has nothing to recommend herself other than her affinity for being out-of-doors?"

All he could do was shake his head and go out for a walk. He was not simply getting away from Caroline because of being angry, however; all this talk about the Bennets made it necessary for solitude.

Charles had no idea that it was this very thing that made his friend seek a similar relief. Darcy gave little credence to anything Caroline said, for he thought too little of her and her opinion for it to matter. But the feelings that were aroused at hearing Elizabeth being spoken against, he could not deny.

"I was not just responding to the unkindness Caroline was directing toward Miss Bennet. No, I could not bear to hear her spoken of in such a manner; my heart moved me to speak . . .

. . . and for me to speak even before impulsive Charles is definitely something to be wondered at! I have denied how deeply I feel for her! To hear such sentiments coming from Caroline Bingley, so similar to those that I had uttered to her myself, confirms to me how repulsive it must have sounded when I spoke them to her. How *long* will such recollections haunt me?"

Darcy would not permit himself to dwell on such remorse, so he declared, "I am not a sentimentalist and I will not permit myself to continue to have feelings for someone who has little regard for me, though this confirms to me why I must make a real change in my view and attitude toward others. Caroline has at least been useful in demonstrating to me the ugliness of it."

By the time the carriage had made the journey to his home, Darcy had again run through every reason for forgetting Elizabeth. But as he exited the carriage, a recollection made him stop -- there *was* the letter and his not knowing what effect it had on her opinion of him.

"This will not do!" thought Darcy. "Am I to reason myself in and out of love this way indefinitely? But what hope can there be for me to ever see her again? We travel in such different circles, it would require my purposefully setting out to see her."

This was a bending of his pride that he was not equal to at this point. "It is to be supposed that, with the passage of time, my feelings will diminish and become mere memories."

And so it seemed that time would be the arbiter of Darcy's heart.

Chapter 26

Bingley felt Darcy had left his home injured by Caroline's cutting remarks. Therefore, wanting to see his good friend as soon as possible, he journeyed early to Darcy's home the next morning. Upon arriving, he moved toward him with a concerned look and entreated, "Darcy, please let me apologize for my sister's conduct yesterday; I fear her comments offended you. It was certainly shameful and cruel."

Darcy tried to smile for his friend's sake, but was not able to manage it well. "Pray, do not make yourself uneasy about yesterday, Charles; I am familiar enough with Caroline's manners so as not to be unduly disturbed by them."

"Yes, but to be treated thus when first meeting after so long an absence is unpardonable!"

"I did not say I pardoned your sister, but there is no need for *you* to be uneasy," Darcy said in a lighter tone, which had its effect on Bingley. "Have you eaten yet this morning, Charles? I was about to move into the breakfast room."

"No, I haven't. I was too concerned to sit down, but it would be a pleasure to join you. You know, Darcy, you should be glad that Georgiana is so much younger than you. When sisters are closer in age like Caroline is to me, they tend to take greater liberties, as you have often witnessed. I believe she inherited a very biting disposition; one cannot disagree with her without experiencing it."

"To be sure, Georgiana may look at me more like a father than a brother."

"Well, I am not giving Georgiana her due, because she is not really like Caroline at all, no matter her age. I could never imagine her being so sharp-tongued; she has such a kind and gentle nature."

"You have a point there, Charles. My sister is quite different from Caroline."

"Sometimes I wonder, Darcy, what kind of man could possibly be attracted to such a person as my sister, or if there will ever be one." Darcy was reflecting on the question when Bingley continued, "I will tell you what sort of man -- a spineless fool with a great fortune! For without a fortune, no one could be an attraction to my sister." This last statement was made with a sense of indignation and a note of sadness. Darcy understood it to be a reference to Jane Bennet.

Bingley, noticing Darcy's introspection, said, "Excuse me, Darcy, for carrying on like this. It is just that . . ." he could not finish his sentence. Darcy could see that Charles had recollected that he also was involved in the business of Jane not being a suitable match. The pain he saw in his friend made him reflect on the part he had played in the matter and wonder.

At that moment, the servant came in with a note for Bingley from Caroline.

It read:

>*Charles,*
>*Louisa and I are going shopping and were hoping to take lunch with you at the Austen Inn. Pray, ask Mr. Darcy if he would like to join us.*
>*Caroline*

Charles informed Darcy of the contents of the note and extended the invitation, hoping very much his friend would accept.

"Yes, of course, it sounds like a splendid scheme. While your sisters are shopping for their concerns, we can be off on our own till lunch." The offer did not really appeal to Darcy, but for the sake of his friend, he was willing to put himself through some inconvenience or disharmony.

Lunch unfolded with little unpleasantness, as it seemed Caroline had determined to be agreeable, especially with someone whom she wanted to be found agreeable. Darcy was not the sort to be swayed by such inconsistent behavior and obvious attempts at putting on a display for his sake. The falseness of such conduct worked against his natural sense of honesty, though he was glad to have lunch in peace and calm.

* * * * *

Returning home, Darcy began contemplating how things had turned out for his cousin Fitzwilliam. When last he wrote, Fitz had said he would tell more when he could, and Darcy dearly wanted to know what more there was to be said about the *'young and beautiful'* lady. He had been waiting for this further communication, but since so much time had passed, he decided to write and inquire.

As he proceeded to his desk, the servant came in announcing that the colonel and a lady had arrived! As they entered the room, Darcy saw the glow of happiness and pride on his cousin's face. He smiled and said warmly, "Fitzwilliam, how good to see you."

The colonel in turn replied, "Indeed, Darcy, I apologize for keeping you in suspense for so long, but now I have the pleasure of introducing you to Mademoiselle Maria Leblanc -- my *fiancée*."

Maria was a picture of loveliness -- dark eyes and strong feminine features in that French way, for she was born in France, but raised in England. Her parents, sensing the serious situation that became the French Revolution, had moved the family to England before it started. Here they purchased property and established themselves on a strong financial footing. But being nobles in France, they longed for at least a sense of it here in England; for with the Revolution, they lost all claims to such titles. Marrying into a family such as the colonel's was a move to re-establish themselves to some extent in that direction. The colonel's family felt the idea of the eldest son bringing up the status of a French family was not quite suitable, but Fitzwilliam's father saw in this an opportunity for his youngest son. All that was needed was to know if the colonel would consider the match, which he certainly did!

As the three talked, it became obvious to Darcy that the colonel was taken with Maria. Darcy had confidence in his judgement; Fitz had seen enough of the world not to be fooled by someone putting on airs. With this and his own observations of Maria in mind, Darcy was disposed to like her, even without his resolution of being more amiable. In the course of the conversation, he asked how she felt about being raised in England.

"My father loves France and he has given me a sense of what was lost there, but he has also taught me just how sad our situation could have been. Having grown up here, I consider this my home."

She spoke with confidence and honesty, and it was clear she had been well-educated. Then, too, when she looked at Fitzwilliam, her eyes sparkled with admiration and fondness. Darcy's good opinion of her grew with each passing moment.

Fitzwilliam, noticing the time, declared they must be off, though he was reluctant to go, as he really wished to visit more with Darcy. Picking up on this, Maria said, "Fitzwilliam, as I will be busy with my mother tomorrow throughout most of the day, perhaps that would afford an opportunity for you and Mr. Darcy to spend some time together."

"Yes, Maria, that is a capital idea! Thank you, my dear, for thinking of it. What do you say, Darcy?"

"There is nothing I would like more. In fact, I was in the process of writing to ask you that very thing when you came in."

"Splendid! Come at your convenience, Darcy; come for breakfast, if you wish."

As the lovers left, Darcy felt a sense of pleasure in this good turn for his cousin. He recalled Fitz's beaming face as he declared, *'This is my fiancée.'* Sincerely, Darcy thought, "If it were a matter of one of us being happy in this way, the colonel deserves it much more than I."

Chapter 27

The next day after breakfast, Darcy met with the colonel, and after appropriate formalities with the whole family, the two cousins excused themselves and ventured out-of-doors to enjoy some time talking together, and soon found themselves at the gazebo.

Fitzwilliam asked Darcy, "What is your impression of Maria?" The question had been asked indoors, but there with the whole family present, the colonel felt Darcy would not speak as openly as he would to him alone, so he felt he could now repeat the question.

"Fitz, my praise of her that was spoken when your mother asked was in earnest. I will say further, however, that her disposition seems kind and thoughtful, and though she is aware of what was lost, she is not resigned to look negatively on her family's situation. I think her mother and father must likewise be excellent people."

"They are indeed, Darcy. Aside from her natural disposition, they have raised her to look on things in as positive a light as possible. This speaks highly of them, since they have reason to think the world a very mean place."

"The two of you seem to get on very well," observed Darcy.

"I would say that Maria and I are very well suited. She is extremely intelligent -- in fact, she reminds me of Miss Bennet in her powers of conversation. Maria's wit does not have the same humorous turn, but when we talk, I find myself intrigued by her view of things."

"May I ask you a question about the marriage, Fitz?"

"Of course, Darcy, ask whatever you would like."

"Some time back, Charles Bingley and I had discussions on the subject of marriage and reasons for marrying, and considering your present situation, I would very much like to hear what you have to say on the matter. Fitz, do you feel you are entering this marriage out of respect for your father, or are pecuniary reasons the primary focus? Or are romantic feelings motivating you?"

"You know, Darcy, when my father first presented the matter to me, I asked if he could put off the introduction for a day so I could be prepared for the meeting. He told me nothing had been settled beyond that we would be introduced. He did, of course, point out the advantages of the match and encouraged me to give it due weight. I thanked him for his consideration and the efforts in my behalf. That evening when I was alone, I asked myself something similar to what you have just asked."

"What did you conclude?"

"I kept hearing my father say, *'Nothing has been settled beyond the introduction.'* I reasoned: just meet her and think no further on it now; but my mind refused to be settled. I wondered, would her fortune outweigh some defect of character or appearance? Could I enter into a lifelong arrangement just to secure some financial stability? This thought began to irritate me; I am no fool in matters such as these, nor am I prone to act on impulse -- were I impulsive, I would have made an offer to Miss Bennet! So instead of trying to calculate how big a fortune it would take to outweigh some negative on Miss Leblanc's part, I decided to trust my judgement and put off such calculations till they might be needed."

Again a comparison to Elizabeth! Darcy had to ask, "You were so taken with Miss Bennet that you considered making an offer to her?"

"Yes, and no. I made my position clear to her so she would not entertain false hopes. Had her circumstances or mine been different, I have no doubt my thoughts would have taken a more serious turn. But I must say, Maria and Miss Bennet are very similar. Both have pride, but it is the kind that engenders respect. They refuse to feel sorry for themselves and have a determination that is not often met with in their sex."

"That is true," said Darcy, "most women seem determined only to make a match."

"Then you see, Darcy, speaking more to the point: after meeting Maria the first time, the thought of having to make any allowance for her appearance was moot -- she is loveliness itself! But I continued this debate with myself, still knowing so little of her character. After the third meeting, I saw there was no defect of character, for as you have observed, she speaks openly and honestly. She has thus revealed herself to be as fine a person as I have ever met. Now I was confronted with the question of whether I should continue to see her, and which of those very three reasons that you presented earlier should carry the most weight. I finally concluded, I am motivated by respect for my father, and rightly so; I do have to consider such pecuniary needs as I have, and Maria answers for that. Finally, however, I found that I admire her in such a way that romantic feelings followed most naturally. So, I suppose it could be said, I have fallen in love with the woman that is perfect for me, as well as one of whom my father approves."

"Well, I must say, I am truly happy for you, Fitz."

"As things have turned out, I am actually glad that I have not been in your situation, Darcy."

"My situation? What do you mean?"

"Well, as I said, *as things have turned out*, meaning with Maria. If I was in your situation, having the freedom to marry whomever I would choose without having to consider such things as we have been discussing, I may very well have chosen to marry some time before this, in which case, I would have missed out on meeting a most outstanding woman. In point of fact, I should say meeting and *falling in love* with a most outstanding woman. You know, Darcy, what are the chances that I, or any other man for that matter, should meet two of the most remarkable women in the space of just a few weeks?"

"You are speaking of Miss Bennet again?"

"Yes, and I must say, the time at Rosings with her made me realize what satisfaction there is to be found in the company of such a woman. I believe that experience made me more open to the possibility of finding happiness in marriage and not just making a good match, as is said."

At this point, the colonel's father was seen approaching, and the cousins rose to meet him. "I have been sent to request you lads join us inside, as your mother has prepared a surprise for you, and she did not want Darcy to get away without being a part of it."

Going inside, the cousins were surprised to find Maria and her parents. The colonel's expression of satisfaction made Darcy know that Fitz *really was* in love, and the look on Maria's face revealed the same. Darcy also noticed her mother and father and how proud they were of their daughter, as well as the pleasure they took in the knowledge that she had made a match with one of the finest men to be found in England.

After Darcy was introduced to the Leblancs, everyone's attention was called for and directed to the adjoining room in which were four covered easels. The happy couple was invited to uncover each one, starting from the left. The two mothers had taken portraits of each of their children, which had been done as they were growing up, and had new portraits made, putting the young people together. To everyone's surprise, the last canvas was blank, to be done after the wedding. The mothers explained, they wanted to evoke the idea that they were destined for one another.

As the lovers hugged and thanked each mother, Darcy watched the two families rejoice, but the sight made him feel a bit lonely. His mother and father are gone, his only family is his much younger sister, and now the thought of such a scene as this for himself or his sister is an impossibility. In addition to this sad thought, his first attempt at securing happiness through marriage turned out to be an exposé of his faults. Mercifully for Darcy, lunch was announced and his contemplations ended; and for the rest, the joy and satisfaction in the drawing-room was taken to the dining-room.

After lunch, the men retreated into the library, and the ladies went back into the drawing-room. At such times as these, men and women are now free to talk of things they might not in mixed company. This segregation did not last above half an hour, and when the two parties became one again, coffee was served. In time, Darcy felt the impulse to be off. He had reason to be satisfied with himself, for in harmony with his determination to be more congenial, he had joined in several conversations about the room. His last gesture in keeping with this was to make the rounds of the room, again congratulating and praising what had already been congratulated and praised for the final time. He then was off.

Chapter 28

Darcy felt a certain amount of relief to be alone again, but there was also a certain restlessness, so when the carriage arrived in his neighborhood, he signaled for it to stop. He wanted to walk -- actually, he wanted to think, but his mind was a jumble, and this created a nervous energy that needed an outlet.

The exercise and open air was having its effect. His mind became less confused. "I am not a sentimental man, I keep saying of myself . . . *why then am I struggling with my emotions?* The happiness I witnessed this day was the happiness of real love -- no pretenses, or trying to make the best of some necessary arrangement. That kind of happiness is to be desired by both the sentimentalist and the non-sentimentalist."

As his mind became more focused, he stopped by a bench. Recalling his conversation with the colonel, he thought: "To think that Fitz would have made an offer to Miss Bennet, if he had been in a position to do so! He described her as one of *the* most remarkable women he has ever met, and he moves in such circles to make that statement carry weight! . . . *I seem to be forever confronted with her.* She appears in locations least expected, and obtrudes into my mind for no apparent reason. . . and then she is mentioned in conversations when least expected . . . Heaven seems determined that I not forget her, just as she seems determined to despise me: *'I could not have made my offer in any way that would have tempted her to accept me'* . . . will that phrase ever stop playing in my mind?!!"

With this recollection Darcy sat down. It was as if this memory was too heavy for him to continue standing.

His mind was taken back to the scene of Fitzwilliam and Maria uncovering the different canvases. Darcy was touched by the affection shown by the two lovers as they declared those portraits did indeed convey the idea that they were meant for each other.

And then his thoughts turned to the last canvas, empty, waiting to be painted. He felt his present situation was like that canvas -- *empty, waiting.*

Chapter 29

The time had come for Darcy and the Bingleys to go to Pemberley, but having some necessary business with his steward to attend to, Darcy went on ahead of the party so as not to be involved with such things with company at home. He had made great strides in becoming more concerned with the feelings of others. With the Bingleys, however, this required some dexterity so as not to give Caroline a notion that she was the object of this change in him, and this he had managed very well for the present. Charles had commented several times on his more open manners.

As he rode alone to Pemberley, he had as company the satisfaction that his efforts had made a noticeable change. Nothing was more abhorrent to him than falseness, and he did not want this most personal scheme to be a facade. To be sure, it still required effort, but he was becoming more comfortable around strangers and his interest in them was sincere.

He also thought of Charles and how glad he was to see him more like his old self, although Darcy could sense that the sadness of a broken heart still lingered inside him. These recollections were doubly troublesome for Darcy, for it saddened him that his dear friend still grieved and that *he* was chiefly responsible for it. This naturally led his thoughts to Elizabeth and her expressing anger and pain for his coming between her sister and Charles, and though such thoughts were vexing, he attempted to turn them to some useful purpose so that his determination to continue his reforms would not waver.

As his trip was coming to an end, for he was now in the familiar grounds of Pemberley, he thought, "Well, at least here from this point forward, I will have no occasion for thinking of Miss Bennet."

With this thought in mind, he dismounted his horse, giving it over to the stable boy. Turning and looking about himself, he drew a deep breath and exhaled in a gesture suggesting that Elizabeth was now out of his system, and then walked toward the front of the house.

As he rounded the corner, he saw something that stopped him in his tracks and took his breath away, for there -- not twenty yards away -- stood Miss Elizabeth Bennet!

He paused, frozen as it were. Then suddenly recollecting himself, he proceeded toward her just as she had begun to quickly turn away, for she likewise had caught sight of him. Seeing him step toward her and pronounce her name, she halted and waited for him. The two were equally flustered, Elizabeth not even being able to meet his eyes; yet had she done so, she would have seen the same flush of the cheek on his that shown on her own.

Darcy's new self now broke through the uneasiness he felt to save him, as he asked after her family and how long she had been in the area. The combination of astonishment and embarrassment made him quite confused, which caused him to inquire again after her family, and even repeat himself *again*; speaking in so hurried a manner, it was no wonder there was little time for his words to register in his mind! His regard for her was so strong that he now spoke with such gentleness as he had never spoken to her before; and such an alteration in manner, however awkwardly done, was nevertheless so pronounced as did not escape her notice.

Which of the two were the most astonished and embarrassed could not be made out. Of course, two persons in equal perturbation quickly had nothing else to say, so Darcy found it expedient to take his leave.

Walking to the house, his mind was in disarray! He was trying to recollect what had been said, but the exclamation, *"She is here at Pemberley!"* kept interrupting. He sat down as soon as he entered the house, and the servants came to attend to him. He simply asked for water and to be given a moment to sit. The servants did not go far, for although he looked well, they could tell something was not quite right with their master.

Now that he had a brief respite to recover from this development, something more like rational thought began to work. *"How long will she be in the area? Will she permit me to see her again?"* Then a thought that brought him to his feet -- *"She must still be here at Pemberley!"* Inquiring from the housekeeper about her arrival, he was informed that they had just now been turned over to the gardener to look about the grounds. After determining which direction they had taken, he followed briskly.

As he proceeded after them, his mind began considering that her being at Pemberley could be an indication that her feelings toward him might have softened, that his letter must have made her think better of him. In any case, the only way to discover any of this would be to see her again and with more presence of mind.

Elizabeth and the Gardiners were now walking by the river. Darcy proceeded after them and could see they were nearby. As he walked toward her, the path took some twists and turns that hid them from his view, but he walked with purpose. His heart would not let him recall that within this very hour he had rejoiced at not having to think of her! As he came from the final turn, he found himself right before her. Elizabeth immediately attempted politely giving her praise of Pemberley, how delightful and charming she found it to be, and then suddenly halted in the middle of her words.

At this pause, Darcy asked to be introduced to her friends. On hearing they were her aunt and uncle, he felt pangs of conscience, recollecting his reference to her relations as *'being decidedly beneath him.'* He could not completely conceal his surprise; it was for but a moment, though, for Darcy was determined to present his new self.

When he was informed that they were just making their way back to the carriage, he proceeded with them, stationing himself by Mr. Gardiner's side. Darcy expected to find her uncle as uninformed and tedious as some of her other relations and was bracing himself for it. He was also a bit nervous on his own behalf, but found himself pleasantly surprised in both quarters. The ease with which they conversed was just what Darcy needed; he was able to relax and enjoy the conversation. They began talking of fishing, and he was pleased to be able to invite Mr. Gardiner to come fishing as often as he liked while in the neighborhood, even looking forward to joining him, if possible.

After walking some time in this manner, Mrs. Gardiner expressed a desire to be supported by her husband, as she had grown tired and Elizabeth's arm was not sufficient. Now Darcy and Elizabeth found themselves walking together, and his nervousness began to return. As he rummaged his mind for some topic to introduce, Elizabeth began speaking of how unexpected his arrival was. Hoping to do away with any impression of having purposefully put herself forward, and to explain her presence, she informed him that they had come only after having been assured that the family was not at Pemberley; that even Mrs. Reynolds told them he would not be home until tomorrow.

Explaining his reason for returning earlier, he related that the Bingleys would also be arriving early the next day. This reference to Charles created a painful recollection for them both. Darcy, wanting to move past this as quickly as possible, attempted to mention anything that would accomplish it.

"Would you permit me to introduce my sister Georgiana to you?" The words had scarcely left his lips when he realized he had revealed more in this application than he otherwise would have.

This request took Elizabeth by surprise, and for a moment she was rendered speechless. Her silence made the words hang in the air for Darcy, not knowing if he was going to regret this or congratulate himself for unconsciously saying something that ought to have been said. Elizabeth's positive response stopped any sense of anxiety that was starting to build in him, but this most unusual conversation had the effect of rendering them *both* silent.

Darcy did mentally consider with satisfaction Elizabeth's willingness to be introduced to Georgiana: "It would not be too difficult for someone traveling to invent an excuse to avoid something they really wished to avoid." This brought a momentary respite to his disquietude. Unknown to each of them, however, their minds were trying to process the meaning of the other's words. The silence was very awkward, as they both seemed to want to talk but were afraid of bringing up the wrong subject. This had the effect of making them oblivious to the aunt and uncle, who were moving slowly and getting further and further behind.

The two soon found themselves at the carriage, and upon turning, they realized just how far they had out-paced the others. Now their silence was pronounced. If they had not been searching for something to say with equal anxiety, each would have seen the same expression on the other's face. Elizabeth was first to hit upon a subject: she remarked on their traveling. But this subject was not sufficient, for her aunt and uncle were moving very slowly. Their feelings were forcing subjects into their minds that could not be expressed here, *now;* so as a consequence, any ordinary subjects were blocked, leaving them both somewhat confused.

When Mr. and Mrs. Gardiner finally made it to the carriage, Darcy graciously asked, "Mrs. Gardiner, would you please come in and take some refreshment and sit for a while? After such a walk as this, surely a bit of rest before continuing would do you all some good."

Their schedule required that they decline, however, which was done with great appreciation for the offer. Darcy did not notice Elizabeth, as the carriage drove away, taking one last look at him as he walked toward the house, yet his mind could think of nothing else but her. "Thank goodness for lack of rational thought and speech! I do not believe I would have proposed introducing Georgiana to her otherwise . . . her willingness to see me again surely must be an indication that her feelings have altered and softened toward me! . . . I know she would never be rude, but her view of me as expressed at

Rosings would not allow her to see me now if it could be avoided."

These pleasant musings were suddenly intruded on by the idea that perhaps her real purpose was to see Charles, for her sister's sake. He thought, "She is just such a person that would work in a cause concerning her sister, even if it meant some unpleasantness for herself."

Now Darcy found himself on a footing that was not so sure once again. "At such a time as *this*, rational thought returns, allowing me but a moment's happiness!" Still, with a sense of purpose and conviction in the sincerity of his new self, he determined to make the most of this opportunity and demonstrate to Elizabeth that he is *not* the same man she turned down at Rosings.

Chapter 30

The next day Darcy roamed the house, anticipating the arrival of Georgiana and the Bingleys, eager at the prospect of Elizabeth meeting his sister. When they did come, the party was welcomed into the saloon where refreshments were served. They talked of the trip and how glad they were to see Pemberley again, and all were expressing high expectations for what happy times lay ahead. Hearing all this talk of happy expectations, Darcy could no longer restrain himself; so calling Georgiana and Charles' attention, he said, "Georgiana, do you recall my mentioning Miss Elizabeth Bennet to you?"

"Yes, of course I do."

At hearing Elizabeth's name mentioned, Caroline looked at Mrs. Hurst with astonishment and distress.

"You will be pleased to know that she is here at the Inn in Lambton, and I have proposed introducing you to her; she expressed a desire to meet you." Georgiana could not have been more pleased to meet the lady that her brother had spoken of so highly.

Charles, at hearing this news, declared with enthusiasm, "It is still early, can we not go now? That is, of course, if Georgiana is not too fatigued." She declared herself to be just as eager with this impromptu scheme. Darcy had been hoping to invent some reason to go into Lambton after the arrival of his guests; hence, he was the first one to his feet as the words were spoken by Charles.

"Darcy, I would never have imagined that one of the Bennets would be here. But pray, you and Georgiana go on ahead in the carriage and I will go by horse; I would prefer the exercise."

"Upon my word, what a stir to be created by such a person as Eliza Bennet!" cried Caroline.

At this, Georgiana looked toward her brother, not knowing what such a comment would do to their plan. But Charles and her brother paid not the smallest attention to it, so she followed their lead and proceeded out of the room.

Darcy and Georgiana were in the carriage straightaway, while Bingley waited for his horse to be made ready. In the carriage, she asked her brother, "Tell me again about Miss Elizabeth." As Darcy began his speech, she noticed the joy of his eyes mingled with something else she could not account for. She loved and respected her brother more than any words could express and longed to see him happy. Even as young as she was, it seemed quite clear to her that Elizabeth must figure in this happiness.

To hear her brother, whom she esteemed so highly, speak with such regard for someone she was about to meet created in the shy young lady a sense of nervous anticipation. As the carriage approached the Inn, Georgiana's nervousness was rising every minute, for she did not want to disappoint her brother. Darcy's thoughts and feelings were not too dissimilar to his sister's, for he was longing to see how *he* would be received by Elizabeth.

He could not help thinking, "If her opinion of me had been founded solely on whatever Wickham may have said, my letter surely would be sufficient to undo her resentment of me. But I know now that I injured her, her sister -- indeed her whole family -- in interfering with Charles and Jane. Why did I feel myself called on to act in such a way?! Is not Charles man enough to determine the pitfalls of love and marriage? Is he not able to weigh the consequences of his own choices? And then for me to disregard all my counsel to him and make an offer to a Bennet of my choosing! What further proof do I need of the absurdity of my actions towards him and Jane?"

He did not want to see Elizabeth with the weight of his past inappropriate behavior fresh on his mind; to that end, he called himself away from such recollections, and thought instead, "What better way to start things anew with her than to introduce my young sister, whom I love and hold in esteem?"

Having this on his mind, they exited the carriage with Darcy feeling proud of his sister and eager to present her to Elizabeth.

Darcy realized that making an unexpected visit, as he was, might wind up in disappointment, as they may not be in. Happily, however, she and the Gardiners were there, and upon welcoming them, they expressed surprise and pleasure at seeing him again so soon. Immediately, Darcy introduced his sister, and so as to let Elizabeth and Georgiana have a moment to talk alone together, he engaged the Gardiners in conversation. In the satisfaction of the moment, he recalled that Charles would be making his appearance at any time, and as he was informing them of this, Bingley could be heard making his approach.

Now this was truly a room with a most diverse sense of feelings and thought, considering all present were agreeable and enjoying themselves:

The Gardiners were very much interested in Charles, of whom they had heard so much with regard to Jane. They were also occupied with the notion that there was more to Mr. Darcy and Elizabeth than just a passing acquaintance, for why else would he give himself the trouble of coming with his sister so soon after her arrival? Darcy's admiration of their niece was clear enough; indeed, he behaved as a man in love! But as for the feelings of their niece, they could not ascertain.

Georgiana, wanting to be acquainted with Elizabeth and seeking to make herself pleasing, would often look toward her brother, who was often looking at her and Elizabeth with such warmth and satisfaction that, even though she was nervous, Miss Darcy felt happy.

Charles, whose open, cheerful nature would not be contained, could not have been more delighted to find, not only Jane's sister, but her aunt and uncle as well. This gave him a sense of somehow being close to Jane, and when he learned from Elizabeth that she was still at home, that feeling was abundantly reflected in his eyes.

Elizabeth, who was more sure of herself when Darcy was the object of her *prejudice*, was being overwhelmed by the mere idea that Darcy might still have feelings for her. She did her best, however, to contain her emotions and enjoy seeing Mr. Bingley again, as well as get to know something of Miss Darcy.

Darcy especially felt satisfaction and contentment on seeing Elizabeth's attention to his sister. After Charles had entered and she made no attempt to speak privately to him, it was clear that her interest was not in advancing her sister's relationship with him, for she continued engaged in conversation with Georgiana. It seemed at this point that his own efforts were having an effect he had scarcely allowed himself to hope for.

Having been there above half an hour, it now seemed proper to take their leave. However, Darcy called upon his sister to join him in requesting the Gardiners and Elizabeth dine at Pemberley before ending their stay in the area, and the time was fixed for the day after next. Charles took great pleasure in this, since he was eager to speak further with Elizabeth and to become more familiar with the Gardiners. Darcy's delight at their accepting was greater than that of Charles, to say the least, for to have Elizabeth at the home he had hoped she would call her own was an overpowering sensation.

Now as Darcy and Georgiana were back in the carriage, that sense of pleasure and satisfaction shown on Darcy's face, and his sister smiled as she took note of it. She asked, "Miss Elizabeth is very beautiful, but I have heard it said that her eldest sister is even more so . . . is it true? What is your own opinion?"

"To be sure, I do not believe it possible to find anyone who would not declare Jane Bennet to be such a beauty."

"But is she really prettier than Elizabeth?" she could not resist asking in a playful tone.

"The first time I saw Elizabeth, I did not even think she was pretty, but as I began to know her, she became more attractive in my eyes."

"How is it, Brother, that getting to know someone would make them prettier? Their appearance would not have changed."

"I can say this, Georgiana, that I have often seen the opposite side of this truth. Let me explain -- there have been any number of ladies I have been introduced to whose appearance would be considered lovely, but on becoming better acquainted, I would find them self-centered, some even *mean*. This has always had the effect of rendering them far less attractive."

"Yes, I catch your meaning . . . it makes me think of Miss Bingley. She is pretty, but I do not find her attractive. I have often seen her be so mean, as she was in her comment about Miss Elizabeth when we were leaving."

"You have stated it precisely, Georgiana. And even though Elizabeth may not have the appearance of her sister Jane, her inner beauty diffuses to the surface in a most splendid way."

"Are Jane Bennet's attractions restricted to her outward appearance?"

"No, indeed. Though I do not know her well, I have good reason to believe that there is nothing about her that would render her appearance unbecoming. She and Elizabeth are quite different, though. Jane is more gentle and Elizabeth has spirit, intelligence, and a sense of humor. She is quite simply the most outstanding woman I have ever met."

Georgiana observed, "It sounds as if you may be forming an attachment, *Big Brother*."

Darcy smiled, for he would not deny it, but simply said, "Well, I am making an honest assessment, that is all." And then he added, with a parental air, "In all of this, I hope you have noted the importance of true character and fine qualities, Georgiana."

During their ride back to Pemberley, Darcy would catch glimpses of Charles riding nearby, which would again cause some pangs of conscience. These painful episodes would be apparent to Georgiana, making her wonder why her brother could have such contented -- even *happy* -- expressions, only to give way to such painful ones.

Chapter 31

When they returned to Pemberley from their visit, they found Caroline full of resentment and cutting remarks against Elizabeth and her low relations. Georgiana recalled the conversation with her brother, on how such conduct renders a person unattractive, and could see all the truthfulness of it. Charles made several attempts to call his sister to a more civil posture but was unsuccessful; so, growing tired of such behavior, he excused himself to take some air.

Darcy, to demonstrate just how ineffective her attempts to shame him for the acquaintance with Elizabeth were, declared, "You will be in a position to make your own observations, Caroline, as Miss Bennet and her aunt and uncle will be dining with us during their stay in Lambton."

Caroline's resentful inclination moved her to respond, "How very thoughtful of you, Mr. Darcy! For no one, especially I myself, would want to miss an opportunity of hearing Miss Bennet's vulgar opinions!"

Georgiana, though she was young in the ways of the world, was growing in her understanding in the ways of men and women. She realized that Caroline was jealous for her brother's attentions, and could likewise see such behavior as this was a futile way to get it.

As the time came to retire for the evening, Darcy was glad to be in his apartment. He realized he had missed his sister, but until being with her again, did not know just how much. There was comfort to be found with her since their mother and father had died, and especially since being with the colonel and his family did this sense of loss become more profound. He felt some humor when considering that, in his sister, there was to be found, at least, one female in whose regard he could be sure of.

"What a contrast in the female sex was to be met with this day," he pondered.

"**Caroline Bingley**, who takes great pains to be in company with me, instead of making herself agreeable, simply brings great pain. Why she is incapable of behaving like the respectable lady she imagines herself to be is perhaps something I should better understand, considering the lesson I had to learn the hard way about what it means to be a real gentleman ...

"Then there is **my dear sister**, young and innocent and full of concern for me; I can see it plainly when she looks at me. How good it would be for her to have the support of our mother -- or at least a good sister-in-law ...

"... then, of course, there is **Miss Elizabeth Bennet**. The satisfaction I felt at seeing her and Georgiana speaking with one another is something that warmed my heart beyond description. I so much wanted Elizabeth to meet her, hoping that she would see some good in me through Georgiana's goodness ... that she might conclude that anyone with such a sister could not really be as despicable as she thought me to be when we were in Kent ... one thing seems certain: the more determined I become to put Elizabeth out of my mind, the more the laws of nature seem determined that I not."

Chapter 32

The next day, Darcy and the other gentlemen at Pemberley met Mr. Gardiner for fishing. They had discussed it when first they met while walking by the river, and then again when they were visiting at the Inn in Lambton. Darcy enjoyed the sport, but he wanted to play the guide for the men rather than participate, hoping to be as hospitable a host as he could, and at the same time get better acquainted with Mr. Gardiner.

Mr. Gardiner was one that enjoyed conversation as much as he did fishing. They considered subjects from architecture, traveling, history, and of course, fishing. He observed to Mr. Darcy that there are those who believe that talking while fishing somehow makes the fish aware of the men on the bank and their objective. Since in his experience he had caught as many fish while talking as when he was silent, he concluded that, "if the fish are aware of our presence, they are certainly not aware of our objective, unless they have learnt the English language." Darcy could not help thinking that, if he had been directed by his previous pride and prejudice, he would not have had the pleasure of Mr. Gardiner's acquaintance.

Elizabeth's uncle sorely wanted to raise the subject of his niece, but felt it not proper. Soon, however, he hit upon the scheme of informing Darcy of something that might do instead: "Pardon me, Mr. Darcy, I was noticing the hour, and recollected that my wife and niece were coming to pay their respects to Miss Darcy this morning, considering her kind attention yesterday. I would suppose they have arrived by now."

He was not disappointed in the reaction that this communication caused! Within moments of hearing this, Darcy expressed a desire of seeing if the ladies had come, and off he went, leaving Mr. Gardiner more sure than ever that Darcy was indeed forming an attachment to Elizabeth. As Darcy walked away, Mr. Gardiner said to himself, "So, more than one kind of fishing is being done at Pemberley this day! Which will have the greater success, I wonder?"

Within the house, Elizabeth and her aunt were forming the opinion that Georgiana might appear to be proud and reserved to those beneath her station; however, to them it was clear she was only shy and in fear of doing wrong in her duties as host.

The party that was gathered consisted of Miss Darcy, her lady attendant Mrs. Annesley, Mrs. Hurst, Miss Bingley, Mrs. Gardiner and Elizabeth. Conversation was chiefly carried on by Mrs. Gardiner and Mrs. Annesley, a truly well-bred and genteel woman, as Bingley's sisters had little to say in such company, and Elizabeth was lost in her own thoughts.

When Darcy entered the room, every eye turned his direction. Before him, he could see that the ladies were taking refreshments from the variety of cold meat, cake and fruits that had been provided. His sister, who had been feeling extremely awkward in such a setting, had rendered herself a non-participant; but on seeing her brother, she valiantly exerted herself. Elizabeth felt she was now in a better position to speak to Georgiana without Caroline so obviously listening in, for *she* now had her attention on Darcy; and therefore, Lizzy took the occasion to try to get better acquainted with the young lady.

However, seeing an opportunity to disgrace and unnerve Elizabeth while also reminding Darcy of matters she knew him to find offensive, Caroline once again showed her true character. In a scornful manner, she asked Elizabeth if the Militia was still being quartered at Meryton. Of course, she was particularly referring to George Wickham, but dared not mention his name; nevertheless, she was aiming her vicious dart concerning him at Lizzy, as well as toward the absurdities of her sisters with reference to the corps in general.

Certainly, Elizabeth understood the meaning of her reference, but she would not let herself be drawn in by Caroline, and therefore simply acknowledged that they had departed. Upon learning this, Caroline taunted how disappointing their removal must be for Elizabeth's family. Out of regard for Darcy and his sister, though, Elizabeth remained calm and collected and let the subject drop.

Although such meanness did not have its hoped-for success with Elizabeth, it did have an effect. Darcy had never let the Bingley family know what had occurred with Georgiana and Mr. Wickham, and he certainly did not want it to become known; therefore, moved by Elizabeth's restraint under such provocation, he looked at her with earnest appreciation. This did not go unnoticed by Caroline, and it vexed her greatly. Georgiana, who likewise understood what was said as being a slight, had become discomposed by such behavior in the presence of her company and was unable to exert herself any longer to take an active part.

Mrs. Gardiner and Elizabeth shortly expressed their need to depart, and after bidding goodbye to everyone, Darcy escorted them to their carriage. "Mr. Darcy, it has been such a pleasure becoming more acquainted with you and your sweet young sister," said Mrs. Gardiner. "My dear husband was thrilled to be asked by you to join in fishing with the men today; thank you for including him in that." Darcy declared the pleasure was all his and that he greatly anticipated having them for dinner the following day.

When they reached the carriage, Mrs. Gardiner was handed in first. Taking Elizabeth by the hand, Darcy, leaning closer to her, whispered, "Thank you, Elizabeth."

Elizabeth turned to look at him and smiled, noting the kindness and warmth that was evident on his face. She paused, therefore, before stepping into the carriage, and as he held onto her hand, they also held their gaze. Then recalling the presence of her aunt, she looked up with a feeling of having been discovered, though she knew not for what.

Darcy walked slowly back to the saloon where the rest of the ladies still were. He was reflecting on how easily he had been able to speak to Miss Bennet in a more intimate way just then, and that she received it with pleasure. At this moment, how he admired her character at not responding in kind to Miss Bingley's imprudence earlier! He was now at the entrance of the saloon and wished to have more time for pleasant reflections of Elizabeth.

Upon his entering the room, however, Miss Bingley was ready to disparage the object of his warmest feelings. She began her attack by commenting on 'how coarse and brown Elizabeth looked, how her face is too thin, her nose wants character' and many other petty remarks. Darcy's cool replies and resolute silence served to egg her on, as she reminded him that his *first impression* of Eliza Bennet was to compare her 'beauty' with her mother's *wit*!

However much comfort Caroline took in recalling Darcy's former opinions of Lizzy, she soon found all comfort vanish, as it drew from him this declaration: "*That* was only when I first knew her, for it is many months since I have considered her as one of the handsomest women of my acquaintance." He then calmly left the room, feeling content at having given expression to his admiration of Elizabeth.

This time his sister followed after him, calling to him. Darcy stopped, and the two walked on together. As she put her arm in his, she asked if he would take a turn with her out-of-doors. He responded by leading her to a walk on the other side of the house from where the ladies were and away from the river, so they could converse alone. He put his hand on hers and looked at her in a way that showed how much he appreciated her act of sisterly kindness after Miss Bingley's ill-mannered display.

Reaching the path, Darcy said, "How I love Pemberley! There is something about being home that refreshes the soul like nothing else."

"How much refreshing is your soul in need of?" were the words Georgiana spoke, taking on an almost motherly tone.

"Oh, sometimes it feels like I don't know where I belong or what I am about, and coming to Pemberley connects me to things both past and present, which has a settling effect on me. And I should add, seeing you has done me a great deal of good. There is something in being with you that brings me comfort, especially now that it is only you and I. How proud I am of the young lady I see you are becoming."

"You are being kind to me, Brother. I do not feel that I am becoming the lady you say . . . I still feel so awkward entertaining and being with company, I believe you would find me a great disappointment."

"Nothing could be further from the truth! Some persons can do the things you mentioned well, but with a falseness that renders them as persons of not much worth. Let us return to our example we had yesterday of Caroline Bingley. There are few women, in my opinion, that can be as gracious a host as she. I have seen her be cordial, even genial, on many such occasions. Then, as soon as the last guest has stepped into the carriage, she proceeds describing what a bore the evening was and generally finding fault with practically all in attendance. And so, Georgiana, though she would be described as a model of what a host should be, you can judge for yourself of what value that is, considering her character."

"Thank you for your praise; I find it very encouraging. And you are quite right -- to be false as she is would be a much greater shortcoming."

"As far as you are concerned, I would infinitely prefer you to be lacking powers of entertaining in exchange for being honest and kind. And besides, you are still young, so I would urge you to continue to apply yourself at learning these social abilities. Lord knows how often I have berated myself lately for not having learned them better! But certainly, put greater emphasis on developing good qualities, as I have seen you already display."

Georgiana smiled with appreciation and then said "I believe, Brother, I am not the only one that brings you comfort; is that not so?"

At hearing this, Darcy looked at his sister, a bit surprised that she had observed as much. He took her to the shade of a tree that had benches placed about it. Darcy was accustomed to measure every word before speaking, and he was now struggling for how to begin. Georgiana could tell this pause was not an indication of his not wanting to talk, but a search for a way to start. So she interjected, "It seems to me that Miss Bingley is jealous of your attention to Miss Bennet. I can understand why any lady would want your attentions, but why must she be so mean just because you prefer another? Surely she must realize such behavior will not be to her advantage."

"You know, I really must spend more time with you, for I find that you have matured so much during our absence, and at this moment it is being revealed to me very clearly! What you say is correct, Georgiana," and again he paused. He did not trust himself to say more. He was at the brink of expressing just how deeply he felt for Elizabeth and did not want to open Georgiana to some false hopes. The memory of his first attempt was all too clear. It was enough that she comprehended the situation as it existed.

Georgiana realized it was now time to change the subject and began to speak of Pemberley. They talked of their individual memories of their mother and father and other such things, and the two grew closer because of it. For that reason, it would be a day they would both remember. As they walked back to the house in contemplation, Darcy felt a great pride in having such a sister.

* * * * *

The master of Pemberley found it hard to sleep that night; it seemed to him that he was at a point that was very critical in establishing a relationship with Elizabeth. It was clear to him that she no longer viewed him on the basis of her first impression, or as the person Wickham had made him out to be. But he believed if he said or did too much too soon, she would respond with the memory of how he had interfered with Jane and Charles. Her regard for her sister was as close a bond as could be, and then there was the matter of the material damage that was caused by his interference.

On the other hand, if he did too little, this opportunity that was before him would be lost *forever*. How that word hung in his mind, with all the weight of its meaning. "If I have lost her because of actions that I took in good conscience in the past, then so be it. But if I am *now* to lose her because of what I do not do . . . this would be too great a regret!"

He recalled the look on her face when whispering his thanks as he was handing her into the carriage earlier. There was no sign of resentment, rather the opposite. It was with this recollection and the sweetness of her eyes that he closed his, knowing full well where he would be off to when morning arrived . . .

Chapter 33

At breakfast, the conversation centered on what was being planned by all. Mr. Hurst spoke of venturing out to the river again to a particular bend that seemed to him to be an ideal location for catching fish. Charles, always one for the outdoors, was to join him, interested in seeing how successful his scheme would be. The ladies spoke of taking the morning air and cutting flowers for the dinner table. Darcy did not have much of an appetite and was paying little attention to what was being said.

Charles, calling to him, asked if he would not accompany Mr. Hurst and himself.

"No, thank you, Charles, there are some things about the place that require my attention."

"Well, then, would you prefer some company yourself?" he asked.

"That is very kind of you, but it is just some necessary business that I must tend to. If I am done early and you are still at the river, I will join you then."

No one could discern from this just what the necessary business was, but as the breakfast room was quitted, Darcy spoke to one of the servants, who promptly left to do his master's bidding, which was to prepare his horse and have it waiting for him behind the stable; from there he could steal away into Lambton undetected. He took great care in choosing his attire, as he particularly wanted to look his best today, and therefore settled upon his green coat, which he felt suited him well.

On the ride, he was going over in his mind what would be the stated reason for his coming to see Elizabeth: "I can simply say I was in town on business and felt I should pay my respects . . . but as they are coming to dinner this evening, that excuse seems a little transparent . . . I believe I have it! I can say my purpose in coming was to inquire if there was a dish that Mr. or Mrs. Gardiner were especially fond of! Well, that is good enough, but what I really wish to say is, *'It was impossible for me to stay away, knowing that you are so near! And yes, I know you will be dining with us tonight, but I was unable to wait and had to make another opportunity to see you!'* . . . Perhaps this is what has kept me from the world of love-making -- the challenge of traversing its roads."

If he had had intelligence of what was happening with Elizabeth, he would have been practicing some other speech, for as he was entering town, Elizabeth was reading two letters from Jane which had thrown her into a terrible state of emotion.

Being unaware of this, however, Darcy arrived, continuing to the Inn with happy anticipation. Approaching the door, he felt certain of one thing: what he was doing now was going to be a turning point in his relationship with Elizabeth.

But as he was entering the room, Elizabeth was attempting to exit. She was in such a hurried state, with a very anxious expression on her face, that Darcy exclaimed, "Good God! what is the matter?"

Elizabeth could scarcely say, *'she had not a moment to lose to find her uncle on a matter of great urgency!'* Darcy could see she was in no condition for walking out and called back the servant, who was sent to find Mr. Gardiner. As Darcy helped her to a chair, Lizzy managed to say she had just had dreadful news from Longbourn. She then began to cry, preventing any further communication for several minutes.

Darcy, now in wretched suspense, was imagining perhaps her father had died, or some other calamity had befallen the family, and was gently trying to bring some relief by offering wine, but to no purpose. She declared herself well, but could manage little more than this assurance. Seeing her this way and having no idea what was wrong was creating in him a great uneasiness, for he was not on such terms as to allow an embrace of compassion or any other expression of comfort of that sort which his nature was urging upon him. He was left to simply look on with heartfelt empathy and concern.

At last, Elizabeth was composed enough to relate, "My sister Jane has written informing me of the most dreadful news. Our sister Lydia has gone away with ... *Mr. Wickham!* ... they have been traced as far as London, but have not been heard from and now appear to be in hiding."

In shock and astonishment, Darcy exclaimed, "Wickham! -- surely this cannot be so!" More with hope than conviction, it occurred to him that perhaps there may have been some mistake. "Is it *certain* she is with him? May she not be with some of her other friends?"

"No, no, notes were written by her ... there is no question they have gone off together, and my father is even now in London trying to discover them! Jane begs that we hurry home so my uncle can join him in the search." Lizzy once again fell into tears.

At this, Darcy began pacing the room. The full episode involving his sister came rushing back to him, and along with it, his righteous indignation. He bitterly thought, "How can there be such a contemptible man! He must on this offense be *made* to recompense -- there must be some way of putting an end to his degenerate actions once and for all!"

Darcy was summoned from his private denouncing of Wickham, as Elizabeth once again spoke through sobs and tears: "I condemn myself for not informing my family, at least, of Wickham's true character. If I had done so, this could have been prevented -- what a horrible mistake in judgement for not doing so!" she repeated against herself. She then reasoned, in the greatest mortification, "It may have been possible to have related some part of what I knew ... but I held back, for fear of saying *too much.*"

It pained Darcy deeply to hear this, knowing her silence had been out of respect for him. Hearing her self-reproach and condemnation made him feel the weight of his own part in the matter, and indeed in his heart he condemned himself, thinking: 'if anyone is to blame, I am the one, for my mistaken pride in not informing the young ladies within the reach of Wickham of his true nature."

Elizabeth then cried out in anguish, "What is to be done? I know very well *nothing* can be done with such a man. And we have no leverage against him . . . not even *money* to prompt him into doing the right thing!"

This scene was almost too much for Darcy to bear as only a bystander. A resolution was forming in his mind: "I will not allow this man to inflict so much sorrow on Miss Bennet and her family! I must try to bring relief to them and stop Wickham from doing further harm in this matter!"

This determination, coupled with all his former feelings against and dealings with Wickham flashing before him, created an appearance on his countenance that Elizabeth mistook as his old prejudice about the lowness and weaknesses of her family's character resurfacing. And with such evidence before him, she could not blame him. Had she only known that his thoughts were running in a completely different vein!

Certain that the Gardiners would soon be arriving, he thought it best not to be present with such news at hand. Fully aware it would not be helpful to express his indignation against Wickham, Darcy exerted himself to refrain from such. Being at a loss to know exactly what to say or how to show his concern, he spoke in an awkward, solemn tone, "I know this situation will prevent your coming to Pemberley. I will, of course, make some excuse . . . I hope as matters unfold they will turn out well, despite how things look now. You can be assured of my secrecy." And with one last, serious look at her, he took his leave.

Now riding on, heedless of the scenery, he immediately undertook the consideration of how best to proceed: the first order of business would be to make his excuses at Pemberley for leaving to London so suddenly. Being in a heightened state of emotion, he realized he could not enter there without giving rise to suspicion, so he slowed his pace.

Darcy began to contemplate the perverseness of this new circumstance. "First, I was unable to put away the feelings I had for her; and after having my proposal turned down in so decided a fashion, it seemed I had no choice but to forget her. . . then inexplicably, she is here at Pemberley at the very moment I am arriving . . . and if that were not enough, it seemed her feelings toward me had softened!"

Sighing, he continued, "Considering just how easily my heart went from *determination to forget* to *determination to please,* I know I would prefer to have her love me . . . it appeared progress was being made on that head -- and now to have this stumbling block placed in the way is frustration at its highest degree! And for Wickham to be in the middle of it is a turn that defies description!"

Darcy arrived at Pemberley to find everyone gathered for tea, he having been quite heedless of the time. Putting on a calm face, he informed the party that he had just heard word that the Gardiners and Miss Bennet would not be joining them for dinner.

Caroline remarked that it would be for the best, since it would allow a more intimate occasion, not having "strangers" about the place. *Charles* declared his disappointment at not getting better acquainted with the Gardiners and that he would miss Miss Bennet playing for them after dinner. *Mr. Hurst* added his disappointment, saying of Mr. Gardiner, "He is a first rate fisherman. I would have liked to have related my success today." *Georgiana* only looked at her brother, feeling for him, knowing above everyone else, that Darcy was the most disappointed at not having more time to spend with Elizabeth.

She inquired with true sympathy, "May they perhaps be able to come tomorrow evening?"

"No, I do not think so; unfortunately their trip is coming to an end, and they will be returning home." Darcy then stated, "There is one more bit of bad news I have to relate. I must be off to London on a matter of business and will be leaving early tomorrow."

"How unfortunate! Let me accompany you," offered Charles.

"That won't be necessary, my good friend. Though I would appreciate your company along the way, I would much rather know that you are here enjoying Pemberley than being in town at this time of year. Besides, I am not sure how long it will take to settle this matter, and my time will not be my own, so we would not be together much at all. Please stay and make the most of being here."

Mr. Hurst added, "Yes, Bingley, you know how these business trips are; they are as dull as a rainy day." Mrs. Hurst also reminded Charles that one reason for their coming to Pemberley was for him to relax.

All of that having been discussed and settled, Darcy shortly left their company to go upstairs and prepare for his departure.

Chapter 34

As soon as he arrived in London, Darcy set about looking for Mrs. Younge, the woman he had told Elizabeth about in his letter to her, disclosing all the information about Wickham's connection with his family, including his scheming elopement with Georgiana. Because of Mrs. Younge's history with Wickham, Darcy felt sure she would be a good source of information regarding him. For that reason, he started his search for her by going into that part of town where he thought she ran a boarding house. He believed he had never even ridden through this area, much less walked its streets as he was now doing.

A humorous thought now came to Darcy's mind: "My short association with Miss Bennet must be having an effect on me, for I have a great desire to tell Caroline Bingley I was walking in this part of town; that may do very well to cure her of any interest in me. I must be sure to remember the name of some street or shop for that purpose!"

Aside from this uncharacteristic amusement, Darcy was becoming aware that simply walking the streets hoping to somehow stumble across them was not productive. So after a few more inquiries, he decided to go back home and think of another way of finding Mrs. Younge.

At home while having tea, it occurred to him to look over the advertisements in the paper, thinking that this in some way was comparable to walking the streets without really doing so. In it, he came across *Apartments for rent* by a *Mrs. Younge* with directions on how to contact her. If it had not been so late in the day, he would have proceeded directly to determine if it were the Mrs. Younge he was in search of, but prudence dictated that he wait for the morning.

After breakfast, he went straightaway and found, not surprisingly, that he had been very near the place the day before. Going to the door, he asked for her and was directed to wait in a small room with two chairs and a desk. Mrs. Younge, upon entering the room, sounded cheerful at the prospect of a new tenant; but the moment she saw that it was Darcy, she stepped back, speaking his name with surprise and shock.

Darcy then said in a calm voice, "Mrs. Younge, I have some business to discuss with you. Would you please give me a few minutes of your time?"

His calm manner lessened her initial anxiety, and she proceeded to her usual seat in the room. Not pretending any civility, she returned, "What is it you want, Mr. Darcy?"

"I am looking for George Wickham. I know he is in London and feel certain you will have knowledge of his whereabouts. Do you?"

"I may have, but it depends."

"It depends on what, pray tell?"

"It depends on whether there is any value in knowing."

Darcy knew that to appeal to her on the plight of the Bennet family would be fruitless, for although she was a woman, such tender compassion as is found in the female sex was not evident in her. So he took the approach that motivated her most: "I will give you ten pounds, but it must inform me as to where he is. If it is directions to yet another person who supposedly knows or has information, I will give you nothing."

She considered for a moment trying for more, but the intensity of his look declared he was in no mood to bargain with her. "I do not know where he is, but I can find out and contact you."

"I will be back tomorrow after lunch," and he rose without another word, departing swiftly.

* * * * *

Returning at the designated time the following day, Darcy once again found himself in the small room. This time he did not sit. "Do you know where he is?" he asked pointedly.

"What will be done with him, Mr. Darcy?" She had begun to wonder if she should surrender her friend, although ten pounds was a tempting sum for just uttering a few words.

"I am not looking to do him harm or have him locked up, if that is your concern. I need to talk to him, that is all; so if you want the ten pounds, tell me, or someone else will have it for the same information."

She knew Darcy was no deceiver, so with her concerns for Wickham being settled, she replied, "He is staying in an apartment two or three miles from here. The building has the name *Travelers Way*. He is on the second floor; the door is marked 217."

Handing her the money, he left as quickly as he came. Wasting no time, Darcy headed off in that direction, and after further inquiries, found the street and the building. Across from it was a coffee shop, and sitting there having coffee, he spied Wickham.

Approaching him, he said simply, "Hello, George."

Wickham, instantly recognizing the voice, stood up, looking startled. When one is attempting to be concealed and is found by *anyone* with whom they are acquainted, it is enough to make them nervous, all the more so if it is Fitzwilliam Darcy! Recollecting himself, he asked, "What are *you* doing in this part of town?"

"I am looking for you."

"Whatever for? What business could you have with me?" He could see no connection between his present situation and Darcy.

"I understand that you are here with Lydia Bennet; is that correct?"

"*Lydia!*" he exclaimed. "What possible interest could you have with her?" To Wickham, who was more concerned with his financial woes and remaining hidden from those to whom he was indebted, this was a strange conversation to be having with Darcy. He cautiously sat down, fidgeting and looking around as if he expected some other unwanted surprise to come upon him.

"I have come to return her to her family. That is, unless you are married."

"Married! Don't be absurd!" Wickham responded, with a mixture of relief and confusion. "I am in need of money -- *she* certainly has none. My intention is to acquire enough funds to leave the country and find a rich woman to marry. Then my only money problem will be how to spend it!"

"If that is the case, then there should be no objection to your allowing me to take her home to Longbourn."

"Just because I have no intentions of marrying her does not mean she is of no use to me."

"Surely you can see there is no advantage to continuing with Miss Lydia Bennet as you are," Darcy returned with a measure of disgust. But thinking it may do some good, he added, "Mr. Bennet would certainly work in your cause if you were to marry his daughter. I know he is not rich, but he would have some connections that could assist you."

"Darcy, since you have money, you cannot possibly understand. I desire wealth, not just a sum to live on."

"Why, then, did you take Miss Bennet with you?"

"TAKE her?! She fairly demanded to come, declaring her love for me when I disclosed that I was leaving." Wickham was now showing how little he felt for her, as well as his own pride in this latest conquest. "She is an amusement, to be sure, in this time of my distress . . . You, of course, would not understand of what I speak, but the kind of distraction she provides is very welcome. It is no more than that on my part, however."

"If that be the case, it will mean nothing to you for me to speak with Miss Bennet about taking her to be with her aunt and uncle here in town."

Wickham paused for a moment and considered to himself, *"How odd that it is Darcy here looking for Lydia and not her father -- if he has an interest in this matter, there may be some way of profiting by it"* . . . he then spoke, "Darcy, for her to see you would be more surprising than it was for me, and to think that she would leave me, whom she has declared her love for, to go with someone so unconnected to her family, surely you can see the difficulty. Let me speak with her first, and perhaps she will be more receptive to you. Come back tomorrow at this same time, and we shall talk again."

Darcy was suspicious of Wickham's seeming to be helpful, but was also aware that there was a certain logic to what he had just stated. Reluctantly, he agreed, saying, "Till tomorrow then," and briskly turned to be off, as it was distasteful to the greatest degree having to deal with Wickham; he wanted him out of his sight immediately.

Making his way back to the carriage, Darcy could not help but wish he had the same degree of influence here as he had when his sister was the one involved with Wickham. That frustration, coupled with his growing hunger pangs, made it difficult to concentrate. He therefore was in anticipation of arriving home, where he could satisfy his hunger and find repose, thinking, "In the quiet of my study I will be able to give this matter proper attention."

In his room while changing for the evening, Darcy considered whether or not he should inform Mr. Gardiner of having discovered Lydia. But in a moment's reflection, he saw the need of waiting till he had something more to relate to him, hopefully something resembling a resolution to this scandal.

After he had taken his meal, he proceeded to his study, feeling better able to look at this more objectively. He began contemplating, "Why is Wickham delaying this till tomorrow? *What is he up to?* Does he fear Miss Bennet is not as attached to him as he led me to believe and is therefore trying to strengthen his position with her before tomorrow? My coming onto the scene is certainly an unexpected development for him, so he may very well want time to consider some way of profiting from my involvement."

Darcy then recalled Wickham's words about Lydia: "*She fairly demanded to come.*" If this was an accurate description of Lydia's feelings in the case, it was something Darcy had not anticipated. It was too easy to envision Wickham luring her into this reprehensible affair for his own gratification, and that she would welcome Darcy's assistance in returning to her family. If it be true, however, this would suggest a stronger attachment to him than he had considered, admitting to there being a grave deficiency in her character. Looking at matters with this in mind, Darcy thought, "He may, of course, be deceiving himself, flattering his inflated ego; but if he is not, this may prove to be a formidable obstacle to resolving this business. How much better it would be to find her wishing to be back with her family!"

By the end of the night's ruminations, Darcy felt he had prepared himself to confront the many variations that could present themselves on the morrow.

* * * * *

That same night, inside the small apartment where Wickham and Lydia were staying, Wickham was attempting to ascertain the strength of her regard for him: "Lydia, if it were possible for you to leave me and return to your family, would that be something agreeable to you?"

"George, dear! Don't say such a thing! Why would I want to go back to that common, boring life?"

"Well, as you know, I may not be in a position any time soon for us to marry . . . would that not be a reason for you to want to return?" he asked surreptitiously.

"What is that to me? As long as I am with you, that is all that matters. What has gotten into your head to ask such things?"

With this confirmation, he now related, "I saw Mr. Darcy today, and he is of the opinion that you want to be back with your family and is coming tomorrow for the purpose of persuading you to let him take you home."

"How dare he! Let him come -- I will not go!"

"He may attempt to work on your feelings for your family to separate us," he returned slyly.

"My feelings are for you *alone*. He can say nothing about my family that could tempt me back into that drab world. Being only one of five sisters is nothing compared to being with you!" Lydia said, for she was truly in love with him, and was determined to remain with Wickham, even if her own father were to come looking for her.

"I told him as much, my dear, but he was insistent on seeing you."

Wickham was satisfied. He could allow Darcy to see her without a danger of losing any leverage he might have. As he took Lydia's hand, he said to himself, "Darcy may like to play the hero . . . well, we shall see just how much he values the part!"

Chapter 35

The next day, Darcy and Wickham were found at the same café and the same table. Since they had dealt with one another on such matters before, there was a certain impatience on both sides to begin with the proceedings that lay before them. Wickham, feeling confident that this time he would come off better than when last they met over a similar matter, and Darcy, trusting his efforts to do the right thing would ultimately turn out good, both were ready for the challenge ahead.

Wickham was the first to speak: "I am sorry to disappoint you, Darcy, but she wants to remain with me."

"Are you saying that you intend to keep me from seeing her?"

"No, of course not, Darcy." Wickham's demeanor was such that Darcy fixed a steady gaze upon him, eye-to-eye, attempting to measure the degree of his confidence. George Wickham felt secure about the matter at hand, to be sure, but he was also a man more accustomed to the ways of the weasel and had to look away from Darcy, continuing flippantly, "Come, come, Darcy, you shall see her -- why such a serious attitude? Come to the apartment after supper. She is not an early riser and would not be ready till then." Making Darcy wait gave him a certain amusement, and he felt it would increase Darcy's desire to settle this, even if it required paying out more than he might at first consider, for he was certain Darcy would lay out money in this case.

Darcy was not going to let Wickham have the satisfaction of seeing his efforts of annoying and frustrating him be successful; he therefore said in a manner that declared he would not tolerate another delay: "I prefer you give me a definite time at which to arrive. Since your lady has such late habits of rising, how am I to know at what hour she takes her supper?"

"Very well, have it your way; come at seven," Wickham replied, and with that Darcy walked away.

Wickham remained seated, furtively looking over his shoulder as he watched Darcy leave. "I am puzzled . . . what interest could Darcy have in Lydia? Why should he care what becomes of her? Elizabeth Bennet has made it plain enough that she despises him, and he cares so little for the opinion of the townsfolk of Meryton, what could be his motivation? . . . Oh, yes, I had all but forgotten his good friend *Charles Bingley's attachment to Jane Bennet*. Well, all the better then! The greater the incentive on his part, the greater my gain . . . this will be splendid indeed! I relish the thought of seeing the look on his face when he presents himself to take Lydia back to her family and she roundly refuses to go! . . . Why some people feel the need to go about righting the wrongs they see, I will never know . . . If his determination to get Lydia back with her family is as strong as her determination to stay with me, I believe I will soon be saying goodbye to this miserable side of town and be well on my way to seeking a lovely fortune abroad!"

* * * * *

Later that evening, Darcy knocked on their apartment door and was let in. It was a small room with little in the way of furnishings; a wooden chair was offered and accepted. Wickham took the comfortable chair and Lydia stood by him with a look of arrogant determination.

"Miss Bennet, let me come straight to the point. I have come to offer my services in taking you back to your family."

Lydia declared, "You will do no such thing! I am with Wickham now. We will be married whenever his circumstances permit -- until then, it does not signify to me whether we are married or not!"

"Come now, Miss Bennet, surely you are not serious about pursuing this shameful course, disgracing your family and worrying them? Did you know your father has spent several days in London looking for you?" She stood defiantly, and Darcy continued, "Miss Bennet, have you given any thought to how worried your family is for you?"

"I belong to Wickham now . . . and who are *you* to talk to me of my family?!"

Turning to Wickham, Darcy inquired, "And are you so far removed from compassion that you will do nothing to relieve her family's anxiety over her absence?"

"You have heard what Lydia has to say," he replied coolly. Moving toward the door, he added, "Let me walk you out, Darcy."

Outside, Darcy made another appeal. "George, have you no consideration of how her family is suffering, and how much they *will* suffer due to this affair, not to mention the lady's own reputation?" Wickham sighed dispassionately. Darcy now attempted a slightly different approach, "Surely whatever regard you had for her sister Elizabeth should mean something to you. Is her opinion of you not some reason to act as you should? Be a man, and send her sister away with me, so that the damage that has been done can be repaired!"

Wickham appeared flattered that Darcy would admit Elizabeth had a good opinion of him, but flattered is as far as it went. "Darcy, something may yet be done. Let us meet tomorrow and discuss this alone; perhaps we can find some arrangement that will suit us both."

Understanding this as a reference to money, Darcy, looking at him with contempt, said, "Very well, then, meet me at my solicitor's office at seven o'clock in the morning. You know where it is."

"So early?!"

"Be there at seven precisely or I will leave you two just as I found you, and you will never hear from me again!"

Wickham, believing the meeting at the solicitor's was a sure sign he was coming into a sum that would put his problems behind him, walked off feeling smug. Darcy, on the other hand, was already planning how best to have this scoundrel duly dealt with: "He believes he has manipulated this situation to his advantage and is now congratulating himself for having Lydia Bennet taken off his hands, and at the same time, in effect, getting paid for using her. I trust that, come tomorrow, he will have to adopt a new point of view!"

Chapter 36

At the appointment promptly at seven, Wickham was introduced into an office where sat Darcy and his solicitor, Mr. Newly. An introduction was made, and all took a seat. Darcy had given instructions to Mr. Newly as to terms, because he wanted him to lay the matter before Wickham, as Darcy had had his fill of talking to him.

"Mr. Wickham, I understand you find yourself in less than favorable circumstances involving your finances. Do I understand correctly?" began Mr. Newly.

"Yes. As you well know, things such as this do occur," replied Wickham.

"And just how stressful are your circumstances?" (It must have been those persons in law who determined that not using the term *money* somehow makes talking about money less disagreeable.)

Wickham knew the sum well, as he had been spending all his time in London working on some way to lay hold of it, and thereby come out of hiding. His not answering at once prompted Mr. Newly to continue, "What will you be willing to do for assistance in that direction?"

"How much assistance are we speaking of?"

"We are speaking of retiring the whole amount, as well as something extra to help get you on good footing. Now again, I put the question to you, what will you be willing to do for that amount of assistance?"

Wickham felt a sense of elation at this, and declared, "On receipt of the money, I will leave London and the girl, and you will be free to do with her as you please."

"That is not acceptable. For this agreement to go through, you must marry the girl. After the marriage, your debts will be discharged."

Wickham went from elation to downcast in the span of one short sentence. He said nothing for a full minute, then ended the silence with, "There is . . . no alternative that you will find agreeable?"

"These terms are chiseled in stone, sir," Mr. Newly said, as only a man of law can.

Having anticipated Wickham's objections, Darcy had prepared Mr. Newly to stand firm. He had considered this possibility and believed Lydia was so determined to have Wickham that, if he were permitted to leave as he was now suggesting, she would be bent on continuing to cause trouble for the family in this matter. It also seemed quite appropriate for Wickham to face the consequences of his actions with regard to Lydia.

"But . . . I have other debts in Meryton. What of those?"

Leaning over, Darcy whispered something to Mr. Newly. "Very well, sir. We will see what might be done on that front, but we will need a list of creditors and amounts, then you will be contacted. But I must ask you again, Mr. Wickham, *will you marry Miss Lydia Bennet*? For we will not proceed another step without your agreeing to that *now*."

Wickham considered just how futile his own attempts at acquiring the funds needed had been, so finally, reluctantly, he quietly answered, "Yes."

* * * * *

There were subsequent meetings, and on each occasion, Wickham made appeals to get out of the marriage or to get more money, but in the end, he was confronted with how to inform Lydia of the happy news:

"Lydia, as you know, I have been very occupied with some prominent men these past few days on finding a solution to my financial entanglements. It happens that this last meeting has presented me with something I have been quite reluctant to inform you of -- not knowing how matters would turn out, you see . . . but, today I am in a position to inform you that . . . we are now able to be married." One can only imagine what effort it required to utter these words, when he had held on to the last, hoping for some reprieve from the altar!

Lydia, rushing over to him, embraced him, declaring, "I knew my dear Wickham would manage it! How *grand* that I should be the first of my sisters to be married -- and to be married to you, above all men!" As she held onto him, she carried on in this senseless fashion, recalling to his mind -- her mother! With this sobering realization, he was only too glad he did not have to face her, for with each expression of happiness she proclaimed, the more crestfallen he became. He, who had always fancied himself using his charms to marry into wealth and a life of ease, was reduced to what he was now holding in his arms.

Chapter 37

Now Darcy felt it was time to see Mr. Gardiner, but upon learning that Mr. Bennet was still in town and would be leaving the next day, Darcy put off the visit so that he could see Mr. Gardiner alone, since he was better acquainted with him than he was with Mr. Bennet. After all, if the uncle felt the arrangement was unacceptable, he could simply send for the father and they could work out matters as they saw fit.

At the Gardiner's, Darcy was greeted with expressions of surprise and pleasure at the honor of being able to welcome him into their home. He was shown into the sitting room and, as tea was called for, Mrs. Gardiner proudly introduced her children to him. Mr. Gardiner then said, "Mr. Darcy, let me say again what a pleasure it is to see you. However, I must admit to my surprise at your being in town, since we left you just a short time ago at Pemberley with your friends. I trust Miss Darcy was well when you left her? Or did she come to town with you?"

"No, Georgiana did not accompany me, but she is well, thank you for asking. Mr. Gardiner, something very particular brings me to see you; may I speak with you privately?" At this, Mrs. Gardiner and the children left the room, and coming directly to the point of his visit, Darcy now informed him: "It has to do with your niece, Lydia Bennet. I have located her, and she is well, but I have some things I would like to discuss with you."

"What?! Mr. Darcy, I am dumbfounded! I hardly know which is the most surprising -- that you have found our niece, or that you are even aware of this pitiful business, *and* have given yourself the trouble of discovering her!"

"Please, let me explain: perhaps you recall that I stopped in to see you at Lambton just as Miss Bennet had finished reading the letters from her sister Jane with the news of their youngest sister's elopement."

"Of course! We were informed of your being there; I had all but forgotten in the ensuing turmoil . . . but I had no idea Lizzy acquainted you with this sordid family business."

"Miss Bennet had been overcome with emotion, and in this state, related to me what had occurred. As you know, Georgiana is close in age to Lydia, so the situation hit a nerve with me, and seeing Miss Bennet in such distress, I felt compelled to do something, especially since I had been connected with George Wickham in the past and knew more about him than your family would. I therefore set off for London the very next day."

"That is more than what is to be expected, Mr. Darcy. We are in your debt."

"No, not at all. You see, my concern goes deeper than just empathy in this matter. I feel myself to blame, since I knew Wickham's character and saw his making himself close to your family of young ladies. I should have alerted them; they then would have been more guarded with him. But my reserve and lack of proper concern for the welfare of the young ladies allowed him to be welcomed into their midst, thus permitting this sad affair to take place."

"Mr. Darcy, your conscientiousness is to be lauded, but I will point out to you that what has taken place is beyond the bounds of moral decency, and therefore, the blame should be put on those whose morality would permit such conduct. But be that as it may, please, what have you discovered?"

"First, let me inform you that bringing her to her family was, of course, my primary intention. Incomprehensibly, however, I found the young woman steadfastly unwilling to leave Wickham. Seeing her determination, and in my private discussions with him, finding Wickham unwilling to marry her as things stood, it seemed the only recourse was to facilitate a marriage."

"You say *facilitate*, Mr. Darcy -- just what was needed to bring about this marriage?"

"I have arranged that Wickham's debts be retired to the amount somewhat less than three thousand pounds, as well as some help be given in purchasing a commission in another regiment. In addition to this, Mr. Bennet is to agree to bestow upon his daughter a hundred pounds per annum during his life, with the sum of a thousand pounds upon the decease of himself and his wife."

"Excuse me, Mr. Darcy, am I to understand you intend to provide the relief for Wickham's debts on this side yourself?"

"Indeed, I believe I must."

"Mr. Darcy, you have certainly gone beyond chivalry in giving yourself the trouble of discovering them and making these arrangements, but it is *my* duty as her uncle to settle my niece's account."

"Mr. Gardiner, I understand your position. But please, as I have mentioned, I feel responsible and cannot in good conscience permit the remedy to come from any other source than myself."

"You are asking me to defer my familial responsibility, and that is something I cannot do."

"Sir, please do not look at this as your abandoning your responsibility, but that you are allowing me to right this wrong involving a man whose acquaintance with me has been of long standing. Indeed, it pains me to say it, but we were raised almost as brothers."

"Mr. Darcy, pardon my obstinacy in the matter, but you did not introduce him to my nieces, nor were you in any way responsible for encouraging an association with him. Rather, it was my niece's actions that created this mess more than any negligence on your part. It is unthinkable to permit you or any other person unrelated to us to bear the burden of it."

The two men showed themselves to be men of honor and real worth as they vied with one another to carry out what each believed to be his responsibility. When contrasted with the two persons over whom this whole business was about, one can comprehend what it means to act on principle. Darcy's high regard for Mr. Gardiner increased in the course of this discussion, and again he was struck with the absurdity of having considered such a person as a degradation for him to have a family association with.

It eventually occurred to Mr. Gardiner that Darcy's reason for being so determined might very well involve his other niece. His observations at Pemberley would certainly allow him to look upon this as a display of fondness for Elizabeth. From this perspective, his sense of honor was beginning to give way for something a little more important: *the love of a man for a woman.* He therefore acquiesced.

The two men shook hands, both filled with more respect and admiration for the other. After Darcy left, Mr. Gardiner felt he could write to Mr. Bennet, explaining the particulars of settling Lydia's sordid affair.

* * * * *

In the carriage, Darcy was occupied very differently. He had a sense of satisfaction that Elizabeth would be relieved of worry for her sister, as well as the stigma over this affair. But it was somewhat of an empty satisfaction, for she would not know that he had been connected with its resolution. He had requested that Mr. Gardiner let no one know of his involvement, for he wanted no thanks or praise; he simply wanted to help Elizabeth. The despair on her face and in the sound of her voice when last he saw her was his motivation, and he could not even reveal to Mr. Gardiner the depth of his feelings in this matter in order for him to understand the reason for his actions. But on this point, it seems, he had underestimated Mr. Gardiner's powers of observation and deduction.

Chapter 38

After the wedding of Wickham and Lydia had taken place, in which no one was happy but the young lady, Darcy took the opportunity to go back and join Charles at Pemberley. He looked forward to being removed from a situation so distasteful as dealing with Wickham and his immorality. Though he was glad to have gotten better acquainted with Mr. Gardiner, to say nothing of being of assistance to Elizabeth, these were the only things he looked on with any comfort during that whole episode.

"I am sorry my business took me away for so long, Charles. It is a great pleasure to be in company with you again."

Charles was not accustomed to hear Darcy speak so sentimentally and wondered what sort of business in London could have affected him so, but felt it best to let it pass without mention and allow Darcy to bring up the subject, if he was so inclined. He responded, "Well, then, what say you to our riding out today and seeing the grounds? I can think of no better remedy for countering the effects of those tedious days of business in London."

Riding out in the environs of Pemberley indeed sounded like a remedy to Darcy, who blithely replied, "That is a splendid proposal. Let us take along some food so we will not have to return early."

The two friends were off before anyone in the house knew anything about it, and that is just as they wished. Darcy was taking Bingley to places he had seen before and told stories that he had heard before, but Charles knew it was somehow doing Darcy good. They stopped to eat at one of his favorite places: close to the river was a location where the shrubs formed an enclosure and the trees were a most elegant ceiling. The light filtering through at this time of day made it an excellent place to rest and cool down from the morning exercise.

"I used to come here often when I wanted to be alone. I haven't been here in quite some time, though."

"It appears to be a lovely place where one can think and just get away from everything," said Charles. Then he added, "Darcy, pardon me, I don't mean to pry, but is all well with you?"

"You've heard, I'm sure, of the common opinion that those with wealth want for nothing?" Charles nodded in agreement. "To own the truth, not too long ago I had not given things of this sort much thought . . . I imagine one could say I was complacent. But last week when I was in town, I had to deal with a person who believed that money could solve all his problems; and considering his want of good character, I could not help but think, if I were without my fortune, what kind of a man would I be?"

"I believe that I have seen just as many men in want of good character, who have position and wealth, as I have in those who lack such. It is certainly not the *lacking* or the *having* that determines character, but the man and what he makes of himself. Our best literature tells us this in many different ways."

"Charles, you are as wise as you are a good friend! You are quite right." They sat silently for a few moments in quiet reflection of what they had just considered, and then Darcy said, "Let us leave here, if you are ready, and I will show you the place my father most liked to take me."

Bingley could tell that this brief retrospective was sufficient to revive Darcy's spirits, and he stood up at this invitation. They rode on away from the river toward rising ground, and Darcy pointed out, "See that small patch of trees at the top of the hill? That is where we are going."

Once there, they dismounted and walked under the shade of the trees. "My father would bring me to this location because from here, as you can see, it affords a view of Pemberley like no other. Sometimes he talked of the responsibility that would one day be mine, and sometimes he would just point to various scenes and tell me stories of his youth growing up at Pemberley."

"I would imagine, then, that this also is one of your favorite places to come?"

"Yes. Unlike any other place, I have come here, often thinking of those times with my father and his words to me. On the day of his funeral, I rode up here at night, needing to be alone with my thoughts of him. As I was remembering some of our conversations on this very spot, I happened to look down at the house, and at that particular moment a servant was extinguishing the lights in one of the rooms. The whole room went dark, and I remember thinking it seemed a bit symbolic. I realized, that with the passing of my father, it was much the same . . . something very significant had gone out of the house, and I wondered if my light would be sufficient to illuminate in his absence."

With empathy, Bingley joined, "I understand your feelings. Of course, my family does not have the heritage of yours, but I have had similar thoughts. I suppose every son that has had a father in the real sense of the word feels that way."

"Do you think, Charles, women feel that same sense of duty of living up to something that the family stands for, or is it just men?"

"You have declared me wise, Darcy, so on what women feel, I will not venture an opinion! Therefore, I will not ruin my reputation as quickly as I have got it."

"Amen!" cried Darcy, and the two friends laughed. They had enjoyed this day together immensely, but soon realized they should be getting back. Putting his hand on Bingley's shoulder, Darcy said sincerely, "It is good to be with you again, my friend."

Chapter 39

Early the next day, Charles hesitantly began, "Darcy, I know you have only just returned to Pemberley, but Mrs. Hurst and Caroline are going into town . . . I must go to Netherfield, and I wondered if you would accompany me there? I would be ever so grateful for your company." He was taken by surprise when Darcy readily agreed, for he felt Darcy might need this time at home, considering his mood yesterday. Now Bingley had reason to rejoice at the prospect, and they all made plans to be off later that afternoon.

How much the two ladies of Longbourn had to do with the decision of these gentlemen is a matter rather obvious. Darcy, though, did try to convince himself that his chief motive was to determine Jane's feelings toward his friend, so as to amend his previous advice, if necessary. And whatever might be said as to motives, suffice it to say the gentlemen found themselves at Netherfield straightaway.

However strong their urge to be closer to the ladies was, the two found that actually *being* closer intensified this self-same urge to the point of considerable distraction. That evening, Darcy was so unsettled it prevented him from sleeping. The image of Elizabeth at Pemberley was a pleasant recollection indeed, and to have had her there on such good terms as they had been was perfection itself. But to have it all dashed by that sordid incident made him feel as if he had been robbed.

"My feeling that happiness with her was in the making is certainly not some exaggeration! I can remember only too clearly how she accepted my attentions, as well as her efforts at becoming acquainted with Georgiana. Surely it should not be too difficult for our relationship to continue from where it was interrupted . . ."

* * * * *

At breakfast the following morning, the gentlemen sat, with Charles very much wanting to talk of Jane and his desire to see her, but not daring to let Darcy know how eager he was to pay the visit. So instead, he spoke of everything else: "I had a dreadful time falling asleep last night, Darcy. I finally came downstairs to oil and clean the guns that had already been oiled and clean for today's shooting."

Darcy offered, "Surely after today's exercise you will be more tired and not have the same problem when you retire this evening."

"Yes, of course, I'm sure you are right." Then continuing to feel the need to say something on any subject that did not involve Jane, he added, "I really should give directions to the housekeeper so Caroline will have nothing to find fault with." Darcy only nodded. Never had the two friends been so like-minded, while feeling unable to talk of what they most wanted to talk about! Thereupon, Bingley restlessly talked about nothing, and Darcy restlessly listened.

They spent the first couple of days at Netherfield shooting, persistently avoiding the subject that was uppermost in their minds. Despite the exercise, they both continued to have difficulty getting to sleep. If they had not each privately put an embargo on the topic that was preventing their slumber, they could have kept each other company in those late hours. As it was, they were completely unaware that when they were both *in* their beds, as one tossed, the other turned; and when they were forced *from* their beds, as one paced, the other sat!

After coming in from their sport on the second day, the two friends were sitting at table when Darcy surprised Bingley by saying: "Charles, do you not think you had better do your duty by your neighbors and call on them?" His desire to see Elizabeth would not be put off another day, and it was evident Charles would not venture to suggest a visit to the Bennets. Of course, Darcy could comfort himself with his avowed purpose of observing Jane Bennet's actions toward Charles, and imagine that his desire to see Elizabeth was not stronger than Bingley's was to see Jane.

"I had been contemplating the same, but knowing your disposition for such things, I did not want to make you uncomfortable."

"Charles, one cannot think of comfort when considering one's duty. I recommend since we have seen Miss Elizabeth in Derbyshire, the Bennets should be called on tomorrow morning. Are you of the same mind?"

Charles agreed quickly, not wanting Darcy to recall the mother and change his mind! Neither gentleman would say anything more on the subject, but a look at their faces would have revealed both relief and great keenness at the prospect.

Chapter 40

Riding over the next morning, Darcy was silent and Charles was nervously talking on, wondering if it would be a convenient time for the Bennets, or would some of the ladies be away from home? The more he talked, the less Darcy listened, but soon both men were silent as they entered the grounds of Longbourn. Their nervousness and anticipation were as high as one might expect when entering a situation that involves matters of the heart, along with that feeling of uncertainty.

If Darcy had forgotten the mother, it was all brought back as soon as they entered the room where the ladies were. Her rudeness to him was all the more apparent by her contrastingly kind treatment of Bingley. In her meanness, she seemed determined to use every opportunity to direct some dart at him.

In particular, she mentioned Lydia having been married to Wickham, and his now going into a new regiment in the north with the help of 'some friends' he has -- and added, with fiery emphasis toward Darcy -- 'though not so many as he deserves!' This was, of all things, unexpected and painful for Darcy to endure. It evoked his former self to come rushing back, despite his recent success at his new self; under such provocation, of course, nothing could be more natural. He turned to a nearby window with the pretense of looking out, for to hear Wickham spoken of in terms of tenderness and himself vilified, when Mrs. Bennet was well aware of Wickham's misconduct in this matter, was shocking to Darcy.

"I know she is unaware of the part I played in bringing this affair to its present conclusion, but is she so lost to common decency as to refer to it without a blush?" he thought; then attempting to rally himself, "Come on, man, you were moved by your feelings for Elizabeth in that matter, not for her mother!" Turning away from the window, he tried again.

As determined as Darcy was, however, this setting proved to be too great a challenge, and the pleasantness and ease of Pemberley now seemed well beyond reach. The rise in his emotions at seeing Elizabeth became more disheartening, given her unanimated demeanor . . . she would scarcely look at him. He had been in keen anticipation of seeing her lovely face display some pleasure at his appearance, but he was unable to discern any such emotions.

Even when Darcy brought himself to ask about the Gardiners, she replied tersely. In addition to all of this, she was making herself so occupied with her needlework that she seemed purposefully to be avoiding any opportunity for discourse. The combination of being assailed by Mrs. Bennet, along with his eager anticipation of seeing Elizabeth crashing in ruins before him, had the effect of driving him into silence, and he could manage little more. During a brief pause of her mother's ramblings, Elizabeth did ask after Georgiana, but by this time, Darcy's disappointment was dominating, and he could manage only a laconic remark.

Remembering his purpose in regard to Charles, however, he would often look at Jane. The serenity of her face that he once believed betrayed a lack of feeling for his friend, he now saw in a very different light.

When she looked at Bingley, there was a depth of expression in her eyes that was not there when she looked at anyone else, and her mouth took on a pleasant aspect, rendering her face with a warmth and glow that unmistakably revealed her heart. Darcy reproached himself for being fooled by his prejudice and not noticing this months ago. A sense of happiness for his friend came over him at that moment, and had he not been looking down, a smile would have been noticed on his face, for Bingley obviously was becoming more captivated by Jane with every moment.

But as for his own happiness, he knew not what the morning's events were revealing. Darcy recalled his words to Bingley: '*One cannot think of comfort when doing your duty.*' . . . . . how prophetic those words proved to be for him!

Before leaving, the gentlemen were engaged to come for dinner Tuesday. Darcy did not know if he should be glad for another opportunity to ascertain Elizabeth's feelings toward him or to dread more discomfort.

Chapter 41

As Darcy was preparing for dinner at the Bennet's, he could not help but wonder: "What should I conclude if she continues silent and avoids me today as she did the morning of our visit? She has not the spirit to be suppressed; she is perfectly capable of letting her feelings be known, that much I know for a certainty... I observed in her sister Jane that she is still partial to Bingley, but on Elizabeth's side I saw nothing that spoke of particular regard for me; rather, that whole visit fairly declared her indifference. She constantly avoided looking at me, and even upon exerting myself and specifically addressing her, she was so succinct as to leave me now in suspense. I can only hope, this being a dinner party and her expecting to see me among the guests... if in this setting she continues as she was, that will tell all."

After everyone had arrived at Longbourn, they were called to table. Darcy noticed Bingley taking his place next to Jane, where he had been used to sit. He, on the other hand -- by some strange oversight, perhaps -- was placed next to the mother, with Elizabeth being so far away conversation with her was impossible. He could scarcely even make out the sound of her voice. Dinner thus passed with Darcy having a sinking feeling; it seemed that as nicely as things were turning out for Bingley, matters were continually going the other direction for him.

After dinner, the gentlemen repaired to the library for brandy, and the ladies into the drawing-room. As the men talked of the weather, sport, the roads, and all other subjects which it is supposed the intelligence of women does not allow to be discussed in their presence, Darcy found it impossible to take an interest. Having placed himself in a reading chair that permitted him to be out of the way, he sat unnoticed in anticipation of rejoining the ladies. He wished he could excuse himself for that purpose, but instead he simply waited.

Finally, the men moved out to the drawing-room, where he saw Elizabeth pouring coffee. His first impulse was to go directly there, but the number of ladies gathered around the table did not permit it. He even noticed one young lady move closer to Elizabeth as if to prevent even the smallest possibility for him to come any closer. Darcy had to take a place on the other side of the room, turning his eyes her direction as often as he could. If only their eyes would meet so that some communication of feeling could take place! But alas, as often as he would turn to look at her, he had just missed her looking at him. Hence, it seemed to him a mystery -- why she could be so amiable when he saw her in Derbyshire so that it seemed there was hope, to this.

Having finished his coffee, with a determination to put himself forward, he brought his cup to Elizabeth. She asked after his sister, he replied that she was still at Pemberley, and then she said no more. Darcy found himself unable to introduce another subject. He stood silently by her for some moments, wishing for something to say; but the hope of love apparently slipping away hung both in his chest and his mind, preventing wit, cleverness, or even a clumsy attempt at conversation with the lady that meant so much to him from surfacing. And when he observed another young lady lean over to whisper to Elizabeth, he became embarrassed; the impulse to leave rushed upon him, and under these circumstances, he moved away.

When next the card tables were brought out, he and Elizabeth were again put apart, as they were assigned to different tables. It appeared conclusive to Darcy: she had been deliberately keeping herself from him all evening. He therefore approached Bingley, even before they took their seats, and declared his need to leave after cards; so the message was sent to their driver to be prepared right away.

While they played at cards, Darcy could not help feeling that this may be the last time he would see Elizabeth as she was. This preoccupation, and the distraction of always looking at her, made him play very badly. At last, the card tables were put away, Bingley's carriage arrived directly, and the two gentlemen were off.

In the carriage, Bingley asked Darcy if all was well. "Yes, you know me, Charles; the crowd was becoming tedious. I am sorry, for I know you were enjoying yourself, and rightly so. Indeed, I thank you for indulging me in leaving so promptly."

"Don't give it another thought; let us relax and enjoy the ride home. Shall I let down the windows?"

"Yes, please, the fresh air will do me good."

They rode on, each one with their minds very differently occupied. Bingley was thinking of Jane and what a lovely time he had just had, although he could not help but ask himself, "What is it that Darcy and my sisters see about Jane that I do not?" All he could see was a beautiful lady that would make his life full and pleasant. He truly felt that she cared for him, but the nagging doubt involving the opinions of his friend and his sisters stood in his way of happiness.

Darcy, on the other hand, felt an emptiness more profound than when his offer of marriage had been refused. "At least then I had my indignation and the need to clear my name. Tonight, I was wanting only the smallest indication that I could hope for love, but none was forthcoming."

Arriving at Netherfield, they had tea and Bingley suggested they walk about the grounds before supper. Despite his low feelings with regard to his own hope for love, Darcy wanted Charles to know about his changed view of Jane and her feelings for him. He thought, "I would hope his knowing this would encourage him to feel free to do as he sees fit to secure his happiness."

He therefore introduced the subject by observing: "Miss Bennet looked as lovely as ever." Unsure of what was to follow, Bingley commented cautiously that he agreed. Not knowing what else to say by way of small talk about her, Darcy said abruptly, "Charles, I believe I was mistaken about Miss Bennet being directed solely by her mother."

"What are you saying, Darcy?" he asked in an animated tone.

"There is no question that Mrs. Bennet is a contriver and is doing all in her power to bring you and Miss Bennet together, but I failed to see that, despite her mother's maneuverings, Jane Bennet seems genuinely to care for you. How strong her regard for you is, you alone must determine."

"I was wondering about this very point on our ride home! It was troubling me that you and my sisters could see something in Jane that I could not. You cannot imagine the relief this is, knowing I have not been indulging in self-deception! . . . but on this matter of determining how strong her feelings are, do you have any advice to give?"

"In this regard, I have no advice to give, but my wish is that, if you should marry Jane Bennet, you and your new family would have all the happiness you deserve."

"Thank you, truly, Darcy. . . but your mentioning my family just now puts me in mind that when you talked to me months ago, your concern was not just that Jane did not care for me; you also described rather forcefully how the connection would endanger the future prospects of my family. How am I to take what was said on that head?"

"My concern was based on Miss Bennet having a stronger attachment for her family than for you. It was her influence, working in conjunction with her mother's schemes, that I feared would be too much for you to oppose. Acknowledging my error in the sincerity of Jane's regard for you, my apprehension about your managing your family's affairs has been done away with. My becoming better acquainted with her myself and the fact that you hold her in high regard have taught me to see her as I should. She is a practical and intelligent young lady and should prove to be a trusted companion for you as a wife. Let me add, lest the horrors of what I portrayed to you that day come back to your mind, you should not discount that, in my zeal to convince you and steer you clear of what I perceived as a danger, I most certainly overstated the evils of the match."

Bingley was speechless at this confession from his friend and was struggling to assimilate it. Finally, he managed to say, "Excuse me, Darcy, but I am caught between the great joy and satisfaction of being able to think about Jane the way I formerly did, and now being astonished at your conceding you were wrong." The latter was said somewhat in jest, yet Darcy could only force a smile.

Charles, putting his hand on Darcy's shoulder, was aware that he was not himself and assumed it had to do with this admission about Jane. They were then informed that supper was ready, but Darcy declared himself not hungry and begged leave to remain out-of-doors.

"Very well, it will be there for you if you decide later." Rather reluctantly leaving his friend, Bingley could tell there was something quite different about him. To say the least, he had seen Darcy in many moods, but none like this. If not for this melancholy of Darcy, he would have been overjoyed at the prospect of having his friend's approval to pursue a relationship with Miss Bennet. Nevertheless, he went in to supper with a happiness he had not felt for some time.

Darcy lingered out-of-doors well into the evening. Out of the darkness, his friend once again approached him: "Darcy, you have me concerned. What could possibly be the matter?" Bingley asked.

"I beg your pardon, Charles, I am quite well." Not wanting to reveal the more personal reason for his sadness, he offered another that was not too far from the truth: "My good friend, I directed -- insisted, actually -- that you put an end to your interest in Miss Bennet these many months ago, causing pain to you and God only knows what on Jane and her family, and I must apologize for that."

"*God only knows,*" Darcy repeated to himself. "I am aware of what great pain I have caused, not just to Charles and the Bennets, but also to myself," he thought, which pain he was now feeling acutely.

Bingley said compassionately, "Darcy, as things have turned out, thus far the worst you have done is delay what had started. So let us think no more about it."

"You are very kind, Charles; please accept my apology," was Darcy's reply.

As they started toward the house, Bingley felt he could now give voice to his happiness. Looking up, he declared, "What a lovely night this is! It does not rival the beauty of Miss Bennet, to be sure, but now that I have your blessing, I believe I would declare the most abominable weather fine."

Darcy half-smiled at his friend's exuberance, and they finished the night with a little more talk about Miss Bennet, which was a most difficult subject for him, but thankfully, he had learnt composure, or better said, he had learned to *appear* composed.

Chapter 42

In the morning as he was dressing, his thoughts turned to the time he had spent with Elizabeth at Rosings, which led to his recalling her asking about him seeing Jane when she was in London. Now Darcy felt compelled to inform Bingley of his withholding this information from him. He believed it important for his relationship with his friend that he hear it from him, and since he would be off to town in a day or two, he wanted to tell Bingley right away.

After breakfast, he began, "Charles, I have something unpleasant to tell you. It occurred to me only this morning; otherwise, I would have revealed it last night." Bingley, not knowing what unpleasant news there would be to tell after last night's *tête-à-tête*, leaned forward with a concerned look.

". . . when we had gone away to London those months ago, Miss Bennet also came into town, and I concealed it from you."

Bingley, looking incredulous, cried, "Darcy, I cannot believe you would behave in such a petty and deceitful manner!"

"It was indeed, but I confess it sprang from my concern for your getting involved in a bad match. At the time, I felt my motives were good; since then, I have come to see them just as you have described. I apologize with all my heart, Charles."

"Yes, yes, that is all fine, but if my memory serves me well, and I believe it does, your argument to me was she did not care for me, and her following me to London was a strong counter to your position! How could you treat me as though I were your child or ward in need of that kind of oversight?"

"You have every right to be angry with me, Charles, at my arrogance and pride. It is certainly abhorrent to me now. My only consolation is that my confounded meddling did not ruin your chance of happiness with Miss Bennet forever."

"Well . . . yes. No one will be more thankful for that than myself, I assure you. But, my happiness has yet to be secured on that head."

"It may seem so. However, no one that sees the way she looks at you could deny her feelings, and you know her mother is doing all in her power to forward the match, so I would say your happiness is secure and depends only upon you."

This speech lessened Bingley's heightened emotions, for he was not made in a way to hold on to such negative feelings, to say nothing of hearing the person on whom he depended most assuring him of the love of Jane for himself.

That day and the next were a bit tense after Darcy's confession. Bingley was compelled to mention it briefly a time or two more, but then that was the end of it, although he did inquire of Darcy what was the motive of his sisters in the matter. Darcy assured him it was from the same mistaken point of view that he had held; and now with all obstacles out of the way, nothing was left but to let the two lovers be together without any further interference.

The day Darcy was leaving for London, Bingley informed him, with a look of nervousness, of his intention of calling on Jane. Darcy replied, "Charles, you are one of the best men I know, and Miss Bennet seems to be blessed with one of the kindest inclinations I have ever seen. If this match goes through, as I am confident it will, I believe the two of you will be very happy together. Your situation is one most men would envy." Darcy, of course, was saying this more about himself than about *most* men.

With a look of deep friendship, they shook hands and bid each other farewell.

Chapter 43

In London, Darcy began calculating the number of days before he would receive news of his friend's engagement. He had not been there a week when that information came. "If left completely on his own, it would have taken longer, but with the influence of Mrs. Bennet, I knew it would be done within the week," he thought to himself.

To Darcy's distress, love and marriage seemed to be blossoming everywhere. The colonel arrived and informed him of the date of his upcoming wedding. "I sent a letter to Pemberley only to find that you were not there. Knowing that you would be coming to town, I decided to call on you with the news myself."

Darcy was truly happy for his cousin, but his own situation was weighing heavily upon him. His response, therefore, had a somber tone, "This is happy news indeed, Fitz. You seem to be as much in love as when I last saw you."

"Darcy, whatever could you mean by such a statement?"

"Fitz, I beg your pardon for my pessimistic mood. A certain melancholy has settled in on me and I find myself thinking of things under its influence. So my first thought was, these matters can start out well, but then turn bad."

"Yes, I have seen it so myself. But I assure you, we are very well matched and becoming more alike each day. However, enough of me -- what is it that has caused you to feel this way?"

By way of an excuse, Darcy suggested, "I suppose I am feeling a bit exhausted from traveling; I have had to do quite a bit of it lately. I am sure a good night's rest will serve me well." Then wanting to move the conversation away from himself, he added, "You are not alone in this lovers' happiness. I have just heard from my friend Charles Bingley. He is engaged and declares himself also to be very happy."

"Isn't that the chap you saved from an imprudent marriage some months ago?"

"Yes, he is the same person, yet my saving him was more a disgraceful interference, for which I have apologized."

"That was very big of you to admit such a thing, considering that you viewed it as such a triumph, as I recall. Who does he marry?"

"A young lady named Miss Bennet."

"You mean Miss *Elizabeth* Bennet, who was with us at Rosings?" the colonel cried.

In his despair over his plight, Darcy failed to remember: "Oh, yes, of course, that is right . . . I quite forgot you are acquainted with one of the Bennet girls. No, it is not Elizabeth, but her elder sister Jane."

"Well, I am glad he was able to make a match after all. Listen, I am sorry to cut this short, Darcy, but I must be off. My other reason for stopping was to invite you to join us for supper tonight."

Darcy felt being out in company would do him good, and as he was looking forward to getting better acquainted with Maria, he replied, "Yes, of course; surely Maria will be there?"

"Not just her, but a number of her relations, all here in anticipation of the wedding."

* * * * *

Later that evening while getting dressed, Darcy began to have second thoughts as to the advisability of being out in company with a group of strangers, but he did not want to disappoint Fitz. "I can always leave early on some pretext, or just honestly admit to feeling out-of-sorts and in need of rest. But perhaps once I am out, the evening air may revive me."

The carriage ride did little to invigorate him, so as he exited the carriage, he gave directions that it should expect an early summons. However, contrary to his apprehension, upon entering the gathering, Darcy saw there was the feel of a warm family affair, as the French are a very active and cheerful people. He was approached by the colonel, who greeted him with: "Darcy, you remember Maria's father, Monsieur Leblanc? . . . oh, please excuse me, gentlemen, but I see I am wanted by my mother." With that, the colonel left to attend to his mother's request.

"Yes, indeed; how do you do, sir?"

"Mr. Darcy, I am very glad you have come; you honor us."

"Thank you, sir, that is very kind. Let me say, it is a pleasure to see you again. Colonel Fitzwilliam and I are very close, and I am only too glad to get better acquainted with his future family."

"Yes, the colonel speaks well of you and wanted very much for us to get to know one another. I understand from him that you are still unmarried, is that so?" Darcy nodded in affirmation. "You two have the right idea on this matter, if you will permit me to say."

"I do not catch your meaning, sir."

"So often I have observed in my time, both here in England and in my home country, that young men are too . . . as it is said . . . too *quick* to make a match, when they themselves have yet to establish firmly what sort of men they are to be. Not so with you and my daughter's fiancé; you have become the kind of men a woman can depend upon before seeking the match. The woman that marries a man like you or him finds a man well worth having as a husband. I hope I am not being impertinent in saying this . . . we French tend to talk more openly of things than the English, and I find that I can say or talk of matters that I should not have, which I am informed of later by my dear daughter."

Though Monsieur Leblanc had a strong manly voice, there was a gentleness in its tone, and Darcy was touched by the kindness in his eyes as he spoke. "No, sir, you have no reason for concern in this instance, I am gratified by your good opinion. In my experience, it is often difficult to know when to speak and when not to. It is a balance that is delicate regardless of our culture or natural inclination."

"Such is the thing that makes up life, learning what is best to be done or said, which can usually only be measured after something has been done or said. For my case now, I will miss having my *faux pas* pointed out by my sweet Maria. And if you will allow me to confide in you, Mr. Darcy, I would sometimes do so purposely, just for the pleasure of her correction."

Darcy nodded, thinking how much that sounded like a loving parent. The father was called away, and Darcy then moved toward Maria. She was standing alone, and he began the conversation, "Will you and Fitzwilliam be traveling after the wedding, Miss Leblanc?"

"Yes, my father has taken a house for us in the country, and we shall go there from the church. Then the colonel wishes to take me on a tour through Sweden and Germany. His description sounds most enchanting! Rarely does one meet a gentleman with such powers of description as he has; he fairly carries me away with anticipation."

"To be sure, my cousin has often entertained us with narratives of his travels."

"And it is not merely that, but, dare I say, most men that are as active as he is rarely make time for reading and those more intellectual matters of life. However, with him I came to appreciate very early upon our acquaintance that our conversations will never be dull. Surely, I can speak freely with you, Mr. Darcy -- some of the gentlemen my father has introduced me to in the past have been as uninformed as a sign post!"

Darcy was intrigued by this comment and asked, "How is it you have come to esteem education and intelligence so highly? I'm afraid I have found many women more interested in good looks or charming personality, although I can say that my cousin also has both of those as well."

"From my youth, I have such pleasant recollections of my father and mother engaged in discussions about how present happenings relate to historical events, or perhaps points of architectural beauty when they were planning some renovation to the home, or an expansion of a certain area of the grounds. I do not believe I could truly be happy with a partner in life that I could not share such times with, and in Colonel

Fitzwilliam, or *Fitz*, as you call him -- I love that, by the way -- I have found such a kind, generous soul that unites all these, including good looks, as you say!"

Darcy was truly moved by this speech and impulsively responded, "May I say, Miss Leblanc, Fitz speaks as highly of you as I have just heard you speak of him. Your prospect for happiness is set on a very solid foundation." She thanked Darcy for his kind words just as the colonel came up to them with his mother, and Darcy now began to feel more acutely just how much he was losing out on in having ruined his chances with Elizabeth.

As things turned out, Darcy did not leave the gathering early, for the festive nature and happy ambience did much to rouse him from his doldrums, and on the ride home he was in very good spirits. After arriving, he requested some port and sat by the fire, thinking over the various conversations he had had that evening, appreciating that his cousin would be connected with such a family.

This reverie led to other thoughts, and he now began contemplating Bingley being happily married, the colonel being happily married, and himself continuing single. "I can see myself the single uncle coming to visit them and their children, bearing gifts, having to endure hearing the children ask their parents again and again, *'Why is Uncle Darcy not married?'* Well, perhaps I can convince myself to be satisfied with singleness by thinking of matters from this point of view: they will be busy with family, being husbands and fathers, while I shall be unencumbered to do as I please . . . however, considering my record of failing to convince myself, I should not get my hopes up."

Chapter 44

About a week after hearing from Bingley on his engagement, Darcy received a visit that would lighten his heavy heart in his situation with Elizabeth, and that from a most unexpected source. Lady Catherine de Bourgh called in the afternoon, and she was in such an agitation, he believed something must be seriously wrong.

She began before even reaching the sitting room: "Darcy, I must speak to you on a matter most urgent, that threatens the future prospects of both our families!" Darcy was quite alarmed and looked at his aunt with deep concern for what she was to relate. "I have just come from seeing Miss Elizabeth Bennet, and could not be more displeased and disappointed -- headstrong, unfeeling girl!"

Certainly the last thing Darcy could have imagined his aunt mentioning after her saying 'the future prospects of their families were being threatened' was Elizabeth. His concern quickly turned into surprise and interest of a different kind, as he declared, "Miss Bennet?!"

"Yes, *Miss Bennet*," she repeated scornfully. "That young woman of inferior birth and of no importance in the world."

Darcy impulsively asked, "What business could you have with her, madam?"

The manner in which Darcy asked this question caught the great lady's attention. After all, on her way to see Darcy she recollected with perfect clarity how he and the colonel reacted when learning of Miss Bennet being at the parsonage while they were staying at Rosings.

Consequently, rather perturbed, she started, "You have heard, I am sure, of her elder sister being engaged to the wealthy Mr. Bingley, your particular friend. Well, as that report reached me, another more scandalous one now being circulated involves *you* and Miss Elizabeth Bennet. I know it must pain you to hear it said, just as it pained me, but after my meeting with her, I found that I must come to see you on this subject."

Darcy was now in great anticipation to know to what she was referring. "What report? -- what subject is being spoken of involving Miss Bennet and myself? And am I to understand you have actually gone to her home?"

"Yes, I have just come from there, and I'm sorry to inform you that a report is being circulated declaring that you and Miss Bennet will yourselves soon be engaged to one another! Upon hearing this malicious rumor, I set off to make my feelings known to that young woman, and Darcy, you cannot imagine the language and coarse manners I met with when talking to her! But, please, let me hear it from you that there is no basis for this rumor."

Elizabeth's actions toward him recently were only too fresh in his mind, so without hesitation he responded, "I am not engaged to her, nor could I consider myself likely to be. What is more, this is the first I have heard anything of this sort. How could such a rumor get started?"

Hearing Darcy express matters this way, Lady Catherine was able to continue in a more calm attitude. "She told me the same, but with people of that sort, one can never be sure of what they are capable. My concern for you, Darcy, was that she used her arts and allurements, and in a moment of infatuation, she may have drawn you in.

"She is obstinate and headstrong, to be sure, but I had her understand, *my* character has ever been celebrated for its sincerity and frankness, and in this cause, I was certainly not going to depart from it. I can assure you, I have not been accustomed to such language as she used!"

This subject made Darcy listen with an intensity he had never given to his aunt when she was speaking.

"I told her, *'Let me be rightly understood. This match, to which you have the presumption to aspire, can never take place.*

No, never! Mr. Darcy is engaged to my daughter. Now what have you to say?' I demanded."

When Darcy heard this, he was concerned, thinking: "If Elizabeth had heard a reference to this since our meeting at Pemberley, this may be the reason for her cool reception of me." He interrupted, asking, "What was her response to this?"

"She declared, with such disrespect, *'If that is so, you can have no reason to suppose he will make an offer to me...'*

'The engagement is of a peculiar kind,' I explained, relating that you two have been intended for each other from your infancy, and that it was the favorite wish of both your mothers."

Darcy began shifting about in his chair, considering the conviction with which Lady Catherine presented to Elizabeth the proposed marriage to his cousin, as his aunt continued: "I appealed to her, *'And now, at the moment when the wishes of both sisters would be fulfilled, are you lost to every feeling of propriety and delicacy?'*"

Darcy asked cautiously, "How did she reply to this information?"

"Darcy, did I not tell you she is an obstinate, foolish girl? She declared with bold audacity, *'Yes, and I had heard it before. But what is that to me? I shall certainly not be kept from marrying your nephew simply by knowing that his mother and aunt wished him to marry Miss De Bourgh.'* She asserted that if you were neither by honor nor inclination confined to our dear sweet Anne, what should prevent you from making another choice? And if *she* were that choice, why should she not accept you?"

"Those were her words?" Darcy asked in disbelief. With this, he was now brought to the edge of his seat.

"I see your shock at such unrefined and vulgar behavior, Darcy."

"Forgive me, madam, but was that the end of it? Did you then come away?"

"I certainly did not! Those who are obstinate have found that they have met their match in me! I spoke with the force of one defending justice and said, *'Because honor, decorum, and prudence forbid it.'* And becoming very explicit, I informed her, if her high-minded scheme were to succeed, she should not expect to be noticed by the family, describing just how she would be treated -- I told her she would be censured, slighted, and despised by everyone connected with you! Her alliance would be a disgrace; her name would never even be *mentioned* by any of us."

Darcy felt some worry at this, and exclaimed, "I dare say, Lady Catherine, I could scarcely imagine more forceful language . . . did she respond, or was she rendered silent by this representation?"

"I wish I could set your mind at ease, Darcy, and say she was silent and repentant, but that was not the case. With her dark eyes taking on a satirical look, she stated, as if talking to some commoner, *'These are heavy misfortunes, but the wife of Mr. Darcy must have such extraordinary sources of happiness necessarily attached to her situation, that she could, upon the whole, have no cause to repine.'* "

The comment on Elizabeth's eyes brought to Darcy's mind the very expression on her face, and he was privately very proud of this woman he so admired still being unaffected by wealth and position. He broke in, "Being thus affronted, madam, what did you do?"

"I told her I was ashamed of her, and reminded her of my attentions to her last spring: *'Is nothing due to me on that score?'* I asked. I gave her to understand that I have not been used to submitting to any person's whims, nor have I been in the habit of brooking disappointment. I had come with a determined resolution of carrying my purpose, and for all her verbal impudence, I was not dissuaded from it.

"I really believed that this might somehow reach her, when thus far she had been unmoved. But again, I was to be confronted with her sharp tongue! She said, as coolly as you please, *'That will make your ladyship's situation at present more pitiable; but it will have no effect on me.'*

"I demanded, *'I will not be interrupted -- hear me in silence!'* . . . and trying to call her to reason, I repeated, 'My daughter and my nephew are formed for each other, and no upstart pretensions of a young woman without family, connections, or fortune is to divide them. If she was sensible she would not wish to quit the sphere in which she had been brought up!' "

Darcy, astonished at what he was hearing, was further astonished when his aunt related Elizabeth's response, which was: *'In marrying your nephew, I should not consider myself as quitting that sphere. He is a gentleman; I am a gentleman's daughter.'*

"Finally, I was at least able to get her to confess that she is not engaged to you, but upon attempting to make her promise never to enter into such an engagement, I was again presented with her perverseness as she declared, *'I will make no promise of the kind.'* . . . Honestly, Darcy, I expected to find a more reasonable young woman, but as I pressed for her assurance of not entering into an engagement with you, again she asserted she *'certainly never shall give it.'* "

Darcy was now obliged to stand, no longer able to just sit and listen, to which Lady Catherine responded, "I see this whole affair has upset you, as well it should. I told her as much when I informed her of my knowing about her younger sister's infamous elopement -- that patched-up business, at the expense of her father and uncle! Persons of such low connections have no sense of what a degradation it would be for a man of your station in life to have such a girl for a sister! Not to mention her husband, the son of your late father's steward, to be your brother! Your regard for Pemberley is too great to have its shades thus polluted!"

Darcy was speculating just how much more there could possibly be to relate, for how could either woman bear such talk from the other? "Was it then that this interview was ended?" he proposed.

"I had planted myself immovable until I got the assurance for which I came; it was she that rudely began to walk away. Nevertheless, till the last I would not leave off, and becoming highly incensed, I declared, *'You are, then, resolved to have him? You refuse to oblige me? You refuse to obey the claims of duty, honor, and gratitude? You are determined to ruin him in the opinion of all his friends, and make him the contempt of the world!'* "

"And did she answer you?"

"By this time, we were at my carriage, and in defiance of all, she retorted, *'Neither duty, nor honor, nor gratitude, have any possible claim on me. No principle of either would be violated by my marriage with Mr. Darcy.'* I gave her one last word of warning before departing, *'Do not imagine, Miss Bennet, that your ambition will ever be gratified. I hoped to find you reasonable; but, depend upon it, I will carry my point.'* "

Lady Catherine, believing all of Darcy's agitation was caused by his being as disturbed as she herself was upon hearing of this said, "Why, Darcy, there is no need for you to be so alarmed. As I have related to you, for all her loud talk, I have settled the matter. And as she sits in her home, my reproofs will have their proper effect, and she will be of no bother to us.

"But, if she should dare raise her impertinent little head this direction, leave it to *me*, Darcy; you need not worry yourself -- she is no match for me! It is fortunate for yourself that you have me to look after you in matters such as this. You are a very good young man, but you are too kind to handle interest needing a firmer hand. Now that she realizes she will have *me* to go around, she will be dissuaded. But alas, Darcy, take this as a warning about women in general . . . you have not yet learnt just how contriving the feminine mind can be! And you cannot live secluded at Pemberley, seeing that you are an active young man -- you must learn a lesson from this."

"As you say, madam, I believe there is much to be learned from this, and one may never know when such a lesson is to be taught. I do, indeed, hope to be benefitted by your coming here today!"

It was only now that Darcy recollected he had not offered tea, and Lady Catherine having arrived in so disturbed a state, the servant had not dared come in to offer it. "Pardon me, madam, I have just realized, I have not even offered tea."

"Yes, please, Darcy. But who could think of refreshments with such news at hand? Now that the initial shock is over, however, tea would do just fine."

While they were waiting for tea, Darcy, in an effort to change the subject, asked, "Do you call upon the Earl and the colonel while you are in town?"

"I believe I shall. Although, I hardly know what the Earl is about . . . what does he think, matching the colonel with a French woman, as if there are not English ladies aplenty? The colonel is as fine an English gentleman as there is to be found. If he had consulted me on the matter, I certainly would have counseled against the match! The prospects of the colonel were always so promising, and now for them to end in this way . . . there is much to be lamented. The French blood runs too hot; no Englishman that marries one will be destined to a peaceful family life. And heaven protect us if they have children with that same hot blood! I would certainly never turn the colonel away from Rosings, but I will dread the day when he comes with that French woman! What a contrast will be seen in your marriage to Anne -- there they will see what true marital felicity is! And with me to give the needed guidance, your marriage will be a true model for respectable couples to follow." Had Darcy ever been inclined to any degree to enter into a marriage with Anne de Bourgh, the image just created by her mother would have driven such inclination out forthwith!

Since the concerns of the colonel were of far less importance to her than those of her own daughter, Lady Catherine recounted the particulars of her meeting with Elizabeth with even more fervor through tea, and, indeed, until Darcy handed her into the carriage. Turning away as she departed, he immediately began trying to comprehend just what he had heard and the significance to himself. Darcy was glad that Lady Catherine repeated everything through tea, for on the second hearing, it confirmed what he thought he had heard.

Knowing Elizabeth's nature, he struggled with two possible reasons for her statements to Lady Catherine: "Was she simply replying in such a way just to be contrary and give a little trouble to a person who is accustomed to always having her own way? Or would she really consider another offer from me? I can well imagine her responding in such a manner to my aunt's impertinence in coming to her home, demanding such things as whom she should marry in such a way as to vex her. But if it is the other, the actual possibility that she would again consider my proposal, why then did she deliberately not speak to me when last I saw her? In which light am I to take this news?

"Surely when being pressed by Lady Catherine time and again, she would have tired of such insolence and acknowledged she had absolutely and irrevocably no interest in me . . . but Lady Catherine said Elizabeth steadfastly refused through their whole encounter to give any assurance of not accepting me if I were to ask! Can it be so? Is there room to hope, where I had thought there was none?

"How astounding to be informed of this by Lady Catherine, of all persons, whose sole purpose was to prevent our coming together! She has given me the courage not to give up hope! . . . it seems I may have completely misinterpreted Elizabeth's actions toward me in our last meetings. I was a fool in coming away so quickly!

"*I must return*, this time to make an honest effort at winning her affections. After all, with Charles and Jane engaged, no lasting harm has come from my meddling, and the last obstacle of our past has been swept away. So now, in truth, my hope for happiness with Elizabeth rests with me!"

Chapter 45

In a very short time, Darcy arrived at Netherfield and found Bingley preparing to leave for Longbourn. Upon seeing him, he said with great pleasure, "Darcy, what a surprise; I was not expecting you till much later! I am on my way to the Bennet's, but of course, I will delay in going and have you settled in. Have you had breakfast?"

"Please, do not let my arrival prevent your leaving, Bingley. May I accompany you there?" Darcy proposed, before even dismounting his horse, not realizing he had not properly greeted his friend.

"Of course you can, but are you up for it? Would you rather not relax and refresh yourself before we leave?"

"No, I am quite ready and the day is fine; besides, I do not wish to detain you from your fiancée." Recalling himself, he added, "Actually, this is my first time seeing you since receiving the news -- please, let me congratulate you and wish you all the best." The two shook hands, with Bingley smiling appreciatively at his friend.

"Thank you for your felicitations, Darcy, and for being so kind as to continue your riding so I may not be delayed in seeing my Jane."

It would not be possible to know which man possessed the greatest desire to get to the Bennet home. Certainly, it is to be noted that each was driven by very different feelings: Bingley's was an emotion that had just been allowed to express itself after months of delay; Darcy's was one looking for release inspired by the newness of hope rekindled.

As they were on their way, Bingley spoke of his own happiness and asked after the colonel's upcoming wedding. This called Darcy away from his contemplation of just how he should proceed, given whatever circumstances they might find themselves in. He had to ask Charles to repeat his question, then was able to give an answer, and further felt it incumbent upon himself to ask Charles about his plans. Consequently, any strategy for the advancing of his own love would have to be improvised. Darcy had, though, formed a resolution with regard to Elizabeth -- this one, unlike the others, he was in a fair way of keeping, seeing that it had the support of his heart.

Unknown to Darcy, Bingley was thinking of his friend as they entered the gate. Feeling for him, he did not want to expose Darcy to the impoliteness of Mrs. Bennet, so he decided he would recommend the party walk out on this fine day. This he did promptly as they entered the house; being nearly family, he could do such things without regard for decorum. Those venturing out were Charles and Jane, with Darcy, Elizabeth and Kitty. The two lovers walked slowly, allowing the others to advance well ahead.

Charles facetiously observed, "Considering what a great talker Darcy is, one can only imagine what lively conversation must be taking place among the three."

Jane laughed, adding, "Kitty is so frightened of Mr. Darcy, I am sure she is silent."

"And Elizabeth?" Bingley asked.

"She dislikes him so, I would suppose she is not giving herself the trouble of carrying the conversation if he is not making an attempt at it."

"Well, my suggestion of going for a walk had as its motive keeping Darcy away from your mother's unkind remarks. Now I wonder which Darcy would prefer: what he is in, or what he has escaped?"

"I do apologize for my mother's behavior toward your friend, Charles, but as for Elizabeth, I know she will not be unkind to him."

"Let us not think of it any further, for I had another reason for going on this walk. It was a more selfish one, to be sure, but I wanted some time with you alone." Jane smiled shyly, and taking his hand, they talked of matters having to do with themselves. Engaged as they were in such conversation, and so far behind, they did not see Kitty leave to call on Maria Lucas.

Of all the circumstances Darcy had time to consider, this was not one. Finding himself alone with Elizabeth on a walk created a struggle in his mind over just what to do now . . . having once declared his love, should he do so again as abruptly as he had before? Or should he proceed with some patience and allow her to see that the changes she had observed when they were in Derbyshire were not the work of a moment? His struggle was not helped by the awareness that he was saying nothing at all. This, of course, did not speak well for making a good impression on her. In truth, his emotions were so strong at being in this most unexpected situation, he was doing well to walk without tripping.

Elizabeth put an end to his struggles by thus addressing him: "Mr. Darcy, I beg leave to thank you for all you have done for my sister Lydia. I learned of your involvement from my aunt, and though the rest of my family continues ignorant, I will thank you for us all. Your actions speak of such great compassion, considering what trouble it must have required and the mortification you were put through to discover them, not to mention your generosity in setting matters right. I cannot even suppose to imagine how irksome it must have been for you to deal with Wickham in all of this! If I were to thank you a thousand times, it would not seem sufficient."

Darcy, showing a bit of disappointment, remarked, "I am sorry you have been informed of this. Of all things, I had not wanted you to be made uneasy, nor could I wish for you to feel a sense of obligation to me . . . I am surprised that Mrs. Gardiner could not be trusted to keep the confidence."

"My aunt is quite trustworthy, I assure you; it was Lydia, in a moment of carelessness -- which for, her is very often -- who betrayed the secret, and having heard that much, I would not rest until being made aware of all the particulars, and so wrote my aunt for the information. I am glad for having this opportunity now to express not only my own gratitude, but to do so in behalf of all my family as well."

"If you insist on thanking me, please thank me for yourself alone, for although I felt empathy for your family in this matter, my actions were driven only by the thought of you. I could not countenance the image of you being made so unhappy as I found you that day at Lambton, and was determined to be of service to *you*."

♥ ♥ ♥ ♥ ♥

Having begun these expressions of his feelings, and Elizabeth having spoken so kindly and sincerely, Darcy was unable to contain himself any longer. What better opportunity could he ever have? The thought occurred to him, "It is fairly obvious I will have trouble recommending my suit by the art of romancing!". . . so he abruptly declared, "I know I can depend on your being candid and not trifling with me: the wish of having you as my wife continues undiminished. Please tell me, are your feelings the same as they were last April? One word from you will render me silent on this subject forever."

Elizabeth was overcome by what she heard. There had been a sense of uncertainty about his regard for her that made this proposal almost as surprising for her as his first, and though it required effort, she responded softly, "I would not wish you to be silent on this subject. . . my feelings are quite the opposite from the time to which you allude."

To be sure, marriage proposals have been asked and answered in a more romantic way. But after all, what is needed at times like this is *the asking* and *the answering*. To those involved, nothing could be more romantic.

Darcy's happiness was unbounded and his emotions began forcing their way into expressions, while Elizabeth uncharacteristically remained silent. There was a look of shy modesty on her face, as she could not even look up at him. It was an exchange of temperament that very much suited the moment.

"My dear Elizabeth . . . *dear Elizabeth* . . . how pleasant the sound, how I have longed to call you that! I must say, of all the people I know and care for, you have come to mean more to me than I had ever thought possible! There is, of course, a unique bond between Georgiana and myself, seeing that it is only the two of us in our family now. And yet, the strength of my attachment to you is such that it defies my understanding ...

... I have spent days and nights recounting your strength of character, your intelligence and wit. There is not another woman that possesses these qualities in such perfect balance! And the loveliness of your face ... I can scarcely *close my eyes* without seeing your face."

Elizabeth still could not bring herself to look up, but finally was able to manage in a hushed tone, "I dared not imagine you would make another offer to me ... I am quite overcome with happiness!"

It struck Darcy how amusing this information would be to Lizzy, so he asked: "Would you like to know to whom you are indebted for your elation?"

"I would say it is owing to your good character in extending forbearance with me and my mistaken views of you," she humbly replied.

"Alas, no; as much as I would like to take the credit. Rather, it is Lady Catherine." He looked at Lizzy to see her expression and was not disappointed; as expected, she looked up at him in amazement, repeating, "Lady Catherine?!"

Enjoying the moment, Darcy laughed, "Well can I believe your being astonished at this, but it is so. She stopped to see me soon after her visit with you, if it could rightly be called a *visit*. She was, as you can well picture, determined to receive a guarantee from me that she was unable to get from you. At the time, I had not the slightest hope of ever being accepted by you, so when asked about some rumor she had heard, I expressed matters as I thought they stood. This proved to be very helpful, since I was able to avoid her asking me to promise something I never could, that of not entering into an engagement with you. All that aside, your words in refusing made an indelible mark in her mind, for she seemed to repeat what you said precisely ... it was as if I was actually there, hearing the confrontation myself."

Looking at her with admiration, he continued, "I believe it had something to do with her being confronted with the one person whose intrepidity would not allow them to be intimidated by her. I can assure you, she spoke with enthusiasm on all your remarks, which she thought would have the same effect on me as it had on her."

Giving voice to more tender feelings, Darcy stopped at this turn in the road, and facing Elizabeth, revealed, "At first I could not believe what was being said, as she was reciting your declaration of having the right to marry me. . . but then, as she unfolded her continued attempts and your steadfast refusal, I was taken from disbelief to *hope*. I knew that in such a moment as that, had you no interest in me, you would have openly expressed it."

Elizabeth, cherishing his sentiments, nevertheless responded in her characteristically lighter tone, "You mean, if I could so easily abuse you to your face, it would be just as easily done to all your relations!" Darcy smiled, then disclosed what an impact her comments to him on the occasion of his first proposal had on him. "I can hardly believe my words to have had such an effect," she uttered.

"That I can well suppose -- your reproof, though founded on mistaken information, was nonetheless the correction of a true friend. Your words, *"Had you behaved in a more gentlemanlike manner"* have haunted me ever since, and I must say, impelled me to look at myself without the bias of self-deception." Elizabeth peered at him incredulously.

"I can well understand your doubting the impact of what you said, but there was also the turn of your countenance when you said that I *'could never have made an offer in any possible way that you would have accepted'*. . . that look, those words . . . yes, indeed, they have had a lasting impression."

"My dear Mr. Darcy, this will not do -- we are just now *engaged*; is it not time for happier reflections?" she laughed.

"You are quite right. But may I ask, and still stay within the bounds of 'happier reflections' -- did my letter soften your view of me? Did you give it any credence?"

Lizzy was initially inclined to tease him here, but sensing the heaviness of his question, she began, "As you might apprehend, my inclination upon first reading it was against you, especially with reference to the part having to do with Jane. But coming to your dealings with Wickham, I was truly humbled, and even ashamed at having been so prejudiced against you. I had prided myself on being this great reader of character and observer of human follies . . . what a rightful joke was being played on me, that the very things I would laugh at, I was heedlessly engaging in. I read your letter so many times, I began to know it by heart, and thus learned to see you as I should have."

"I hope the letter has been destroyed," Darcy said earnestly. "There are things I would dread your having the power of reading again. Having gained your good opinion now, I would hate to lose it by your being reminded of those things."

Elizabeth responded that she would burn it, though she did not believe it could possibly have such an effect, and added, "Mr. Darcy, I would suggest you learn to forget such troubling recollections, and consider more pleasant things, as I do."

"I dare not forget, given the fact that I have had much more practice at my former ways. The reminder of what it could have cost will serve to admonish me never to go back to that conduct again. My parents brought me up with good principles; however, being spoiled by them encouraged me to be selfish, and even worse. I learned to care about those who were close to me, and to think meanly of everyone else."

To that, Elizabeth observed, "I am convinced my sister Mary would offer a commentary such as, '*We humans too easily learn a negative lesson, whereas the positive ones are more trouble to learn.*'"

"I am in complete agreement with such a statement, although I would hasten to add, *you* are the only person that could have taught me such a positive lesson. My dearest, loveliest Elizabeth, my debt to you is beyond my ability to express, for how do you thank the person that has been the means of altering your life in such a wonderful way? To be sure, it was more trouble to learn it -- being humbled always is -- but you also taught me that to be worthy of such a woman as you, I had to be a better man than I was."

It was now Elizabeth's turn to bring up her own question, as she ventured, "Dare I ask what you thought of me when we met at Pemberley? I was mortified when I suddenly encountered you out on the lawn! Surely you felt it quite inappropriate of me to be there?"

"No, no, I was surprised, indeed *astonished* may be a more accurate word. I'm sure you can recall how disconcerted I was in my efforts to talk to you. But after the initial flush of emotion, I was truly glad to have an opportunity to behave in a more gentlemanlike manner. . . I was eager to make a new beginning with you."

"Your change in manner was quite obvious, and I was at a loss to determine the reason you had been so altered. Now being given this account, the events of that day make perfect sense."

More was said involving their past dealings, some of which were too painful to speak of at length, such as the matter with Lydia. But when the subject turned to Jane and Bingley, there was happiness for them both to express.

At last noticing the time, they knew they should start back. At the Bennet home, there were questions about where they had wandered off to, but no one had a suspicion. The rest of the evening passed with Darcy and Elizabeth restraining themselves from showing any partiality for one another, for they felt it best to inform Charles and Jane first, then make an application to Mr. Bennet, instead of announcing it to the whole family at once.

Chapter 46

Later that night at Netherfield, Darcy introduced the subject of his engagement in this manner: "Charles, I have some news for you. As I am informing you, very likely Elizabeth is doing the same with Jane."

The thought that Darcy and Elizabeth could have something in common to relate to Jane and himself could not have raised his curiosity to a higher degree, so Charles leaned forward and listened with great interest.

"Miss Elizabeth Bennet and I are engaged." Charles looked at Darcy with a smile and chuckled, suggesting disbelieve. Darcy then responded, "I understand your difficulty, but it is true."

"Darcy, may I suggest you retire your efforts as a humorist; you do a poor job of it. You and Miss Elizabeth would have had to wander far longer than *that* for such a thing to take place!"

"No, actually, I have been in love with her for some time, and I came back for the sole purpose of making my feelings known to her. Do you not recall my defending her before your sister on many occasions?"

"Yes, but I am sure you were simply responding because Caroline can become so tiresome," Charles replied, still doubting.

"That is true, to be sure, but I am in earnest: Elizabeth and I are engaged. I asked her on the road during our 'wanderings', as you put it, and she said yes."

"I am sorry, Darcy, but this just sounds too fantastic a step, considering . . . well, considering you and your feelings, not to mention her own feelings for you."

"Charles, I know this must make me sound like a hypocrite of the highest order after all the difficulty I have given you . . . I must say, I still cannot look back at my conduct in that matter without abhorrence."

Charles was much too happy in his engaged state to hear anything about the past; besides, the present subject was far too interesting to hear of anything else. "Please, Darcy, let us not talk of that, it is all forgotten on my part -- although it does me good to hear it still troubles you," he added in a lighter tone, continuing, "so, please, tell me once again if this is all to be believed, and I will accept you are in earnest."

Darcy's face broke out in a broader smile than Bingley had ever seen, as he said with conviction, "Miss Elizabeth Bennet and I *are* engaged."

Bingley rushed over and taking hold of his friend by his shoulders, declared, "Darcy, I could not be more surprised, to be sure, but I honestly could not be more happy! Let me heartily congratulate you! Nothing could be better than Elizabeth marrying you and Jane marrying me. This is indeed a capital development! May our friendship and that of the ladies be ever as strong and close in marriage as it has been before." With great curiosity, he inquired, "But Darcy, you say you have loved Elizabeth for some time . . . just how long have you loved her?"

"Charles, to own the truth, I had resisted and denied my feelings for so long, it is hard to say when admiration turned into love."

"But why should you fight such feelings? Your wealth and consequence -- surely you have no one to answer to, or whose opinion matters."

"You are correct except for one thing: I do answer to myself, and you will not find it hard to believe that my pride and prejudice were such that I felt she and her family were beneath me." Pausing to look directly at his friend, Darcy spoke sincerely, "As I have said before, such feelings and the way I interfered with you are disgusting to me now, but at that time I reproached myself for being attracted to her."

"How did you reconcile yourself to it all, so that you would go as far as making an offer to her?"

Darcy had to think a moment before answering. He was not sure just how much he felt like revealing on this point, even to his good friend. Finally, his respect for Bingley moved him to say, "Believe it or not, Charles, this is the second time I have asked her. The first time was when I was at Rosings with the colonel and she was visiting Mrs. Collins at Hunsford."

Charles could not contain himself. "You have asked her once before?! This is more inconceivable than you asking at all! I don't know what to make of it. *What happened?*"

"Well, as you may have deduced, she turned me down," Darcy said matter-of-factly.

"But Darcy," Bingley said, objecting to the notion, "how could any woman decline an offer from you? Especially someone in the situation of Miss Elizabeth Bennet? Are not all women interested in making a good match? And there are very few that could equal you as one."

"You are very kind, Charles, and you honor me more than I deserve, but if you were to consider the young lady you have the privilege of being engaged to, you might recant that last statement. She is making a good match to be sure, but it is a good match with a good man. If you were only wealthy, I do not believe you would have this happy prospect ahead of you."

"Darcy, I have known you for many years now, you are a good fellow. What possible objection could there have been to you?"

"Again, you flatter me, but there were objections solidly based. As you know, I am not eloquent, and in the ways of love and romance even less so. But I can assure you that it was not a want of sweet words, but rather, a want of proper feeling, or as she justly described, a lack of behavior becoming a gentleman. My rudeness and defamatory statements in making my suit were such that even a woman violently in love with me would have recoiled."

"Darcy, surely you are exaggerating!" Bingley responded sympathetically.

"No, Charles, it is absolutely true. My pride and prejudice were in high form that day. I do believe, though, that only

Elizabeth would have had the spirit to tell me so in such a way that even I could not deny it. She taught me the greatest lesson of my life that day, and I will always be thankful that I at least had the good sense to fall in love with *her*."

In amazement, Bingley listened to all of this, and then asked, "But if it was as bad as all that, how is it possible for matters to have turned out as they have?"

"As you might imagine, my initial response after leaving her that day was one of trying to justify my feelings and way of thinking. However, going over the events again and again, I realized that what she had said about me was correct. And so I set about on this great reworking of my character, to do away with such petty pride and prejudice. I will say, having such fine examples as the colonel and yourself gave me excellent models to work by."

Stopping in reflection, he went on, "There was a sadness in all of this, though, because I thought my improvements would never be seen by the person who inspired them, since I believed we would not see each other again. Indeed, it was in this belief that I tried diligently to put her out of my mind; and yet, time and again, we were thrown together inexplicably. For instance, when she was seeing the country with her aunt and uncle and happened to be at Pemberley just as I was arriving. From that point to here, you are acquainted with how things have unfolded, though you have been unaware of my feelings for her."

"I have noticed quite a change in you, but I had no idea to what to attribute it. This account you have related is enough to make even a skeptic believe in the power of love!"

As the night went on, they continued talking of their experiences of falling in love and what happiness marriage would hold for them. There was a moment of serious reflection, though, as the talk turned to how Mr. Bennet might take the news when approached for his blessing.

In whatever way the morrow would unfold, everyone concerned in the business would have to wait, but until then, at

Netherfield, and in at least one room at Longbourn, there was great joy.

Chapter 47

The next morning as they were riding over to the Bennet home, Bingley was in high spirits. His happiness at his own engagement, coupled with that of Darcy's, made him feel his cup was overflowing. Darcy, on the other hand, felt as close to happiness as his situation permitted, because unlike Bingley, there was still the application to Mr. Bennet to be made. He had no doubt of Elizabeth's feelings for him, but one thing his experience with her had taught him was not to be overconfident. How would Mr. Bennet react to this engagement, given Elizabeth is his favorite? Darcy had no idea, no way to even suppose, how the man felt about him.

His thoughts on this were interrupted by Bingley asking, "When do you propose to speak with Mr. Bennet?"

"It is difficult to say. Unless some other convenient opportunity presents itself, it will be done in the evening."

Once the gentlemen were in the home, Mrs. Bennet, wanting to get Darcy out of the way of Jane and Charles, suggested that Darcy take the opportunity to walk to Oakham Mount with Elizabeth and Kitty. Bingley, scheming in a similar way as Mrs. Bennet, suggested the distance was too much for Kitty, to which she admitted she had rather stay home. All was arranged, then, for both the acknowledged lovers and the unacknowledged lovers to be alone for the morning.

Darcy and Lizzy needed this time together to enjoy their engagement in this private way, which seemed appropriate, since each in their own way kept their feelings for the other a secret, even to some extent, from themselves. Now alone, it was as if all the world's pride and prejudices which had worked to keep them apart were very far away.

As they walked, Elizabeth related the conversation between herself and Jane the night before: "What pleasant sport I had in trying to convince Jane of our engagement! She, of course, did not accept it as true when I first informed her, and the more I assured her of it being so, the more she would not believe it."

"I had the same reaction from Charles."

Struck by what seemed odd to her, Elizabeth began, "On my side, I can see the difficulty: I am always teasing, and last night the temptation was too strong! I started in earnest, I assure you, but her initial reaction took me from earnestness to teasing in a moment, and Jane is sometimes so serious, it is often a challenge for her to know when I am having fun at her expense. But you are not the sort to be doubted -- I am surprised at hearing Mr. Bingley needed assurances from *you*."

"What you say is true, but like you, my not being believed did have something to do with my nature. I am speaking of my tendency to keep personal matters to myself. You see, I confided my feelings for you to no one, neither my growing attachment nor my later disappointment at first proposing. In fact, I concealed my feelings so well that not even the object of my admiration was aware of it, as you can testify. Consequently, Charles considered me indifferent to you at best. But, of course, he had good reason to believe my feelings were stronger than just indifferent, remembering my actions involving your sister and himself."

"Poor Mr. Darcy," Lizzy stated sympathetically. "Through all your disappointments, you have been alone? What a sad picture to consider . . . if I had not had Jane for support and comfort in my times of trouble, I can scarcely imagine how well I would have managed."

"Your sympathy for me does you credit, and I am grateful for it, though it is more than I deserve. But my keeping Bingley in the dark was only half the reason for his difficulty in believing we were engaged." Lizzy's curiosity thus piqued, she stopped and turned to him, wanting very much to know what other reason there could be?

Finding himself with the rare opportunity of teasing her, Darcy answered, "Though he was ignorant of my true feelings for you, he was not ignorant of your feelings against me, so to him it seemed we fell in love and got engaged in the span of yesterday's walk; and this, I am sure, you will grant is too much for anyone to accept."

Elizabeth laughed heartily and remarked, "We are probably the only two lovers who have had to produce proof even before being believed about their engagement!" Then in a more serious tone, "Though I can't prevent myself from seeing the humor in it all, there is the matter of my father's approval. If our two best allies were having trouble with this, what might his reaction be?"

"Do you foresee his disapproving of the match?"

"I ... do anticipate his being uneasy, but I truly cannot fancy his disapproving," noting wryly, "It seems my outspokenness and your quiet reserve have thus created a very curious dilemma!"

"I must say, I have come to know very little of your father, and though there is a bit of nervous uncertainty, I am looking forward to getting on with him. I feel you are much like him; therefore, I am disposed to think well of him. And if it works in the other direction, in that he would think well of me as you do, there is every reason to be positive." Darcy had learned not to be haughty, proud and overconfident, but he was still *Fitzwilliam Darcy of Pemberley,* and dealing with matters of weight was not new to him. He therefore undertook his interview with Mr. Bennet with due seriousness, but not undue nervousness.

After determining that the application to Mr. Bennet should be done in the evening, Darcy turned the conversation back to his discussion with Bingley. He professed how much good it did him to recount to Bingley the events leading to their engagement. "I think in some ways I was still unsure of it being true until the retelling. Though there is something for which I feel I must apologize to you."

"For what, pray tell? If on the beginning of our second day of engagement you find yourself called on to apologize, this is foreboding indeed," she said with a smile.

"No, it is nothing like that. But being here with you now, I see I did not do you enough justice in talking to Charles. Your beauty makes words be of no account, and your spirit is such that it has carried me and inspired me in ways I would not have believed possible. So, yes, I want to apologize for not speaking highly enough of you. And what is more, I believe I will often find myself deficient, because the reality of you is always greater than my memories." Elizabeth, rendered speechless to hear him speak so of herself, could only take his hand and, as they had often done, walk on together in silence the rest of the way.

There was much to be admired at Oakham Mount -- the natural beauty and serenity that seemed to have existed since the beginning of time was a perfect setting for these two lovers who had gone through every range of emotion with each other, to finally arrive at this strong sense of abiding love.

Chapter 48

Once they were back at the manor and evening had come, Darcy waited for Mr. Bennet to move to his library. Elizabeth suggested this to be the most propitious time, and as anticipated, Darcy saw him soon withdraw into the library. After stealing a glance at Elizabeth, thither Darcy also went.

Mr. Bennet was taken back at being petitioned for an audience by Mr. Darcy. What could he have to say to him in private? Nevertheless, he invited him in and signaled that he take a chair near the desk. Settling in his mind that Darcy must have some recommendation to make about the place or the grounds, not understanding, as is often the case with rich men, that not everyone has their means to do what they please with their homes or grounds, Elizabeth's father was prepared to listen politely and thank him for his interest.

However, because Mr. Bennet struck Darcy as a man who did not care for small talk or beating around the bush, he felt it best to get right to the point, and said forthright, "Mr. Bennet, I have asked your daughter Elizabeth to marry me, and she has accepted. I have come now to ask for your approval and blessing."

Mr. Bennet, prepared to utter as pleasant a '*thank you*' as he could muster and close the subject as quickly as it had been opened so that he could have his library to himself, sat staring at Darcy for a moment, stupefied. Then recovering, he said in disbelief, "Forgive me, Mr. Darcy, did I understand you correctly? You have come to ask for Elizabeth's hand in marriage?"

"Yes, sir, I have. If the suddenness of it is a concern to you, I can assure you this is not the work of moment. Rather, I have had feelings for your daughter for some time." Then wanting to make certain that Mr. Bennet had heard what he said about

Elizabeth's response, he repeated, "and as I said, she has accepted me. So I now make my application to you."

Mr. Bennet was silent, considering how to answer this extraordinary request from such a formidable man. Darcy exerted a great measure of self-control here, for the silence and steady gaze of Mr. Bennet was having an unnerving effect on him, despite his being *Fitzwilliam Darcy of Pemberley!* After all the twists and turns he had been through to get to this point, he could not be sure whether this was going to be another one.

"If you will pardon my asking, Mr. Darcy, you say that Elizabeth has *agreed* to marry you?"

"Yes, she has."

"And she was absolutely clear that you were making a marriage proposal?"

"Yes, sir, I assure you, there was no misunderstanding. We spoke again on the subject today."

"And how long have you been engaged, sir?"

"Only since yesterday when we were walking; we both agreed that you should be made aware of it and your approval sought as soon as possible."

Mr. Bennet determined it would be best to speak to Elizabeth about his concerns rather than to Mr. Darcy, so at last he said dismissively, "Thank you, Mr. Darcy, for coming to me as soon as you have on this. It would be pointless to talk of your ability to provide for my daughter. As to anything else, let me just say, if Elizabeth has agreed to enter into a marriage with you and does not have a change of heart, you have my approval. Please, when you go out to the drawing-room, send Elizabeth in to see me."

Darcy thanked him and, upon leaving the room, paused to reflect on the interview ending so quickly. Being asked how sure he was that Elizabeth understood he was making a marriage proposal threw him off balance. Not knowing Mr. Bennet's disposition, he had been unsure of what to expect when asking for her hand, though there was a certain anticipation of a father explaining the serious nature of marriage, and even some pointed remarks on what the father expected by way of behavior toward and care of his daughter. Darcy wished he had been given the opportunity to express his willingness, indeed his *eagerness*, in caring for Elizabeth with all the love and security that were his to give. In truth, for a moment he felt the impulse to go back in and do so, but thought better of it, considering how summarily he was sent out to summon her.

He therefore took comfort in knowing that his joy rested with Elizabeth not changing her mind. Regarding her father, he thought how unlike Mrs. Bennet he is on the subject of marriage for his daughters; in fact, he could not help but smile at how like her father Elizabeth is. Money and prominence mean very little to either of them -- their view of the world and society are unique, to say the least, and how glad Darcy was for that! To know Miss Elizabeth Bennet truly loved him and was not seeking an advantageous match was something of which he was certain.

Remaining but a moment in the hall for these reflections, he proceeded on to the drawing-room. Upon entering the room, he smiled at her, considering there could not be such a woman as she without such a father. He did realize Mr. Bennet's statement, *'If she does not have a change of heart'* suggested there might be some effort on his part to dissuade his daughter from the marriage, which made him wonder what objection Mr. Bennet might raise against him. However, determined to have the matter settled, he walked quickly over to Elizabeth under the pretence of looking at something and informed her of her father's desire to speak to her; and just as quickly, she left for that purpose.

* * * * *

Elizabeth remained away for some time, causing Darcy to wonder how matters were working out. Unknown to him, not all the time she was away was spent with her father. To be sure, it took some persuading for her to convince Mr. Bennet that she really loved Darcy, which was his sole concern. But after the emotion of the interview, she went upstairs to her room to compose herself.

When she returned, Darcy looked at her with an expression that showed his keenness to know the outcome of her meeting with her father. Her calm composure and tranquil expression let him know all was well. With the application to Mr. Bennet being concluded to everyone's satisfaction, these two lovers could now relax, though they kept up pretences for the rest of the evening, until Elizabeth could give the news to her mother. It had been decided this would be done after the gentlemen left, so as not to expose Darcy to her mother's initial joyous effusions.

Chapter 49

That night at Netherfield, Bingley said to Darcy, "So starting tomorrow, the world may know that Mr. Fitzwilliam Darcy and Miss Elizabeth Bennet are engaged! I suppose you will be happy to be able to acknowledge your love for each other openly?"

"I am sure you are right, Charles, but there was a certain pleasure derived from being alone with our secret. I cannot account for it precisely, but I suppose my private nature was more comfortable with being thus secluded. It now feels as though we have to share what we have with everyone."

"To be sure, living in a world populated with people can be most inconvenient at times," returned Charles, adding, "but Darcy, what a romantic you are becoming!"

Darcy laughed at this image of himself. "Yes, perhaps you are right. There is something you have reminded me of, though, Charles. I must write Georgiana, and if you will excuse me, I will retire to do that now." Departing to his room, he sat down, and taking pen in hand, recalled how he had anticipated writing *this* letter months ago:

My dear sister,
Forgive the brevity of this note, but my eagerness in what I have to communicate will answer for it, as I am sure you will understand after reading it . . . indeed, I have happy news to share with you! You will, I am sure, remember how highly I spoke of Miss Elizabeth Bennet, as well as your own first impression in being acquainted with her. I pray your pleasure will be increased, as mine has, with the news of our engagement. It happened only yesterday, and today we received the blessing of her father, so I am writing promptly to you, that you may have

the earliest information of it and share in our happiness, though it be from a distance.

I have long been troubled at your being without a mother or older sister. To be sure, I know no one could replace our mother, but I do believe that in Elizabeth you will find a sister worthy of your love and admiration. How I long for the two of you to become better acquainted and establish a bond that can only exist between sisters!
Your loving brother,
Fitzwilliam Darcy

With the letter sealed and the happy thought of Georgiana soon rejoicing with him, a satisfying day was thus brought to an end.

* * * * *

The following day at Longbourn, Elizabeth and Darcy were talking over matters when the subject of informing Lady Catherine was introduced. Elizabeth asked, "When might you have the courage to do so?"

"Courage is not what is wanting. I admit I am torn in my feelings about informing her, but I am not afraid of her; as is obvious, neither are you."

"You may be speaking too hastily, Mr. Darcy, on *my* part -- I am not frightened by her when being confronted with a demand on whom I should marry, but without that sense of righteous indignation, I just might find her very terrifying!" she said playfully. To understand what he had said, she then asked, "However, you say you feel torn? In what way?"

"Her feelings are so strongly set on the match between Anne and myself . . . as she informed you, it has been something she has planned for since we were children, so I know it will cause some pain, and this I do regret. And, of course, there is Anne: as you know, she is not out in society, so the initial news of my engagement to you may seem to sink her prospects for marriage substantially." Observing Lizzy's concerned look, he quickly added, "There is no need to feel uneasy about this -- Anne was as much against the match as I was. I believe, at least for her, this news will be a relief, and with all of Lady Catherine's resources and determination, I am certain there will be little difficulty in procuring a husband for Anne who will undoubtedly be better suited for them both. This is part of my consideration, however."

"Yes, but you spoke of being *torn*."

"Indeed, though I am not as exuberant as Charles, I am nonetheless filled with happiness, and there are moments I could wish the news declared from the rooftops! So, though I am not wishing to make my aunt unhappy, neither can I wish my happiness to be contained."

Elizabeth said softly, "What a dear man you are." Providing him with paper and pen, in his typical fashion, he got directly to the point:

Lady Catherine de Bourgh
Dear Madam,
You have often reminded me of the wish of my late mother and yourself that our two houses would be united by a marriage between Anne and myself. This, I must inform you, is a hope that can no longer be entertained. I have, as of two days ago, entered into an engagement with Miss Elizabeth Bennet.

I imagine this will surprise you, considering our conversation of a few days past. I stated then that I had no hope of being engaged to Miss Bennet because I believed she would not accept me, having refused a prior offer from me. Your communicating the particulars of your meeting with her inspired me to renew my offer, which, as I stated, has been accepted. I hope, Aunt, you can see from this her feelings for me are genuine.

I have no wish of injuring someone so close to me as yourself and Anne. I know it sounds trite, but I love Elizabeth and have come to understand, over the course of several months now, that love should be the foundation of marriage. Please understand, these feelings of which I speak have been of long duration and have sprung from my own admiration for Miss Bennet. The truthfulness of this is to be found in this fact: what other love could bear the disappointment of a refusal and be rekindled into action at the first glimmer of hope?

I believe this news will not initially meet with favor on your part, but do hope in time you will come to be happy for me, as I feel my mother would have been. I know you have always wanted the best for me, and since my mother's death you have felt that urge more strongly. For this, I will always be grateful.

Having done all you could in this matter, and since I am not an inexperienced young man, I beg leave to make my own choice of a marriage partner with one I consider to be best for me. Miss Bennet's deserving of your good opinion is something I hope time will manifest. Your kind forbearance in this is my strongest wish. Please be assured of my continued felicity for you and my cousin Anne.
Yours sincerely,
Fitzwilliam Darcy

Elizabeth asked if she could read the letter, which, of course, was allowed. Taking a moment to reflect on it, she commented, "This is such a kind letter, my dear. I was thinking, though, that the part she played in advancing our match may be difficult for her to read. Do you suppose you should really leave it in?"

"I think it is an explanation that is needed to account for some of my remarks in the conversation I had with her. It is not meant to affront her, but rather to explain my actions."

"Yes, and to be sure, it does not have a tone of meanness. I do not believe you capable of that."

Darcy thanked her for her expressions, and while getting the letter ready for mailing, concluded with: "I will certainly be glad when all this informing of others is over and we will not have to concern ourselves with other people's feelings, but are able to rejoice in our own."

His *fiancée* agreed: "You and I are truly alike in this regard . . . we care little for the good opinion of the world, but find comfort and satisfaction in each other. Perhaps this is the payment for happiness in marriage, in which case, we should prove to be very happy."

Chapter 50

With the news of their engagement being common knowledge, Mr. Darcy and Elizabeth found that the world often intruded into their comfort and happiness. When that intrusion came from Elizabeth's relations, it was particularly mortifying to her. She sheepishly brought it up one morning in this manner: "Mr. Darcy, how sorry I am that you must be exposed to the particular foibles of my family . . . I hope the constancy of it has served to make you less sensitive to it."

"Please, Elizabeth, do not make yourself uneasy. Yours is not the only family with persons for which there is a reason to blush -- you have only to think of Lady Catherine and Caroline Bingley to make you less concerned! Besides, it is not as bothersome to me as you suppose. I really have learned to think better of people in general, and to take myself less seriously."

This was welcomed news for Lizzy; she was now able to relax, which made the bustle of these days in preparation for their marriage much more enjoyable. She was even able to take some delight in the time spent with her mother in this regard, as Mrs. Bennet's changed attitude toward Mr. Darcy was apparent in her humble tone and address. Seeing the two of them putting forth the effort to tolerate one another did Lizzy's heart good.

There were many happy days spent with Georgiana, Charles and Jane leading up to the wedding. And what a lovely reunion it was when they all went into town to shop for their wedding and had the pleasure of seeing Colonel Fitzwilliam and Maria.

* * * * *

At the wedding, on the astonished lips of many it was heard:
"Mr. Darcy fell in love!"

It was also observed that, for a man whom they had seen smile very little, the town had never seen a groom smile so much.

And for a man that used to be known for his *pride and prejudice*, everyone marveled at how the love of a young lady named Elizabeth Bennet could produce such a change in the man named Fitzwilliam Darcy.

The end . . .

Extension of Chapter 20

Darcy, putting the letter aside, realized he was very tired, though the agitation remained. Thus was the beginning of a fitful night's sleep.

The next thing he knew, Miss Bennet was before him, saying, "Mr. Darcy, after reading your letter I implore you to *forgive me*. My family and I are unworthy of you . . . please allow me to acknowledge the undeserved kindness of your offer of marriage!"

Caroline Bingley now stepped forward before Darcy could utter a word, and taking him by the arm, said sarcastically, "So, Miss Eliza, you have come to your senses! I, for one, have *never* seen the attraction of your eyes. It is about time you see yourself as others who are superior to you do! What nonsense, for a woman who is talked of as having sense, to be throwing away this opportunity of a most eligible match."

Darcy was shocked to next hear *Mrs. Bennet* speak -- he had no idea from where she came -- "Oh, Miss Bingley, there is no need to scold Elizabeth, she will ruin any possible marriage opportunity on her own! You need not worry about her being a rival of yours." Then turning to him, "But, Mr. Darcy, if you will but take a commission and don a red coat, one of my other daughters would do very well for you . . . Lydia or Kitty will take you, but you must be an officer."

"I do not understand -- what is the meaning of all this?" Darcy demanded.

Suddenly, he was relieved by the appearance of Charles, until *he* spoke, "Don't worry, Darcy, leave it all to me. I know what is good for you; you need not bother yourself. You know how incapable you are at making decisions without my help.

All you need do is allow me to talk you into doing the right thing for yourself, regardless of how you feel on the matter."

Elizabeth then declared, "If you had behaved like a *gentleman,* all of this could have been avoided, Mr. Darcy. It is too late -- since you have now hesitated, you cannot make an offer to me in *any possible way* that would tempt me to accept you!"

"You need not fear, cousin Darcy," Anne said as she pushed Caroline away. "I am a match that would be no degradation for you. No one of your acquaintance would find you marrying me repugnant. From our youth we have been meant for each other -- let us now seal our affection with a kiss."

The others came closer, repeating, "Kiss her, Darcy . . . kiss, her! There will be no shame with her as a wife!"

Bingley was saying loudly, "Leave it all to me; I know what is best for you!"

Mrs. Bennet, holding an officer's red coat, approached crying, "Look, Mr. Darcy, I have found an officer's coat, it will do for now! Let me bring you one of my other daughters. It will be wonderful, you know, for you will be able to introduce all my girls to very rich men."

As the others were coming toward Darcy and he backed into a wall, preventing himself from retreating another step, he saw Elizabeth walking slowly away, shaking her head and saying, "If only you had behaved *in a gentlemanlike manner* . . . but now, you cannot make me an offer in any possible way that I would accept. It is *too bad* you are not a gentleman! You could be receiving a kiss from me instead of your cousin Anne, sealing an engagement with her. It is too late now, Mr. Darcy; if only you had behaved like a *gentleman!*"

As Anne drew closer, the others continued repeating, "kiss Anne, kiss Anne!" Darcy tried to run, but his feet would not move, and when he tried to hold up his hands to conceal his face, his arms would not move. He wanted to scream, *"Stop!"* but he could not speak. Everyone else in the room was getting closer while Elizabeth was slowly moving away -- he wanted to call out to her, but still he could not speak.

Finally, in a rush of extreme panic, he exerted himself and lunged forward, only to find himself sitting up in bed, looking about himself, gasping for breath.

* * * * *

Just having a bit of fun here...

* * * * *

ENDNOTES

Why I wrote this book

Because of our love of **Pride and Prejudice**, my wife Cindy and I read this Jane Austen classic almost every year. We never tire of reading about those unforgettable characters. For some time, Cindy urged me to write an account of the story from Darcy's point of view, and eventually I did take up her suggestion. I used as my model for further developing this character, as well as the events in his life, these words of Jane Austen, where Darcy says of himself:

> "I have been a selfish being all my life, in practice, though not in principle..." **and** "I certainly have not the talent which some people possess of conversing easily with those I have never seen before. I cannot catch their tone of conversation, or appear interested in their concerns, as I often see done." **He also later says to Elizabeth,** "I hoped to obtain your forgiveness, to lessen your ill opinion *by letting you see that your reproofs had been attended to.*"

This gave me enough of his character to begin, as well as the spark toward what I wanted to tell from his viewpoint. Of course, telling the very same story from another character's point of view created a dilemma. There is an inevitable overlapping in his story with the original, told from Elizabeth's point of view. I struggled with the notion that for me to rewrite what Miss Austen wrote was like someone trying to repaint the Mona Lisa.

All praise to **JA** aside, I still had to decide how to handle my story at those overlapping situations. In my first draft, I took the position that I would simply summarize what was in **P&P**, feeling that anyone who would be interested in reading my book surely has already read the original and would therefore know what was being referred to at any given point. There was a problem with that approach, though -- it created a feel of something more akin to a newspaper article than a novel.

It was clear that those occasions where Darcy and Lizzy meet as described in **P&P** are *necessary* for the reader to understand why Darcy feels the way he does about Elizabeth. As a possible solution, I figured I could just copy those sections straight from the original, inserting my account of Darcy's perspective and feelings around that. As you read my book, those of you who are very familiar with **P&P** will see I have tried to make a very limited use of this option. In Chapter 44 especially, nothing would do but to copy portions of Lady Catherine and Elizabeth's conversation, and where I did, you'll see the direct quotes italicized. (In the digital version, their words are in color instead of italics.)

It was on one of my edits - I can't remember which - that I opted to rewrite the **P&P** narrative in the overlapping sections to flesh out my story. The advantage to my doing so is that those who are familiar with the original will feel like they are not just rereading that great book, and those not so familiar will have a more complete story.

A further incentive to my writing this book was that wish to know *just what did Darcy say to Bingley to convince him that Jane Bennet did not care for him?* or about *the conversation with Lady Catherine and Darcy when she had just come from talking to Elizabeth . . .* and most importantly, *what was it like for Darcy to wrestle with his feelings, from first admitting Elizabeth possessed some attractions, to actually falling in love with her?* As I pondered those questions, I wanted to give voice to the answers that I thought were not only my point of view, but possibly also his.

This is a story begging to be told -- the story of how **_Mr Darcy falls in love_** with Elizabeth Bennet, and how that love had a transforming effect on a man that seemed to have everything. My intention was to be as faithful to **Pride and Prejudice** as I could; I did not want to take artistic license and ignore the story timelines or take any other liberties with what Jane Austen had written.

To the best of my limited abilities, I have tried to capture the feel of **P&P** in writing this 'mirror image' of it. In doing so, I am in no way suggesting *that* excellent story is somehow incomplete -- it has stood the test of time as only a work of genius can. Reading one of the best novels ever written, though, makes you wish it would go on and on. I suppose it is for this reason that so many have taken up the story of **Pride and Prejudice** and expanded on it in one way or another. My effort was embarked on out of affection for the story and its characters, as well as respect for Jane Austen. I hope you enjoy reading this book as much as I enjoyed writing it.
Noe

Editor's note

Did you catch the spelling of *judgement?* Looking it up in the dictionary and online, you'll find the spelling <u>judgment</u> or <u>judgement</u> is mostly a matter of preference. It can also have to do with where you live and speak or write English. I just like the way it looks with that "e" better than without it.

Like the word "engagement."

cindy

*Please visit our **Amazon Author's** page at*
http://tiny.cc/s1r8ew for our other e-books.

Also visit our website for more at
noeandcindywrite.blogspot.com